HARD FOR A HARPY

FOLK HAVEN
BOOK 5

LAUREN CONNOLLY

HARD FOR A HARPY

Zara plans on finding a magical mate, starting a small family, and living a quiet life as a harpy in the town of Folk Haven. She does *not* plan on dating a sensual witch who hates magic.

When Zara's ex messes up her chance for happily ever after, she decides to organize her approach to love. The best way to find the perfect mythical partner in life is through a thorough research and vetting process. But once she finds the right man to spend the rest of her life with, there's the problem of seducing him. But maybe the hot new witch in town can give her a helpful boost...

Anthony Shelly avoids all things magical, but when his three siblings move to the mythic-filled town of Folk Haven, he settles in for a long visit. And what better way to pass his time than flirting with a tightly wound harpy in need of a little fun? When she asks him for a favor that would have him in her bed for a few months, the answer is an easy yes.

But as Zara uses Anthony's temptation skills to find herself a mate, the magic-rejecting witch can't help wondering if he could be the one to make her dreams come true instead ...

For the readers who wish they could live in Folk Haven. Thank you for continuing to visit.

Visit my website at laurenconnollyromance.com
Cover Designer: MoorBooks Designs
Editor: Jovana Shirley, Unforeseen Editing, www.unforeseenediting.com

ISBN-13: 978-1-949794-30-4

CONTENT WARNINGS

This book contains scenes with a snake—but he's friendly—discrimination, drugging a person with a potentially harmful substance, breaking and entering, and physical assault, but not sexual.

This book contains discussions of diet and exercise in relation to maintaining a certain body type or figure for work, parental neglect and abuse, microaggressions and racism, pursuit of pregnancy and possible infertility, and loss of a pet—but no pets come to harm during this story, only in the past.

PROLOGUE

ZARA

When researching monsters, I figure the best place to go is a mythical library. Luckily, my town has one of those.

Despite the fact that the Folk Haven Public Mythic Library is a newer creation, everything about this refurbished Victorian —from the rugs on the ground to the books on the shelves— has an aged feel. In a pleasant way. Like I've stepped through time into a cozy, magical hideaway.

This isn't the first time I've visited, so I know to bypass the grimoire section. As a harpy, there's nothing useful for me there. Nothing I can even read if I want to. The witch's language is indecipherable to any who don't have witch blood.

Would a baby born from a witch parent and another mythical parent be able to read the witch's language? Would they still maintain enough of their witch lineage for the knowledge to remain in their blood?

Maybe I can find a part-witch monster and ask them?

Technically, mythics call all crossbreeds monsters. But that's just a label born from fear. When a mythic mates with their own kind, they tend to make more of that mythic. Harpy with harpy makes another harpy. When mythics mate with humans, most often, a mythic is born, and on a rare occasion, a human is. Harpy plus human means harpy or maybe human.

But I'm not looking for a human partner. Not after what happened with the last one.

If I were to procreate with a dragon or a werewolf ... the result would be an odd combination of the two.

Hence, monsters.

As I ponder the intricacies of monster-hood, I slip an interesting title off the shelf and tuck it under my arm, heading to my favorite seat in the house. There's an overstuffed wingback chair situated by a window with a gorgeous forest view. Perfect reading conditions. Settling in with a contented sigh, I set to studying.

Some of the words have faded with age, and I lean closer to a nearby lamp to make them out just as a floorboard lets out a loud creak, alerting me to a new arrival. When I glance up, I barely manage not to gasp.

One of the handsomest men I've ever seen stands not too far from me. He's tall and lean, white skin and crimson hair, with a face that is sharp enough to cut. But his eyes—a beautiful dark green—widen with something like vulnerability.

He looks like he's been caught.

The guy must be another library patron. Maybe a curious resident of Folk Haven, like me. Maybe a professor from the local college, here for research purposes. Whatever reason, he seems unsure of himself in this space.

Probably not an academic then.

Once I get over the brief surprise of his good looks, I offer the stranger a friendly smile, wanting to put him at ease.

"Hi there," I say, watching as he attempts to ease away the candid expression in his eyes, drawing on an aloof mask.

"How's it going?" he asks as if the answer doesn't mean

much to him. Still, he leans the top half of his body my way. He reminds me of a cat who wants his ears scratched, but doesn't want *you* to know he wants his ears scratched.

The image has me giving in to the urge to tease him. To play with him.

"That all depends on your perspective." I lay my book flat in my lap and smooth the pages down so I don't lose my spot.

He shuffles a step closer. "My perspective on what?"

Here, kitty, kitty.

I let my smile widen. "On what you mean by *it*, obviously."

He props a shoulder against a shelf, affecting a casual stance as he smirks. "I'm interested in multiple *its*."

"Well"—I draw the word out—"why don't you list them then?"

His eyes track over my face, and I try to remember if I've ever seen him before. The man seems familiar somehow.

"Okay," he purrs. "How's your day going?"

I fiddle with the edge of a page and decide to meet his attempt at disinterest with blatant honesty. "No dogs died today. So, better than yesterday."

His face slackens with shock, and I take pity on him, softening my smile.

"I'm a veterinarian at the clinic in town. A day without the death of a pet is better than I can hope most times."

Yesterday, I had to put two furry family members down because of age and illness. It was terrible.

"Oh." He massages the back of his neck, as if he can physically feel the stressful weight of my job on his shoulders. "If I saw a dog die, I would cry."

The candid answer warms my heart and has me revealing a truth of my own.

"Sometimes, I do. But in my office so I don't upset the owner."

He grimaces. "That's rough."

"It is." I'm not about to lie and claim it's not. There are parts of my job I hate. My eyes drop to my book, but I realize I don't want to get back to reading just yet. I return my gaze to the handsome stranger. "You said multiple its."

"I did say that." But he doesn't ask any more questions. Just frowns.

Look at that. I started out teasing, then immediately ruined everything.

Maybe I'm not ready to get back out in the dating world.

After I broke up with my long-term human boyfriend last month, I thought a few weeks of mourning the end of what could have been was all I needed. Turns out, I require additional time to relearn how to flirt.

"If I made you uncomfortable, you're free to say you forgot the rest and retreat." I wave toward the doorway leading to the other rooms in the library, hiding how disappointed I would be at his abrupt departure. "I'm not very good at small talk. The animals don't usually require it."

But the man doesn't run. Instead, his lips curve into another devilish smirk as he settles in the chair next to mine. "Can't do it. Got more *its* to cover. How's your reading going?" He nods toward the book in my lap.

"Just started, so I'm not sure yet." I close the volume and show him the worn cover so he can read the title.

MONSTERS OF THE FAR EAST

"What made you pick that up?" His ginger brows tick up, and I hear the unspoken question.

I answer it. "I'm not a monster."

"Okay."

He nods, and since he shows no signs of utter relief that he's not talking to a mythical mixture, I decide teasing is back on the table.

"But I might make one."

His eyes look ready to pop out of his head at that, and I stifle a chuckle.

"Sorry. That sounded Dr. Frankenstein-ish, didn't it?" I give him a rueful grin. "I swear I don't have a bunch of random body parts I'm stitching together to form the perfect monster man. Your limbs are safe."

His body relaxes, and his chin tilts down as his face turns into a mask of mock reproach. "What, none of my pieces are good enough for this dream monster man?"

More like he's already perfectly formed and there's no way to improve.

My eyes drag over the redhead, taking in every inch of arrogant beauty. "Maybe I spoke too soon. What would you suggest? Pitch your pieces to me."

Long fingers, meant for an artist, smooth over his lips, pressing away a grin. "Well, there's no ignoring my face."

"No, there's not," I murmur involuntarily.

His voice has an enticing deep note when he speaks next. "My chest could fetch a good price at auction."

Now, I'm the one trying to suppress a smile.

"But what you really want," he continues, "are my ... toes."

"Your toes?" I choke on the question, almost breaking and giving in to the laughter.

Goddess, it's been so long since I did this. Flirted with someone. Played this silly back-and-forth game that is so much fun if done right.

He nods sagely. "They're wily toes. I can pick stuff up with them. Could probably type a dissertation with the things."

I bite my bottom lip until I have my urge to snicker under control, then keep my voice as dry as an academic's. "Fingerlike monkey toes. Got it."

When I grin wide at him, the stranger blinks, as if my expression surprised him.

"But," I clarify, "as I said, I'm not building a monster."

And I really should get back to my reading. I resettle the book in my lap and open the worn cover.

"Enlighten me." His voice tempts me to ignore what I came here to do. "How do you plan to make a monster then?"

My attention stays on old words as I give him a summarized version of my mission. "I plan to date a mythic. Then fall in love with that mythic. Then mate and/or marry them. Then have one baby with them."

Silence descends for a moment, but I keep my eyes on the page.

"That's a very specific to-do list," he says at last.

I nod. "I know what I want." And I'm not changing my mind.

"And you don't want another witch?" he asks.

That surprises me enough that I glance up again. Then, I figure out the conclusion he must have drawn, finding me in a library run by witches.

"Oh. No, I'm not a witch. I'm a harpy." As if he needs a demonstration, I flap my arms, miming the wings I sprout in my secondary form. Then, I tuck my arms back against my sides and try not to be extremely embarrassed by that odd display. "Males of our kind are rare," I explain, moving the topic along. "The only one I know is gay, so he's not in my dating pool. And humans ..."

I try not to clench my teeth as a certain face flashes across my mind.

We loved each other at one point, but now, the memory of my ex just pisses me off.

How I could never be good enough for him.

"Humans are not an option," I simply say. I'll never risk that kind of rejection again. "So, it's another mythic. And if we have a child, like I want, it'll be a monster." My finger taps the book cover. "Best to know what I might be getting into."

There's a handsome new kappa—a mythical water creature more common in Asia—in town, who I've considered asking out for drinks. In fact, he's renting a room on the upper level of this house-turned-library. Would have been convenient to run into *him* and exchange a few flirtatious remarks.

Although, the kappa is nowhere near as good-looking as *this* guy.

Still, despite my body's obvious interest in this stranger, not once in this exchange have I considered if he'd be a good candidate for my future plans. His overall demeanor has a *I'm doing my best to seem like I don't give a fuck* vibe. That might work for some people, but not a thirty-year-old harpy who's looking to find love and start a family.

I want my partner to give all the fucks.

As if hearing my silent rejection, the man doesn't press me for anything. "I'll leave you to your reading."

He peels himself off the chair, no doubt coming to the same conclusion that I did—our flirting is going nowhere in the end.

I nod, eyes on my book so I don't watch his ass as he walks away. "Nice to exchange odd conversation with you, man who still hasn't properly introduced himself." Couldn't help that last bit.

"You haven't told me your name yet either," he points out.

"I'll introduce myself the next time I see you." Some part of my brain thinks it's best I never learn his name. That'd give me one more detail to get stuck on.

"I'm not staying in town long."

Weird how that sends my gut on a disappointing drop. But I keep the reaction to myself and shrug one shoulder. "Then, I guess you don't need my name."

Whether he agrees is answered only by him leaving the room without another word.

And I never expect to see him again.

1

ANTHONY

Four Months Later

THERE'S a weight in the bed next to me, but I don't remember bringing anyone home last night. This isn't the first time I've woken up next to a stranger. Most of the people I sleep with are humans I don't know well.

Rubbing the sleep from my eyes, I stare at an unfamiliar gray wall. My walls being unfamiliar isn't odd either. Half the time, I'm in a new city, in some ritzy hotel my agent booked for me.

The view outside of the cracked curtains finally has me remembering that this isn't my usual displacement. I'm not on a world tour, hawking an expensive liquor or clothing line.

I'm in Folk Haven, a small town in northern Georgia.

"Damn it, Broderick." I mutter the curse at my brother even though he's on the other side of this town and he can't hear me.

He's committed the unforgivable sin of setting roots in this place. I could blame my sisters too, who moved to Folk Haven first, but I've never been as close with them. Getting mad at Ame and Mor feels wrong.

But my twin? Yeah, I'll get pissy with him, no problem.

Though this still leaves the question ... who did I hook up with in this tiny town?

Gods, they'd better not think this means we're dating.

I don't date. For the good of the population as a whole. No one should be stuck with someone like me for any length of time.

Some*thing* like me.

"Hey," I start to say as I roll over, ready to let the woman or guy down easy. Only the rest of my pathetic morning-after speech lodges in my throat when I see the body in the bed beside mine.

Long. Lithe. Dark.

Curled in a perfect circle on top of the covers.

There's a snake in my bed.

"Fucking hells!"

As I scramble away from the massive black creature, the sheets tangle in my limbs, and I end up sprawled on the hard-wood floor. An ache in my elbow and hip means I can expect bruises on my pale skin, which means my agent will berate me for marring what she considers my "perfect, sexy ginger" look. But there's a *giant-ass black snake in my bed.*

I snatch my phone off the bedside table and sprint into the main living area of the apartment, dialing my brother as I go.

"You're up before noon," Broderick greets me. "I'm so proud."

"There's a snake in my bed!"

A pause, then, "Is this a euphemism for your dick? I'm at office hours. Students could show up at any time. I can't trade dick jokes with you right now."

"No, fucker. It's a real fucking snake. This town has snakes, and they break into apartments and feel you up while you're sleeping!" I pant and pace and keep my eye on the bedroom doorway, waiting for the reptilian demon to appear and try to swallow me whole.

"It got fresh with you?" Broderick does not sound as concerned as he should be.

"I'm sure it would have!"

"True. You are a handsome devil." Broderick only compliments my looks because we're identical, and we both know he's actually bragging about himself.

"What the fuck do I do? Do they, like ... sell snake repellent spray or something?"

There's a cough and a snort on the other end of the line, and I hold my phone far enough from my face to glare at it. Not that Broderick can see.

"Stop fucking laughing!" I yell.

"Okay, okay. I can tell by your copious use of *fuck*s that this is serious. Hang up with me and call the police."

"You want me to call the cops on a snake?"

"Folk Haven is a small town with almost no crime. They're probably bored over there in Town Hall. And if they don't handle this kind of stuff, I'm sure they can direct you to who can." His voice softens. "You're not in some metropolis anymore. People care about each other here."

I'm used to people envying me. Wanting to be me or to live the extravagant lifestyle I do.

But I don't know how I feel about strangers *caring* about me.

Nope, I decide. *I don't like it.*

Still, won't mind if some hottie in a police uniform shows up for a snake wrestle.

"Fine. I'll call them."

"Great. And just so you know ..." Broderick loves a dramatic pause and draws this one out.

"What?" I snap.

"I'm never going to let you live this down."

The line disconnects.

"Fuck," I grumble, glaring at my phone.

Then, I look up the website for the Folk Haven police department. It's a simple single-page website, but there's a number for nonemergency calls. This feels like a dire circumstance to me, but I don't want to tie up the 911 line if someone is dying. The snake hasn't tried to kill me ... yet.

The officer I speak to is much nicer than my brother, meaning if the guy thinks I'm dramatic, he keeps it to himself.

"We'll send over animal control. Please don't try to engage with the animal before they arrive," he instructs me in a deep voice that leaves no room for argument.

"Believe me, I won't."

The moment I hang up, I realize I didn't ask how long they would be.

Do I have to be here when they show up?

Probably. And it's not like I can go out. Glancing down at myself, I imagine walking down Main Street in what I'm wearing—skintight black briefs and nothing else covering my pale ass. All my clothes are in my bedroom, and I'm *not* going back in there.

I pace to the front door and unlock it, wondering how the snake even got into my place. The apartment is on the second story, above Fresh Feathers, the local dry cleaner. The only entrances are a set of metal steps on the outside of the building and the windows. But late March in Georgia is still chilly, so I didn't have anything open.

Pondering the puzzle, I wander back into the kitchen.

Where the snake is waiting.

"Fuck!" Without thought, I leap onto the kitchen island, the marble cold against my bare feet.

The snake doesn't lunge at me, but it does raise its head, flicking out a forked tongue, as if it can already taste me.

"I'm a shitty meal." I pat the six-pack my agent insists I maintain for shirtless shoots. "I'm gamey. Full of bitterness and alcohol."

The creature continues to stare at me, as if it understands what I'm saying. Or is looking for an opening to attack.

If one of my siblings were here, I doubt they'd be stuck on a kitchen counter. The other Shellys would have spells for this. A little finger wiggle, some of the enchanted red powder our family is known for, and the snake would be on its way. Or transformed into a feather boa.

But me? I don't mess with that shit.

Which puts me at the mercy of the snake.

Ten minutes later—just as I'm considering making a run for it—there's a knock on my door.

Thank the gods.

"It's open!"

My relief dries up immediately when the door swings wide, revealing my savior.

Please tell me it's not her.

But it is.

The woman who strolls into my apartment is tall, curvy, and altogether too gorgeous. She has her dark hair in a messy bun, which lets me see the slope of her neck and every sharp, lovely angle of her face. But there's softness too. In her brown eyes, a few shades darker than her dusky-gold skin. And those lips. There's an adorable birthmark sitting above the top curve, which is slightly fuller than the bottom, giving her a natural pout that disappears as she smiles up at me now.

"You're taller than I remember," she says, her voice husky and teasing.

The sound does things to me, and I cup my hands in front of my briefs to hide my body's reaction.

This is the woman from the library. The one I met months

ago. The same one I've been hoping to run into ever since I returned to Folk Haven.

Even though I shouldn't let myself want that. In a single conversation, I learned that no matter how attractive I found her, anything between the mystery woman and me would be doomed.

I can offer her a hot hookup. But that's not what she's looking for. This lovely harpy told me she wants to find a husband and start a family in this magical small town.

All I want is to peel those jeans off her long legs and lick her pussy until she tells me her name and then shouts out mine.

Stop thinking dirty thoughts.

Even if I was the *settle in a small town* kind of guy, I wouldn't have a chance. She's funny, intelligent, and standing there, looking sexy and cute in her tight purple sweater. I, meanwhile, am crouched on my kitchen island in my underwear, waiting for her to come save me from the big, bad snake.

Not a good look.

The only thing that would make this worse is if I got hard in front of the harpy.

2

ZARA

I ALLOW myself one surprised chuckle. But that's it.

When Carl, a merman who works on the Folk Haven police force, called me about a snake removal at the apartment above the dry cleaner, I didn't prepare myself for a familiar redhead wearing only underpants and taking refuge on a kitchen island. Odd as Folk Haven is, this is not a sight I see every day.

"So, you're here to rescue me?" His rueful smile is entirely too endearing, as is the blush that spreads over his porcelain skin. Which I can see a whole hell of a lot of because, again, he's in his drawers.

I also enjoy how he doesn't bluster and get defensive and try to pretend he was doing anything other than hiding from a snake, which I now spy patiently waiting on the floor. It does seem awfully interested in the man.

Black rat snake. Maybe four or five feet, but hard to tell with it curled around itself.

"At your service. You found yourself a new friend, huh?"

Leaning out the door, I pick up the nonlethal trap I brought and consider the best way to coax the snake into it.

"I'm not looking for any new friends. Not poisonous ones anyway." He cringes as the snake shifts and lifts its head higher.

The gesture comes off more curious than aggressive.

"Black rat snakes aren't poisonous. They can bite, but only if they feel threatened." Which is why I'm going to do my best not to frighten the little one.

Lots of people think snakes are scary and creepy. Not me. I've always found their flat heads and flicking tongues to be adorable.

When I step forward, intending to set the trap down close, but not too close, to the creature, it uncoils and slithers around me, almost too fast to track.

"Hells!" the redhead yelps.

But there's no reason to worry.

In fact, the snake does my job for me, slipping out the open front door and disappearing, either down the steps or around one of the stair's metal support beams.

And then it's just me and the handsome out-of-towner.

"You're welcome, I guess." Smiling up at him, I watch as the guy slips off the counter, his movements almost snakelike as well—they're so smooth.

"Didn't think to just leave the door open," he mutters, that blush returning to his cheeks. "Sorry to bother you."

I shrug. "No problem. I'm glad you called." When his brows creep up, I clarify, "Instead of trying to hurt it. Animal control isn't my official job, but I offered to handle situations like this so fewer wild critters get injured or killed. You might not like the snake, but they're a beneficial part of the ecosystem here, and it seems wrong to kill something just because it stumbled into a place it shouldn't have and ... I'm rambling about animals. Sorry. Habit from my job. I'm Zara." I thrust my hand forward. "Last time I saw you, I promised I would introduce myself next time we ran into each other. So, here's me, introducing myself. Zara Ironfeather. Harpy. But I think I told you that last time."

He accepts my hand, his palm smooth, fingers long and strong, nails so clean and evenly cut that I wonder if they're manicured.

"Zara. I'm glad we crossed paths even if I'm not at my best." His smile is dangerous this time, filled with teasing temptation. "I'm Anthony."

After giving his hand a firm shake, I release him and try to ignore the tingle in my palm.

Then, the name clicks, paired with the red hair and where I first met him.

"Oh, *Anthony*! Anthony Shelly. You're Ame's brother. She works at Folk Tails, the veterinarian office, with me."

Our witch receptionist mentioned she had two brothers, one named Broderick who moved to town and got a job at Ramla University. I haven't run into him yet, spending almost every day at the clinic for what feels like months.

"You decided to come back?"

When we spoke last, Anthony planned to leave town. I never thought I'd see the man again. Still, I thought about him from time to time.

He leans back against the counter, bracing his hands on the granite, his full body on display. The guy might blush easily, but he doesn't seem to have qualms about giving me an eyeful.

Not that I'm complaining.

"Only to visit. Came to see my brother and sisters. And I needed a break from work."

"What do you do?"

His long-fingered hand comes up to rub his throat. "I'm an influencer. On social media. Companies pay me to advertise their products."

"That's so interesting."

I'm not blowing enchanted smoke up the guy's ass. Whenever pet owners are willing to chat about what they do, I love to listen. The animals are great, but it's nice to get a break from all the howling and whimpering and angry meowing. Plus, when owners talk about themselves, their pets tend to calm down, just from hearing the sound of their loved one's voice in a casual conversation.

"Sometimes, I feel like a generation behind because I never do much with social media. But Ame set up an Instagram account for the practice. She has me write the content, and she does the pictures and posts things. We just got to three hundred followers. How many do you have to do it professionally?"

His gaze tracks away from mine. "A bit more than that."

I roll my eyes. "Of course." Slipping my phone from my pocket, I click on the app Ame downloaded for me. The feed is full of cute animal photos and pet care facts because we just follow other vet offices. "What's your Instagram name? I want to see what you do."

When Anthony doesn't answer right away, I glance up to find him frowning.

I'm being pushy.

This guy just had a scare, he's still in his underwear, and I'm trying to engage him in some good old-fashioned Southern neighbor chatting. When I'm around the animals for too long, I forget a little thing called tact.

"Never mind." I offer him an easy smile. "That would mess up your algorithm, right? Ame was trying to explain it to me. How I should only like and follow vet and animal-related things. I don't want to confuse your fans."

I start to close the app, but fingers pluck my phone from my hand.

"That's not it. I'll bring it up."

He swipes over the screen, much faster than I could ever manage, fingers well trained in the art of modern technology. Also, he doesn't have to worry about talons popping out and scratching his screen. Normally, keeping them sheathed is easy enough, but when I get excited, they can make an appearance.

"Here."

Anthony turns the phone back over to me, and I look at the name first. Not his. Instead, it reads, *Crimson Dread.*

My mind can't decide if it's funny or sexy. Maybe both. Then, my eyes drop to the image, and I forget about the name.

The picture is … erotic.

Taken from a low angle, the photo shows Anthony in dark pants and a suit jacket—no shirt—lounging, legs spread, one hand holding a glass, filled with a golden-tinted liquor, that's resting on his knee. His other hand is busy tangling in some guy's hair as their mouths meet. Then, I notice on the table beside him, there's a bottle, label turned out.

"Is that what you're advertising?" I point to the bottle.

"Yes."

I squint to read the name. "Is it good?"

"If you like tequila."

"I like Margarita Mondays at Marlin's Marina." Making note of the brand in my memory, I give him a big smile. "You got yourself a customer. I'll ask for it next Monday."

"Oh." His pale cheeks flush a deep, tantalizing red, almost as dark as his hair. "It's six hundred dollars a bottle."

My fingers fumble on my phone as I slip it into my pocket. "Six hundred?"

If that's how much a single bottle costs, how much are they paying the guy who gets people to buy it?

"Yeah. It's … some people like to spend money on that." The man looks embarrassed, and the sight is endearing.

"Sorry. Lost yourself a customer. But feel free to sample cheap tequila with me at the marina sometime. And I promise we don't have to make out for me to treat you to a drink."

His emerald eyes meet mine and hold for a second too long. "My loss."

Oh, wow. Is he a phoenix? Because it's suddenly feeling very hot in here.

Anthony shakes his head, eyes breaking from mine. "How's your research going?"

"My ... oh, you mean, the Monster Baby Plan?"

He huffs a laugh. "The what?"

"For the record, I did not come up with that name. My friend Mary Jo gets the credit for it."

I cross my arms over my chest, suddenly self-conscious. Should I be talking about this? I want to be honest, but do I come off as strange when I tell people, like men standing in their underwear in their kitchen, about my quest for love and a baby?

But he asked.

"Monster Baby Plan." He chews over the title. "Sounds like step one in the pursuit of world domination."

A smirk tugs at the corner of my mouth. "I do like the idea that my uterus could produce the next Antichrist."

Anthony's eyes drop to my belly, and I wonder if he's imagining me gestating a Godzilla, like I sometimes do. A very cute, lovable Godzilla.

"Please remember to tell your progeny I was totally on board with the Monster Baby Plan."

That has me grinning wide.

"Will do. But to answer your question, not much progress has been made." I tuck my hands in my pockets as I talk. "I mean, I have a list of prospective partners. Men I think would be compatible and possibly open to dating a harpy. But I haven't approached any of them. Work has been hectic. Everyone's pets eat things they shouldn't around the holidays, which means stomach-pumping extravaganza. Then, Keith—the other vet I work with—had the flu, and we're just catching up on the backlog of appointments and surgeries now. So, soon, hopefully."

Not that I even know how to go about dating anymore. My ex, Christian, and I were together since high school, and we bonded in Chemistry Club.

How do I approach a man when I'm not riding high on teenage hormones?

Then, there's the fact that I'm old enough to know exactly what I want.

Do I tell him outright?

Do I date him and try to parse out through clues if he'd be amenable to a mixed-mythic—and if he's not Indian, mix-raced —family?

How do I even know if someone *likes* me that way?

Reflecting on my relationship with Christian, I cringe at some of the behavior I put up with because I convinced myself he loved me as I was. But now, with distance, I can pick out the many small, hurtful acts. The clues that showed me my ex only cared for certain parts of me, but not the whole woman.

I want love and a family, but I don't want to go through that again.

Sometimes I feel like I need a class in human behavior.

Another example, spending an extended time around animals seems to have dulled my ability to pick up on social cues.

Which is why it takes me until right now to realize I should have left Anthony's apartment on the tail of the snake. The guy probably wants to get dressed and start his day, and here I am, trying to social media–stalk him—which I could easily do later, when I'm alone—and chatting about procreating.

Get your shit together, Zara.

"What will—" Anthony starts, asking another question I'm sure to be polite.

But I cut him off, "Anyway, glad I could open your door and let the snake out for you. If you run into any more animal issues, feel free to call the clinic directly. Or call Ame—she usually knows where I am."

Scooping up my snake trap, I head to the door, then pause when I remember a common service some Folk Haven residents pay for.

"There should be a spell too. Ame or Mor would know what it is. A version of warding to keep out unwanted critters. A customer told me about getting it done when a raccoon came in through her dog door. You could cast that, if you're worried about the snake coming back."

Maybe I shouldn't have been concerned about Anthony being uncomfortable before. Because as I watch him now, I see true discomfort. The man's entire body goes rigid, bones and muscles and joints turned to stone.

"I can't cast spells," he says, voice brittle.

He can't work magic?

Ame never mentioned her brothers being adopted, and they look *so* much alike with their bright red hair and pale complexion. If he's a Shelly, magic is in his blood.

"Aren't you a witch?"

He scowls. "No, I'm not."

3

—————

ANTHONY

THE REST OF THE DAY, I berate myself, regretting the cold tone I used with Zara after she went out of her way to help me. The harpy was only making a suggestion. She doesn't know about my hang-ups with magic.

Ones that I have to face yet again as I turn onto the gravel drive of the Folk Haven Public Mythic Library—aka my sisters' home. The Victorian house comes into view through the trees, and I can't help gritting my teeth at the sight of it. Objectively, the place is beautiful. Multiple stories, dramatically sloped roof, plenty of windows, and an air of elegance.

But the building is also steeped in magic. The power calls to me. Reaches for me.

"Fine, yes. I'm coming inside," I mutter to the house as I put my car in park.

The luxury vehicle was not meant for Georgia back roads, but I get to use it for free because I did a whole week of images with me in the driver's seat, leaning on the hood, and plugging it into charging stations. The company's stock shot up.

Wasn't until I arrived in Folk Haven that I realized bringing a fully electric car here might leave me stranded, but turns out, the local recycling company sponsored a few charging stations around town.

I park next to Broderick's SUV, glad he's already here. I love my sisters, but sometimes, I struggle to talk to them. Mor's main interest is magical texts, which is not a topic I want to discuss. And Ame has been Mor's sidekick since she could walk.

And am I even their brother?

I shake my head to clear away the question that's bothered me since I was ten, back when my mother had an informative chat with me that tore apart my understanding of the world and how I fit in it. If I even did.

Helena Shelly is a powerful witch. So powerful that she managed to form a child purely out of magic. Broderick, Mor, and Ame are all real, but am I?

To this day, I still don't have a clear answer. But I do know my family would be better off without me. The brother who turned away from magic, only to do fuck all with his life.

Still, they called, so I came.

I find the three of them inside a room with a view of the lake. My mind takes me back to the last time I was here. Zara, though I didn't know her name then, was sitting in the chair by the window where Ame is perched now. The harpy had a book about monsters in her lap, a sweet smile on her plump lips, and her dark hair in two braids I wanted to tug on. Just a gentle tug. Enough to make those sweet lips open on a gasp.

Stop thinking about her like that. She's not for you.

"Here he is, our fearless brother!" Broderick grins at me from the cushy chair beside Ame's. "How'd your pest problem turn out?"

Mor and Ame stare between the two of us as I scowl at my brother.

"Fine," I mutter. "Ame's boss came over, and when she opened the door, the snake went out on its own."

"Impressive." He smirks, and I barely manage not to flip him off.

"It was Zara's day off. I didn't hear about that. You had a snake problem?" Ame powers down the tablet she was typing on, giving me her full attention.

Suppressing a sigh, I run through my morning, leaving out all the embarrassing details, which Broderick realizes, if his shit-eating grin is anything to go by.

"Where's Jack?" I ask to change the subject when I'm done with my story.

Ame's grumpy werewolf mate is usually wrapped around her, growling at anyone who makes even the most casual comment about too much PDA.

It was me. I made the comment.

Then, he challenged me to a wrestling match.

And I immediately retracted the comment.

Who am I to talk anyway? Half my social media content involves me in some type of amorous situation with another person. And I'm lucky if I get to know their name before the pictures are taken.

The thing is, those are all business. Soulless images meant to tantalize.

When Jack pulls Ame into his lap and kisses behind her ear, their love is palpable.

And apparently suffocating to a soulless creature like me.

"He has to work late," Ame explains. "It's midterms, and a few students tried to spell school computers to help them with assignments. But they've already been enchanted to prevent that, so now, the whole system needs to be rebooted."

"Tried to swing by his office on my way out," Broderick adds. "But from the amount of growling and cursing, I got the feeling he didn't want to be disturbed."

The two of them grin at each other, and I watch as my brother knits himself tighter into the weave of Folk Haven.

He's never going to leave.

"She's here," Mor announces to the room, and we all turn to look at our oldest sibling.

I hear the crunch of gravel, indicating another car coming down the drive.

"Who's here? None of you said why you wanted me to come over." I assumed it was some kind of family dinner they'd established.

When I arrived in town three days ago, I let the three of them know I'd be here for a few months. No way can I set down roots in Folk Haven, but it's been weird, traveling for work, knowing my siblings are all here, bonding without me.

Maybe that's how it should be.

Still, after my last job, the idea of jetting off to another city to spend a string of nights in clubs sounded exhausting. As much as Julia insisted I do one more shoot before my break, I finally turned her down. It's always *one more* with my agent. Well, that *one more* can wait a few months. I'll be back at it come summer, when all the partying is happening. I told her not to book anything before Memorial Day. I'm sure my calendar after that weekend is nonstop, but at least now, I have some time to relax.

Not that I'm feeling very calm at the moment in this magic-filled house.

"One of the local witches requested to speak with all four of us," Mor explains, setting aside the thick book she was reading. "This isn't a woman you say no to."

"You called me here for magic stuff?" I try not to grit my teeth.

Mor rolls her eyes. "I'm not asking you to *do* magic. I doubt that's what this is about. But she could make life tough for all of us if we piss her off. She just wants to talk."

"About what?" I ask, crossing my arms over my chest, as if that could protect me from spells.

"I'm not sure yet." Mor strides out of the room toward the front of the house, going to greet the guest I feel tricked into meeting.

Fucking witches.

I throw a glare Broderick's way for not warning me, but he's too busy petting Lucky—Ame's black cat familiar—to notice my betrayed scowl.

Fucking unhelpful twins.

Mor returns with a stranger one step behind her. The room seems to shrink the moment the witch joins us.

The woman is shorter than Ame, but her face is maturer and yet somehow ageless. She could be thirty or sixty. I'm not about to guess. Her long brunette hair spills around her shoulders, and despite her designer pantsuit, I spy dirt caked in her nail beds.

If I learned she just buried a body with her own hands, I wouldn't be surprised. That's the aura she gives off.

"Violetta Radeva. We're happy to have you." Mor speaks to the woman in a respectful, curious tone. "I believe you've met my sister, Ame. Next to her is my brother Broderick. And this is my brother Anthony." She waves my way. "Is there a reason you wanted to meet with all of us?"

"Hmm. Isn't this house cozy?" She meanders to the table Mor was sitting at and pages through the discarded book.

"I don't consider it a house anymore," my older sister says. "Now that it's a library, it's a public space."

"But you live here," she points out, wandering over to the shelves.

Mor's posture doesn't change, but I get the sense her defenses are going up. "With The Council's permission."

Violetta turns a toothy grin to the room. "Don't worry, dear.

I'm not upset about it. I think a little chaos in the town is good now and then."

I watch my sister frown. Obviously, she doesn't want her library to be considered chaotic.

"I'm here to talk about the Folk Haven coven."

That gets a reaction from Mor. She stands up taller, and if she were wearing a tie, I'm sure she'd be straightening it.

"Of course. Is there anything the coven would like to know about us? Bloodlines?"

I barely suppress a scoff. Yeah, our bloodlines look good on paper. But meet the individuals we came from, and there's nothing to brag about.

"No. We know everything we need to." She continues to meander around the room, eyes darting every which way, taking the shelves in.

"Then, what would you like to discuss?" Mor turns her body to follow the woman's movements.

"You're interested in joining, correct?"

"Yes," Mor says. "I am. Ame and Broderick would be honored as well."

Violetta stills.

"We don't invite individual witches into the coven." Her blue eyes track over the four of us before landing on me, and I wonder if anyone ever fashioned a dagger out of sapphires because I feel her gaze sliding like a blade into my gut as she continues speaking. "We invite families."

Hell no.

"I ..." Mor starts, then stops. Then, she squares her shoulders and continues, "Anthony doesn't practice magic. He doesn't consider himself to be a witch, and while I'm sure he's honored to be included"—I bite back a snort—"he has no need of a coven."

While I can speak for myself, I appreciate Mor taking a stand for me.

But Violetta doesn't nod in understanding. She continues to stare at me.

"Calling yourself a human does not make you one. You are a witch. A bad one, no doubt, but a witch nonetheless. And your disdain for magic means you are untrustworthy. Covens require a modicum of trust to function properly." Her eyes stay on me, though the next words seem directed at the whole room. "If any Shelly witch of your generation wants to join the coven, all of you have to. And Anthony will have to declare himself a witch and report to me for assessment of his commitment." Finally, she releases me from her gaze, turning to my older sister. "Without his cooperation, you will never join the coven. You may continue to live here, but you shall always be outsiders. The decision is his."

Without waiting for a response, the witch turns and strides from the room. When the sound of the front door closing echoes through the house, out of the corner of my eye, I watch Mor's shoulders droop.

Rage and fear fire through me, and I brace myself for the pleading and the fight that will follow. I'm ready for my forceful sister to push me and demand I fall in line.

But ... she doesn't.

Instead, Mor crosses to the table, scoops up the book she was reading, and turns toward the hallway.

"Thanks for coming over," she murmurs so low that I almost don't catch it. Then, she's gone, and I hear the back door open and close.

I won't feel guilty. I won't.

Having nothing to say and regretting coming here in the first place, I stalk out of the house myself, ready to leave all this behind.

I shouldn't have come to this town. They were better off without me here.

I'm almost to my car when Broderick calling out my name

stops me. Whirling on my brother, I hit him with an unrelenting glare.

"They can't seriously expect me to change my mind about all this because some stuck-up witch wants me to prove my loyalty. I won't do it."

He comes to a stop in front of me, the same eyes I see in the mirror every morning digging into mine.

"Mor and Ame will never ask you to."

"Good, because I won't."

"But *I* will."

I flinch back, as if he struck me. "What?"

"Mor wants to be a member of the coven. She won't say it to you, but she does. She wants to become a part of this community, and joining the coven is a way to do that. Honestly, I can take it or leave it. But I also think it would be helpful for Ame. There's an element of protection, and she needs it."

"She has Jack."

That werewolf is scary as fuck when he wants to be, and he's mated to my baby sister. Anyone who messes with her will lose their head.

Literally. He tore a guy's head off because the man had hurt her.

"Jack will protect her from physical threats, but not from people asking her to do things. She says yes. She always does."

"Well then, I'll lead by example. Show her how to say no." I spread my arms wide. "No."

"Damn it, Anthony!" Broderick shouts, making me stumble on my retreat.

My brother isn't the type to get mad. Or yell. Or curse.

And definitely not at me.

I look at him—really look—and see a pain in his eyes.

"Why can't you do this for them? We never ask you for anything. Why is this so impossible?"

"You grew up in the same house I did," I growl.

"I did. Our parents are twisted. But that doesn't mean magic is. It's only a tool."

Maybe for you. For me, it's so much more.

"And I choose not to use it. If this is so important, then I'll leave. I'll change my name. I won't be a Shelly anymore, and you all can join your coven. Build yourself a new witchy family."

"Anthony—"

But I'm already stalking away, escaping the clinging presence of the library and the disappointed gaze of my brother.

4

———

ZARA

Animals might be adorable, but they are also smelly.

Luckily, this town has a top-notch dry cleaner that can remove any unwanted scent from a set of scrubs. Having access to magical cleaning supplies has many advantages.

"Here you go. All set for the next few weeks." Esme, a harpy like me and owner of Fresh Feathers, grins at me from across the counter as she slides a bag of clothes my way. "Try not to get peed on too much in the meantime."

"As far as I know, there are no appointments with incontinent cats in my schedule. But the day is young."

I'm currently wearing my last set of clean scrubs. Clean-ish. This morning, we had a Lab who was shedding their winter coat, and tufts of yellow fluff are still clinging to my pants. I made sure to get to the dry cleaner on my lunch break so I could grab my clothes before the shop closed this afternoon.

Errand finished, now, I can go eat.

At least, that's the plan until I step out onto the sidewalk and almost plow into Anthony Shelly.

"Zara." The handsome redhead clasps my shoulders to steady me as I clutch my clothing haul, keeping them from falling to the ground.

"Sorry. I was watching my feet." I try not to think about how firm and warm his hands feel on me and that he hasn't removed them even though I've regained my balance.

As if reading the thought in my mind, Anthony drops his hold and tucks his fists in the pockets of a black peacoat. The jacket is unbuttoned, revealing a knit sweater with a dramatic white-and-black pattern that is probably all the rage in New York. He also has on a set of black jeans that fit him *real* well.

I'm glad the winter chill is hanging around. Anthony Shelly looks equally good with and without clothes on.

"No, it's my fault. I saw you coming out of the shop, and instead of saying your name, I just walked straight into you. I don't know what's wrong with me." He untucks a hand, only to drag it through his hair and tug at the strands as his eyes meet and hold mine.

"No harm done. Did you want to talk to me?"

The idea of him seeking me out sends a happy tingle across my shoulder blades. My wings are hidden away, and I have the urge to spread them wide. But unlike sirens, whose transformation only involves sprouting wings, a harpy's second form is so much more.

Full-body feathers. Talons on fingers and toes. My face even takes on birdlike qualities.

I adore my other form, but I know plenty find looking at it disconcerting.

Christian did.

I shove away thoughts of my ex when Anthony responds.

"I do." He gives his hair another tug, then drops his hand before continuing, "Can I ask your opinion about someone who lives in town?"

Interesting. "I won't gossip, but go ahead and ask."

"Violetta Radeva."

Even more interesting. Now, I'm kind of regretting my no-gossip policy because I'm suddenly rabidly curious about why Anthony's asking.

Does he want to date her?

The thought erases all my wing tingles.

The witch is old enough to be his mother, but she doesn't look it, and as long as two people are consenting adults, age is just a number.

Still, the idea twists my stomach in an uncomfortable way.

No. Nope. You cannot have a crush on this man. He is not for you.

I'm a small-town harpy, looking to start a family. After spending my night scrolling through his social media, I can tell that is *not* the lifestyle he lives. Anthony Shelly spends his days —or more accurately, nights—in clubs, drinking high-end liquor, driving luxury cars, flying in private planes, staying in penthouses, even walking in the occasional fashion show.

Meanwhile, I'm picking up my normal outfit of scrubs that usually—but not today because Esme is magic—smell like dog vomit.

So, if he wants to have a fling with the older but more elegant witch, that makes more sense than flirting with me. And I'm not going to disparage the woman out of jealousy.

"She's a sea witch. Powerful. Mother of Levi Abadi, who's the monster council member on the Folk Haven Mythic Council. Formally mated to the Leviathan of legend, but single now, as far as I know." Those are all pieces of information he would've picked up from living in town long enough, and they're facts, so they don't feel like gossip to me. And because I'm generous, I add a piece of my own knowledge. "She has beehives and asked me out to look them over. They were well maintained and cared for. I often judge people by how they treat animals."

Anthony frowns. "Do bees count as animals?"

"Of course they count. Without bees, we'd all die, magic or not. Pollinators are precious."

The redhead stares at his shoes. "I guess I ranked pretty low on your judgment then. Didn't bother making friends with the snake."

His dejected stance has me chuckling.

"I'm sure it was scary for you. And when I came in, you didn't immediately start screaming, *Kill it! Kill it!* So, that's a point in your favor."

Anyway, why would he care about the opinion of a small-town vet? This man makes the world fall in love with him every single day.

The thought sticks with me, and I study Anthony Shelly. He has a skill set that could come in handy.

He lifts his chin, meeting my eyes with a rueful grin as he combs his fingers through silky red strands.

Hell, I'm halfway gone for him after just a handful of conversations.

He's exactly what I need.

"Thanks for the Violetta insight. It was helpful."

"You're welcome." I shift my dry cleaning to my other arm, the load getting heavy. Or maybe I'm hesitating over my idea. It's bold, but I think that's what I need.

Go for it. The worst he can say is no.

"I have another forty-five minutes of my lunch. Would you want to grab something to eat with me? My treat." I square my shoulders, imagining my wings are extended to give me confidence. "I have a favor to ask."

5

———

ANTHONY

DESPITE THE CHILL in the air, I don't mind that Zara chooses a food truck with only outside seating for lunch. Ever since the interaction with Violetta yesterday, I've felt cornered. Trapped.

I spent all morning walking on a trail along the shores of Lake Galen, the lake that Folk Haven had been built on, trying to work off some of the energy that had kept me up all night. My designer loafers did not appreciate the dirt and stones. Neither did the soles of my feet. I need to buy some hiking boots.

Wait, what?

I've never owned hiking boots in my life. I can't remember a time I even went into an outdoor supplies shop. That's a different kind of influencer. The wild-adventure ones. I'm all about luxury products and experiences.

But right now, all I want to do is sit at this picnic table in the Chattahoochee National Forest and eat food from a truck with a harpy wearing medical scrubs that do nothing to show off her deliciously curvy figure.

"Here. You said choose my favorites, so I got an everything bagel with garlic hummus, turkey, and cheddar cheese. And if you'd rather go the sweet route, I got a blueberry bagel with cream cheese, honey, and strawberries. Which sounds good?"

And so this dance begins.

I'm not a turkey fan, and I have an intense sweet tooth, but I know what's going to happen the moment I point to the blueberry bagel. Zara's face will fall because she'll suddenly realize that's the meal she actually wants. It's inevitable.

So, I point to the everything bagel.

"Good choice." Zara slides the food across the table, grinning broadly as she settles on the bench opposite me.

But ... that's not right.

"Wait." I study her face, searching for that flicker of jealousy. Of craving. "Don't you want this one?"

Instead, there's amusement with a tinge of confusion. "I like both of them. I don't care which I have. They're both good."

What's happening?

"But you're sure you don't want *this* bagel, the one that I'm about to eat?" I speak slowly, giving her time to catch up.

Zara looks at me like I'm being odd, which, to anyone who hasn't lived my life, I am. "No, Anthony. I don't want to take your bagel from you. What's up? Do you not like either choice? Mary Jo has others."

Maybe *now*, she does. But that line of customers at her truck window will find themselves all craving a sweet bagel the moment I join them. I'll get to the front, only to learn she's sold out.

There are side effects of having other people covet the things I have and the things I want.

"No," I assure her. "The ones you got are fine."

Zara leans her elbows on the table and stares into my eyes. "What's going on, Anthony?"

I'm on the verge of giving her a charming smirk, a disinterested shrug, and biting into the food in front of me. But something about Zara has me wanting to tell her the truth.

"I want the blueberry bagel," I admit.

"Okay. You changed your mind?"

Agreeing would be easy, but also a lie. "No. I thought you would."

Zara pauses in the act of sliding the sweet treat across the table. "You thought I'd offer you a bagel and take it away from you?"

Fuck. I should've just eaten the everything bagel.

"Can we not talk about it?" Self-conscious, I feel a flush overtake my cheeks and wonder why it is I blush so much around this woman. "You said you have a favor to ask me."

The harpy doesn't respond at first. She finishes pushing the blueberry bagel in front of me and takes the savory one for herself, then pauses. "This is the end result you wanted, correct?"

"Yes," I mutter.

Great. Why do I always have to act like a weirdo around her? Normally, I'm smoother than this.

Also, normally, I don't care what people think.

But I realize with Zara, I do care. A lot.

She takes a bite, then smiles as she chews, her eyes closing in bliss. At least I didn't ruin her lunch. Also, we're going to need to drag this talk out because watching her take so much pleasure from eating her food is making me hard.

After Zara swallows, she fixes her warm brown eyes on me. "I want your advice on how to make myself desirable."

MORE desirable? Please, gods, no. I can barely handle what you've already got going on.

"The thing is, I haven't dated anyone other than my ex since high school. I'm not sure how to go about it. And I think it would help if the men I'm potentially pursuing are attracted to me to begin with. They might even approach me first, which would be fantastic. Would save me a lot of effort in trying to pick up social cues I'm not sure I'd recognize. If we were birds, I could just show off some colorful plumage or something. But we're not birds. Well, I kind of am. But on my current list, I have a bear shifter, a kappa, a dragon, a merman, and two werewolves. I don't think any of them would be attracted by my plumage. So, what do you think? More cleavage? Men like boobs, right? At least Christian—" Her teeth click—she snaps them together so fast.

Christian. Who is this Christian who loved her boobs?

Can I murder him?

I'm not sure where that impulse came from. I'm not a violent man. Normally, you have to care about something to get into a rage about it. But I've spent my life doing my best not to care about anything.

Why would I bother if I could disappear at any moment?

"Anyway," Zara says, "what do you think? Any influencer tips you could give me about making myself more appealing?" She leans back in her seat, arms spreading wide. "I know I'm not a six-hundred-dollar bottle of tequila, but if I were the product, how would you sell me?"

I wouldn't. I would keep you for myself.

Instead, I keep that thought to myself. "That's not ... exactly how it works."

Her arms fall, and she picks up her bagel.

"Never mind. Silly idea." Zara bites into her sandwich and stares at the table between us rather than meeting my eyes.

Her disappointment guts me. And as much as I hate the idea of her pursuing dragons and mermen and all those other fuckers she listed, I can't *not* help her.

"It wasn't silly. It's just ... you're giving me more credit than I deserve. What I do, there's no real skill behind it."

Zara meets my eyes then, her black brows furrowing. "Of

course there is. Even if people threw a bunch of expensive stuff at me, I'd never be able to make the photos you do."

"Yeah, well, I have a team that helps usually. But what I'm trying to say is ..."

Shit, I don't even like admitting this to myself. Much less out loud. But the beautiful harpy is gazing at me with those big eyes that I want to sink into and share all my secrets with.

"It's magic."

Just the word has me cringing.

She looks perplexed. "But you said you're not a witch."

"I'm not a practicing one." I pick at the paper my food is wrapped in, the topic of the conversation making me twitchy. "I refuse to use my abilities. But there are some that are innate."

"Like Ame sensing desires?"

"She told you about that?"

All witches have a specialty skill, a kind of magic they are particularly good with. In the Shelly family, the skill tends to be related to emotions, and my younger sister is a desire witch. That sounds sexier than it should. She's not like a succubus. Ame can sense and influence other people's desires, but she rarely does so.

Zara nods. "Soon after she started working, I asked if she was uncomfortable making eye contact because she was always avoiding mine. I didn't want to make her uncomfortable by trying to catch hers. She explained about the magic, and, well, Ame is lovely, but I'd rather her not hear everything I want. A woman's got to have some secrets, you know? So, I chatted with Mor, and she gave me a few mental exercises she used so I could build a barrier in my mind to block Ame out." The harpy gives a triumphant smile, tapping her forehead. "Now, it's super easy. I pretty much do them all the time without thinking about them."

I lean forward, fascinated. "Are you doing them now?"

"Yep."

"The bagels," I mutter, realizing what must have happened.

Zara glances at our food. "Are we back to that? I'm not trading again."

"No, sorry. I mean, it's all connected." I realize I'm tugging my hair, so I drop my hand and affect a nonchalant air. "My magic is covetous. Or jealousy. When I express interest in something, other people tend to want it."

Zara's eyes widen. "Seriously?" She glances at our food. "So ... you thought when you said you wanted one bagel, I'd go for it, and you'd be left with the other." She points to the blueberry in front of me. "The one you actually wanted."

"It's sneaky," I admit. And I blush again, damn it.

Zara doesn't appear offended, only thoughtful. "Kind of, but I get why you do it." She takes another bite, chewing and studying me.

I eat while I give her time to think, and I groan at the delicious bagel.

Hell, this is as good as any from New York.

Fuck that ridiculous diet Julia had me on. If food this spectacular exists in the world, I'm not about to deny myself the chance to taste it just so people can count the muscles on my stomach.

"Delicious, right?" Zara smiles as she pats her lips with a napkin. "Mary Jo says the trick with bagels is the water quality. She's friendly with a water nymph who purifies a batch for her every few days. My week is not complete without a Mary Jo bagel. Also, she's my best friend, so if I didn't patronize her shop, she'd give me shit." Zara glances over her shoulder toward the truck, where a white woman with ombre-green hair is serving customers.

And also staring at us.

"Can you make people want things they don't want?" Zara asks, bringing us back to the uncomfortable original discussion.

"I'm not sure." I don't test my magical limits. They terrify me. "Maybe, if I practiced the craft. Cast spells on people. But if you're asking if my picture with a six-hundred-dollar bottle of tequila has someone who buys boxed wine changing their mind on a trip to the liquor store, I doubt it. I think they have to partially want something already, and I direct that craving. Or amplify it. My followers want a luxury lifestyle, so they get the products I pose with. Does that make sense?"

Zara nods thoughtfully as she wipes crumbs from her lips.

I wish I could do that. With my mouth.

"And you think because I'm shielding myself from your sister, I'm also shielding myself from you? And if I wasn't, because I was already in the mood for a bagel, you would have influenced which one I chose, just by expressing interest in it?"

"Precisely."

I take another bite of my food, savoring the sweet berries, mixed with rich cream cheese and chewy bagel, which has just a touch of salt. Magnificent. Mary Jo has herself another devoted customer.

"Darn." Zara shoots me a rueful smile. "Wish that could work for me."

I swallow. "What do you mean?"

"Amping up interest in me is what I am looking for. Giving someone who might want to date me the little nudge they need. Especially in this town, where so many mythics live and you're never sure if someone else is open to an inter-mythical relationship. Having that extra push would be nice. I'm not looking to trick a guy into dating me. Just knocking down some of the social barriers that get in the way."

As I absorb what she said, Zara gathers her trash onto her plate and makes ready to leave. "My break is almost over. Keith needs a chance to eat too. He's grumpy if he misses a meal."

Zara doesn't realize that while she talks, my mind is turning over a possibility I shouldn't let myself consider.

But I want it. I want her. Just for a little while.

Just a taste.

"We could do that," I announce.

She pauses, glancing my way. "Do what? Feed Keith?"

"No. That guy can find his own food. I meant, we could use my powers for you."

I shouldn't be doing this for so many reasons.

Magic is a corrupting force that I should avoid.

I'm leaving this town, and I shouldn't develop connections with people.

And I shouldn't help a woman find a husband when I'm the one who wants her in my bed.

But my mouth decides to go off without me, forming a plan that gives me the chance to stick close to Zara.

Maybe touch her.

Maybe kiss her.

"We could pretend to date. Go to places where the men on your list would see you with me. See me wanting you. If any of them are interested"—and why wouldn't they be? She's funny, intelligent, and gorgeous—"they'll feel the urge to pursue you themselves."

As Zara mulls my idea over, I finish my bagel and try not to look too eager, even as my knee bounces under the table.

But after a moment, she shakes her head with a frown, and my gut plummets.

"That's generous of you, but I don't think I can. It feels too much like a trick. I don't want to lie to the person I plan to marry." She gives me a rueful smile. "Five years from now, I don't want to say, *Oh yeah, I pretended to date Anthony Shelly to make you magically jealous.*"

Damn her noble heart. Now, I want to kiss her neck, tell her she's a good girl, then have her ride my cock as I whisper naughty words in her ear.

Fake dating wouldn't give me that chance. But something else might ...

"Then, let's really date."

My libido is immensely proud of this decision. People dating get to fuck.

Zara blinks at me. "What?"

"Temporarily," I clarify. "I'm in town until the end of May. We could date while I'm here. The real deal, only with an end date. Not a lie." Excited by the prospect, I lean forward, pressing my point. "Think about it. This would work on multiple levels. You get more dating practice since you said you've been out of the game. My magic will encourage already-existing interest. Plus, your prospects will know you're open to an inter-mythical relationship."

Because despite my not practicing magic, people will still think of me as a witch. In this case, if it gets me time with Zara, I find I wouldn't mind the label so much.

The harpy's eyes go unfocused as she considers my proposal, and now, both my knees are bouncing, and my hands are sweating as I think about holding her, touching her, kissing her.

Might make me want to extend my stay.

But I won't. A little over two months, and I'm gone. Zara will go on to get married and have her monster baby and live the happy life she dreams about.

The one I can never give her.

But I *can* give it to her. Like this. By making the men of this town stand up and pay attention to the jewel among them.

"That's a kind offer," she starts, and I can see it in her face. The refusal.

I'm out of my seat, around the table, and at her side in the space of a breath.

"It's not," I murmur, gently pinching her chin with my

fingers, relying on the seduction skills people claim I have. "It's selfish really."

As my eyes hold hers, I watch her pupils dilate.

"Selfish how?" she whispers.

Leaning in, I place my mouth against her ear. "Because dating you means tasting you." I trace my tongue along the shell of her ear and enjoy the way her body shivers in response. "And I'm so fucking hungry."

"Goddess!" The gasp has us pulling apart, and I glance over my shoulder to see the bagel maker has left her truck to gape at us. "Sorry to interrupt. But ... are you two dating?"

"Uh ..." Zara flicks her eyes from her friend to me, back to Mary Jo.

I leave the decision to her, trying to look encouraging rather than desperate.

The harpy swallows hard.

"Yes. Yes, we are."

6

———————

ANTHONY

Before parting from Zara, the woman I'm now dating—and I have to keep repeating that fact to myself until I believe it—I ask her for Violetta's address. I figure if she went to check on the woman's bees, she knows where the witch lives.

The house I pull up to looks more like a beach house than a lake house, but I guess that makes sense for a sea witch.

Why am I here?

There was something about my talk with Zara that had me reconsidering my immediate dismissal of the woman and the coven. Maybe there's another solution. A compromise we could reach. If I can get Mor what she wants, maybe I won't feel like such a shitty brother while I stay in Folk Haven these next few months.

When I reach the front door, I intend to ring the bell, but before I can press the button, the door swings inward. As if welcoming me.

Creepy.

"Hello?" I call out into the house, not about to enter someone's home just because the door is open. "I'm looking for Violetta Radeva," I add.

"In the kitchen," a voice responds. "And wipe off your shoes."

I look down at the front mat and don't know whether to laugh or be unnerved by the words displayed.

Go away.

"Believe me, I don't want to be here," I mutter.

I clean the soles of my shoes off the best I can manage before stepping inside. The door starts to swing shut before I'm clear of it. I jump out of the way, and it snicks closed.

Extra creepy.

I find the witch in the kitchen, stirring a large pot that's boiling and steaming.

What kind of potion is she brewing in there?

"Sorry to disturb you in the middle of casting. I can come back another time."

I'm backtracking when her voice stops me. "Creamy carrot and ginger."

"Excuse me?"

Violetta turns with a smirk, her sharp blue eyes taking in every hint of my reluctant stance.

"I'm not brewing potions, you skittish little rabbit. I'm making creamy carrot soup." She affects a thoughtful expression. "Although you're not the rabbit, are you? The one they took from the sorcerer is. A rabbit. A firebird. Lovely feathers, I've heard. Wouldn't mind a few for myself. Mythical feathers have power, you know. If you ever get your hands on some, keep them close. Firebird, phoenix, siren ..." A smile curls slowly over her lips. "Harpy."

Okay. Violetta Radeva officially knows too much and is scary as hell.

And I've put myself directly in her path.

But if I act like the scared rabbit she described, she'll probably hunt me down just for the fun of it.

"Thanks for the tip." I put on my *bored at the club* tone and stroll farther into the kitchen, leaning a hip against the butcher block island. "I'll make sure *not* to do that because, as I said before, I don't use magic."

The witch snorts and strolls to her fridge. She pulls out a pitcher of brown liquid, then plucks a glass from a cabinet and fills it.

"Here. Sweet tea." Violetta presses the glass into my hands. "Southern hospitality requirements fulfilled." She leans in, whispering, as if she has a secret, "I'm not actually Southern, but my son says I scare people."

Her son is right.

"Nothing wrong with being a little scary," I say aloud.

Violetta steps back, stare curious.

As she studies me, I let my gaze wander around the kitchen. The place is a cottagecore wet dream. All wood and windows, plants with vines dripping down the cabinets, copper pots and pans neatly hanging from the ceiling beside drying herbs.

"Your aura is all over the place," Violetta says, calling my attention back to her. "I've never seen the like."

The words cut into my gut. Of course she hasn't. I'm like no being she's met before.

"Look at that." She waves at the air around me. "More spikes and loops spilling everywhere. You're a mess."

"Thanks so much," I deadpan. "My head will explode with all these lovely compliments."

Violetta snorts, then squints her eyes at me. "Why are you like this? Your brother isn't. Neither are your sisters. They're powerful—a touch untamed, but put together for the most part."

Instead of answering, I sip my sweet tea. The mixture is thick, coating my tongue with sugar.

And so freaking delicious.

The witch watches me, the weight of her gaze heavy. Or maybe it's the weight of her power. Violetta is not a woman to be underestimated.

"I'm hoping we can find another solution," I say to fill the stretching silence. "One that allows my siblings to become members of the Folk Haven coven without my participation. I'm only here temporarily. When I'm gone, I could swear never to return."

Hopefully, Broderick, Ame, and Mor would be up for visiting wherever I am. Even though I don't want to live in this magic-filled town, the idea of being barred from it chafes. Still, I'm here to compromise for my family.

"Why don't you want to join the coven? We're an impressive group. Largely because I'm a member." She speaks so matter-of-factly that I find myself fighting a smile.

But the humor flees as I give my normal answer. "Like I said, I don't practice magic. Never have. Never want to."

Violetta tilts her head, studying me like a bird of prey. "Why?"

"I don't need it. Living life as a human suits me. I have an impressive bank account without it."

"Oh, silly boy." She returns to her stovetop to stir her soup. "Keep your secrets—for now—but don't lie to me. We both know you have all that money *because* of magic."

I bristle, setting my glass down on the counter, the sweetness turning in my stomach.

"I don't know what you're talking about."

Liar, liar, designer pants on fire.

Violetta spoons out a sample of the mixture, sipping the hot liquid, then tosses the used utensil into the sink, all before turning to me.

"You have a pleasant face, fit body, sinful smirk, but none of that draws people to you like your magic does. You know that.

And you hate it. But you keep letting your magic use you. You're right. You don't practice the craft. You're like a child with a grenade." She smiles, but the expression reminds me of a shark. "You're dangerous."

"I'm not," I protest.

I'm no one. Yeah, I have millions of followers, but I might as well be a pretty cardboard cutout to them.

"Oh, really? Let's test that then. Make a post." She drums her fingers on the wooden countertop. "Tell your followers you love … ivory. Straight from an elephant's tusk." Her blue eyes clutch mine, making it impossible to look away. "How long before their population is decimated? How many vegans will tear apart their morals to please your out-of-control magic?"

"I-I'd never do that. That's not how I work." I hope not anyway.

I thought I was telling Zara the truth—that I can't make people want something they don't already have a small craving for.

But what if I'm wrong? What if my magic is growing, getting stronger?

What if I'm dangerous?

Violetta keeps smiling. "Really? Doesn't sound like fun?"

"No."

Her face goes hard. "One day, you *will* do that. Maybe not on purpose, but you'll say something, and you'll change the world. Your magic is wild, and you've put yourself on a stage in front of millions. You are dangerous to your audience." She circles the counter slowly, and I feel like I'm being stalked. "You are dangerous to *us*. Your own kind."

"I'm not your kind." My voice is desperate as I take in her words.

"You're a Shelly. You're a witch. Say it. Admit it."

"I'm *not!*" My hands slap down on the counter, and the

whole room shakes. "I'm not real! I'm just ... I'm just ..." I pant, the confession on the edge of my tongue.

The blue of her eyes seems to glow.

"Tell me," she commands. "What are you then, Anthony Shelly?"

Don't say it. No one can know.

I haven't told anyone. Not even my brother.

He's not my brother because I'm not real.

"I'm a copy!" The confession roars out of me. "I'm a fucking duplicate! A magical replication of Broderick!" After all these years, the truth spills from me. "I. Don't. Exist."

I still remember the day my mother told me. My tenth birthday. She was being kind, attentive, caring. All things she normally was not. Not that Helena Shelly was cruel exactly. More like dismissive. Her children didn't interest her unless she could use them.

Starved as I was for her affection, I convinced myself she was being nice because it was my birthday. Then, she took me for a walk through her workshop until we came upon a fish tank with two beautiful clown fish.

"See those, Anthony? I've had them since they were little eggs. In fact, I only had one egg at first. I used my magic to make a second. Now, I have two fish. A real one and a magical copy. Watch this."

She pressed her palms to the glass and pulled in deep breath after deep breath. I watched in fascinated horror as one of the clown fish broke apart into sparkles and shimmering scales, all drifting toward my mother, infusing her hands with a subtle glow.

"That's you, little Anthony. I only had one baby in me, but I wanted to see if I could make another." She rested her hand on my head. "I made you with magic. Every little bit of you. Isn't your mother amazing?"

When she smiled down at me, her hands still shimmering with the fish she'd absorbed, terror infused my body.

Could she break me apart as easily?

Do I truly exist?

"Ah." Violetta's sighed word brings me out of the recollection. Her smile has lost the sharp edges, but I wouldn't call it comforting. "Now, we're getting somewhere."

7

————

ZARA

I HAVE A BOYFRIEND. An almost-but-not-quite-a-witch boyfriend.

Or wait, do I? We're dating, but that's a label he might not want to use right away. It's just that Mary Jo left a long rambling voice mail along the lines of:

"You got yourself a hot-ass boyfriend! Is he down for the Monster Baby Plan, or are you just going for a fun ride? Oh my goddess, please tell me he's as good in bed as he looks. If he's a bad lay, I'm going to burn this entire town to the ground because the world doesn't make sense anymore. He's just too gods-damn gorgeous. I need to know more about your lickable boyfriend—who I will not lick, of course, because he's yours. Call me and tell me all the deets, pleeeease!"

So, yeah, I've got the B-word on my brain.

There's a knock on my front door.

Anthony texted ten minutes ago that he was on his way over for our first date. Which is also my *first* first date in years. I had a hell of a time trying to pick something out to wear.

53

I figured cute floral dress. Then, I looked outside, saw it was raining, then looked at the thermometer, and saw it was still not spring temperatures.

Hopefully, jeans that make my ass look peachy and a sweater that gives good cleavage will do. And since I never wear these clothes to work, they smell nice and have no stains. *Go me!*

As I hurry toward the door, I check to make sure the low neckline doesn't show off any of my lacy bra. Good to go.

Is Anthony a boob guy?

He never answered when I brought it up at our lunch.

All he said was …

"Dating you means tasting you."

So, oral? He wants to go down on me? Or just kissing?

We didn't clarify any of this, and the lack of answers has my nerve endings tingling, feathers threatening to pop free as I reach for the door handle.

Dating at least means kissing. Boyfriend means sex. Maybe? But is that what he is? Gah! I don't know!

I want more control in this situation. Parameters so I know where we stand, what he plans to do to me, and what I can do to him.

"What do I call you?" I ask the moment I open the door, which is good because once I take the man in, I need to relearn how to speak.

The redhead's tousled hair looks as silky as usual and seems to glow in the light of my porch lamp. He has on the same black peacoat he wore before, but this time, underneath, he has on a shimmering red shirt that's molded to his chest, which has me recalling the morning I walked in on him in nothing but briefs.

I kept dirty thoughts to myself that day because I was there in a professional capacity.

And also, he hadn't talked about being hungry for me yet.

"Anthony works. Did you forget my name already?" He smirks, props an arm on the doorframe, and leans toward me, holding my eyes with his smoldering gaze.

Oh goddess. Can our first date be in my bed?

No. No, we need to go out. I need to practice dating someone new, and we need to be seen for word to get around that I'm open to inter-mythical relationships and if his magic is going to work.

"I didn't forget your name, Anthony Shelly. I meant, are we just casually dating, or should I call you my boyfriend for the next few months? Whatever you're comfortable with—"

"Boyfriend," he says, adding a definitive nod. Then, his mouth gets a devilish curve. "Or lover, if you'd like."

Oh, yeah. We're definitely having sex at some point.

Guess I'll be able to give Mary Jo an answer.

"How about shmoopy-poo? Or snuggle bear?" I ask while locking my front door.

"Please yes." His voice is dry. "And definitely call me those in front of Broderick. I don't think my brother has enough in his mockery arsenal."

I turn to find him smirking down at me. My whole body responds to his sarcastic words, tensing and tingling. "Got it. Snuggle bear shmoopy-poo lover it is."

Anthony slips his hand into mine, lacing our fingers together and tugging me toward a car I think might be worth more than my house.

"You'd better stop that dirty talk now, or we're never going to make it out," he mockingly scolds, then opens my door for me. He even goes so far as to gently cradle my head as I climb in so I don't bang my forehead on the low roof.

Why is that so hot?

GPS tends to malfunction in Folk Haven, so I guide Anthony to the bar we're hanging out at tonight. Local Brew, owned and operated by the werewolf pack. Though mythics of all kinds and humans are welcome, and plenty go because it's one of the few places to hang out in our small town.

"How do you like the car?" Anthony asks as he guides the smooth driving machine down the two-lane road that heads from Of the Wing territory into town.

"It's nice. Pretty." I glance over my shoulder. "Would never work for me though."

"Why not?" Anthony tilts his head my way, listening closer.

"There's no backseat. Or much of a trunk." When I choose a vehicle, I don't care what it looks like, other than not white because those show dirt so easily. "I want space. Can't haul things in this. Can't have a pet in here. Or a car seat for a monster baby."

His eyes skip to the side, then back to the road. "You make a compelling argument."

"But you look great, driving it." I don't want Anthony to think I'm passing judgment on his car choice. To each their own. "I'm sure your followers love it."

"They did," he agrees. Not elaborating.

"Past tense?"

"I posted about it last month. Pictures went viral. The company's stock went up."

"Sounds like a job well done."

He nods, again staying quiet. That seems odd to me. Wouldn't a guy who's constantly doing new things, visiting amazing places, and tasting high-dollar food and liquor want to brag about it a bit? Or maybe he gets his fill of that online.

Or maybe he thinks I can't relate, so what's the use of telling me?

That thought doesn't offend me. It just makes me ... sad.

Anthony and I live such different lives. This small overlap of time we have, it might be fun—possibly the sexiest moments I'll ever experience—but temporary is all it can be.

We're not meant for each other.

The rest of the car ride is quiet, broken only by me handing out the final few directions, but when Local Brew comes into view, my excitement for the evening rekindles.

I'm on a date! With my sexy, funny boyfriend!

As long as I focus on those facts, there's no reason to mope.

Anthony acts the gentleman, helping me out of the car, again guarding my head, and when he places his hand on my lower back as we head into the bar, I hope the padding in my bra will hide the jagged mountain peaks my nipples have become.

After the drizzly chill outside, the interior of Local Brew is bright, warm, and welcoming. There's a decent Friday night crowd, but the place doesn't feel overly full, and I recognize a good deal of the faces. A lot of people in town have pets, which means they come to my office regularly.

Hopefully, I can make it through the night without having to discuss animal ailments people think they can get treated for free when I'm not in my scrubs and on duty.

"What can I get y'all?" Griffith, a werewolf and the bartender, calls out.

"I'll have whatever wheat beer is on tap," I tell him, then expectantly turn to Anthony to find him chewing on the corner of his lip, indecisive as his gaze flicks to the other people lining the bar.

A lot of them are glancing his way.

Is it because he's new to town?

Because he's here with me?

Then, I remember the bagels.

Are they all waiting to see what he orders?

I tap him on the chest, capturing his attention. "Let me treat? You get the next date. And I'll order you something. A surprise. Just tell me what you definitely *don't* want."

His gaze warms, and he leans down. "Not a fan of IPAs. And

don't order anything you'll want to drink later because there's a good chance the keg will be kicked."

The heat of his breath on my ear has my skin feeling too tight, and I want to strip off all my clothes. But I stay dressed.

"Got it."

When the wolf returns, I ask for their red ale. The color makes me think of Anthony's hair, and he looks good, holding the glass when I pass it to him.

"Do you want to play pool?" I ask, spying two open tables in the back.

"Pool sounds great. But I should warn you: I'm terrible."

"Perfect, because I love winning by a large margin." But when I move toward the pool tables, I watch as other patrons converge, claiming both before we're halfway across the room. "Wow. Those filled up fast." I glance up at Anthony to see his face fall. Then, I realize what happened. "You wanted to play, so now, everyone does?"

He grimaces my way. "Sorry."

"Don't be. You can't help it." An idea comes to me. "Close your eyes."

He flicks a curious look my way but then follows my instructions. I wrap an arm around his trim waist, enjoying the warmth of his skin through his shirt.

"Wha—"

"Trust me. Keep your eyes closed. Hold your beer. Let me guide you."

"That was a lot of instructions, and I'm a simple man." Anthony smirks, and, goddess, I want to kiss those sassy lips.

"I believe in you," I say instead.

Once we reach our destination, I let my arm slide away from his waist.

"Can I open my eyes now?"

"So impatient. Not yet." After setting my beer on a tall table,

I grab all the darts from the dartboard I led him to. Now, no one can claim the board if Anthony says he wants to play.

Technically, I could tell my date to open his eyes now, but I decide to be bold.

Rising up on my toes, I press a quick kiss to his mouth, enjoying the slight gasp he makes before breaking my rule and opening his eyes to gaze down at me.

"Darts." I hold the feathered objects up to show him. "Wanna play?"

Anthony stares at my mouth, then glances around the bar, realizing that we have control of the board even if someone else takes interest.

He turns a grin on me. "Get ready to get spanked."

"You're that good at darts, huh?"

His eyes flash with desire. "Who said I was talking about darts?"

He sips his beer after the heated comment, and I scoop my drink up, needing a big gulp to cool me down.

I haven't been this horny in public in ... ever.

Well, maybe in high school, when my hormones kicked in for the first time. I definitely got distracted in a few classes, fantasizing about—

Nope. Not going to think about *him* when I'm on a date. A date with my new boyfriend, who can make my nipples hard just by grinning.

"Here." I shove the green darts into his hand. "You go first. Try not to get distracted by my spankable ass."

"Impossible," he murmurs. Then, he lets the first dart fly without breaking eye contact.

8

ZARA

Anthony is terrible at darts.

He only gets one on the board, and it's in the farthest circle. But what I love is his ease with being bad. He doesn't bluster or get frustrated or make excuses.

Instead, he jokes and teases, and, well, he does make *one* excuse.

"How do you expect me to stare at the target long enough to aim when you're wearing those jeans? And that top? I require ten more darts to compensate for these distracting conditions."

He says all this to me while I take my turn.

Heat flushes through my body at the compliment. Guess my date outfit was a good choice even if it's not as high fashion as that snazzy red shirt he has on. The thing looks like pure silk, and I want to run my hands over the material.

Instead, I focus on the game.

"It's entirely fair." I throw one dart, and it sticks one loop out from the middle. "You're over there with that gorgeous hair"—another throw, just as close—"in that tight shirt"—

another dart almost kissing the red center—"when I know exactly what's underneath"—final dart hits the center—"and I'm still dominating."

With a triumphant grin, I turn to Anthony, planning to taunt some more, only to find the man up in my personal space, stern expression on his handsome face.

"You're not doing it right."

"I just got a bull's-eye!"

"Did you?" He saunters up to the target, as if he needs a closer look, then bends over to pluck one of his pathetic darts off the floor. "Well, let me show you how to hit the *right* spot."

"You're ridiculous," I tell him as he curls my fingers around the dart.

Then, the tempting man moves behind me, wrapping one arm around my waist to rest on my belly, and the other drags down my right arm until he covers my hand with his and guides me into a throwing position.

"Now, what you want is a firm grip." His breath teases against my ear, making my shoulder blades tingle.

"Firm grip. Got it." I bite my lower lip to hold back a smile. "Then what?"

"Then, you aim exactly eight inches above the target."

"Eight inches? That's oddly specific. I'm not sure I can judge that without a ruler."

"Really? I happen to know exactly how long of a distance eight inches is." At that moment, Anthony pulls me tight against his body, and a hardness presses against my ass. "Just know that if I tell you something is eight inches, you can trust me."

My cheeks hurt from trying not to smile. "Of course. I would never doubt you. Any other dart-throwing wisdom?"

His teeth nip my ear, and he guides my hand into a gentle arch. "Chuck it."

My dart thunks against the wall and falls to the ground.

"Perfect." The word rumbles with a chuckle, and I don't know if I want to laugh with him or drag Anthony to the restroom and get on my knees for him.

Turning in his arms, I gaze into the face of a devilish man. I imagine him lying in a bed, surrounded by rumpled sheets, reaching for me.

"You're thinking dirty thoughts." He cups my cheeks, thumbs brushing light strokes over my skin.

Kiss me. Kiss me. Kiss me.

"Completely innocent. You can trust me."

His lids lower until I know all he's staring at is my mouth.

"Hey, do you mind if we have a turn? I've been dying to play darts all night."

Reluctantly turning away from Anthony and the heated tension between us, I spot two mermen standing by the board, our darts already in their hands.

Well, shit.

I'm a second away from scolding them for cleaning up our game—what if I were keeping score?—when I catch sight of Anthony's tense jaw and downcast eyes. Gone is the confident, flirty man from a moment before. His whole posture screams, *This is my fault!*

I don't care about the game. All I want is to have a fun night with my magical man. I only have a limited number of nights before he leaves town.

"Yeah. We're done." Scooping up our beers, I stroll across the bar to an open booth, as if this were my plan all along.

For a man who has a lot, he seems to get plenty taken from him.

"Sorry about that," Anthony says the moment he settles onto the padded seat beside me.

"I'm going to need you to stop apologizing. About the magic. I don't get mad at people for something they can't control."

The not-quite-a-witch stares at me. "I'm going to kiss you. It's out of my control. You can't get mad."

Despite his claims, he waits for my response.

"Oh no. Poor me."

Sliding my hand up to the back of his neck, I pull him close. Then, I pray to The Winged One that Anthony takes over because I've only kissed one man in my life, and I'm not sure if I'm any good.

What I discover surprises me.

Anthony kisses with his teeth. In a good way. In a *very* good way.

He tricks me into thinking he's soft with gentle strokes and presses. Then, suddenly, he's biting my lower lip, and the pricks reverberate through my body until I'm sure he's somehow pressed a second mouth between my legs.

What kind of magic is this?

But it's not magic because he doesn't practice the craft. This is just him, rocking my world in public.

Public.

"Curse it," I mutter, managing to pull back far enough to speak, even as Anthony tries to chase my mouth with his. "We need to stop."

He does, but his eyes stay on my lips as he licks his, and he is a fucking hell-dimension demon for doing that. "Why exactly?" he asks.

"Because at least six different people in this bar have pets, and I will not be able to look any of them in the eye if they see me orgasm in public," I mutter, low enough so only he hears.

Anthony jerks his head back, and then I watch the most self-satisfied smirk spread over his face.

"Oh, no. Neither of us wants that." He picks up his glass and drinks deep, eyes on me the entire time.

I grab my beer, take my own big swallow, and realize I'm almost out. Good. I need an excuse to get some space from his sexy orbit. My skin feels tender, ready to burst out in feathers.

"What do you want next?" I tap a short nail against his glass. I always keep mine cut low so I don't accidentally scratch an animal when handling them. "Whisper it to me. No one will know."

Anthony stares at me for a moment, then leans close, bringing the subtle scent of his cologne with him.

"Your cunt."

"By The Winged One!" I exclaim, shoving him back against the booth seat and pinning him there with my hands on his chest. "Anthony Shelly, you have a dirty mouth."

He gives me a wicked grin that sets my shoulder blades tingling. "You can shut me up by sitting on my face."

I have to walk away now, or I'll be at risk of doing just that.

Next up on Veterinarians Gone Wild ...

With a glare that has no heat because I'm also fighting a smile, I climb out of the booth. On my short walk, I suck in a few bracing breaths. Being with Anthony is like nothing I've ever experienced before. The man radiates sensual energy, and I want to bask in the sensation.

When I reach the bar, Griffith steps over to take my order.

"Do you have any red ale left?" I ask, hopeful.

"Sorry." He offers an apologetic smile. "That one's been selling well all night. Ran out 'bout fifteen minutes ago."

Of course you did.

I'm browsing the other selections that aren't IPAs, considering the honey lemon sour, when I feel the presence of someone behind me. Not wanting to hold up the line, I point to the sour, and the bartender gives me a thumbs-up.

It's not my cunt, but I think Anthony will like it.

"Zara. Can we talk?"

The familiar voice leaches away all my good humor, and I turn to find the last man I want to run into while on a first date.

My ex.

9

ANTHONY

My eyes haven't left Zara since the moment she walked away from the table—when you've got an ass like that to watch, why look anywhere else?—which means I see the moment her relaxed posture goes rigid in response to some guy approaching her.

This is how it starts.

All my brief relationships inevitably end when another person comes along and woos my partner away from me. They can't seem to help themselves when my interest makes my lover so much more tantalizing than they were in the past.

I knew by coming here, somewhere public, people would see Zara with me, and if any of them had even the slightest attraction to her to begin with, it would amplify until they wanted to approach her. Shoot their shot.

Please turn them all down. I want my full time with you.

As I watch, Zara shakes her head, and relief washes through me. For tonight, she's still mine.

But the guy doesn't take the hint. He takes a step closer.

"Fuck that." Moving faster than I knew I was capable of, I'm out of my seat and across the bar, just in time to hear his next sentence.

"You're wearing my favorite sweater," the big blond asshole says with a knowing smile.

That trips me up. There's familiarity in his tone. As if he *knows* Zara. Knows what's under her sweater. Like he's seen all her sweaters and gotten to peel every single one off of her.

Note to self: buy Zara new sweaters.

But whatever claim he might have had on her, that's in the past. This guy is not part of the Monster Baby Plan, nor is he her temporary boyfriend.

I am.

"Hey, shmoopy-poo." I slip in beside Zara and press a kiss into her hair. Gods, she smells good. Like a crisp breeze in spring when the flowers have just started to bloom. "Thought you might want help carrying the beers." Turning, I eye the suddenly surly white guy, who's glaring at me and my arms around the beautiful harpy. "Who's your friend?"

Maybe I shouldn't antagonize the man. He's fucking huge. This guy could grind my bones to dust and make me into a loaf of bread. He's a fucking giant.

Do giants still exist? I thought they died off centuries ago.

Either way, in a fight, I would lose. Badly. One punch from his meaty fist, and I'd be in the hospital, trying to remember my own name.

But I'm not about to let the threat of an ass beating stand in the way of supporting Zara. With my body pressed against hers and a close view of her face, I realize now how uncomfortable she is around the man.

"Anthony." There's a hint of relief in her voice that solidifies I'm not leaving her side. There's a touch on my back, and I realize she's fisting a hand in my shirt. "This is Christian Trader. Christian, this is Anthony Shelly. My boyfriend."

Fuck yeah, I am.

The guy's frown digs deep ridges into what is normally a handsome face. "Can we talk?" He doesn't look at me again even though I feel animosity radiating my way.

"We've said all that needed to be said," Zara tells him. "I think it's best if we move forward. If we both move on."

A muscle flexes in the guy's jaw. "All I want is to talk. I think I deserve that much."

Zara's shoulders hunch forward.

No way am I about to stand here while this guy guilt-trips her. I don't care if she murdered his entire family; he's not getting anything from her she doesn't want to give.

"Sorry, Christian. Zara's schedule is all filled up. Got to book with her *months* in advance. And I'm signed up to publicly make out with her for the next two hours, with a generous side of heavy petting. Then, there's the private stuff we've got planned. Trust me when I say, she might not be able to talk for a few days if I do things right. Anyway, I'm sure my snuggle love bear is flattered by your attention"—I cup her shocked face and rub our noses together like the most sickeningly cute couples do—"but I refuse to give her up for even a moment."

The bartender arrives with our drinks. Perfect.

I push one glass her ex's way, hoping it's whatever Zara ordered for me. "Here's a beer for your trouble."

The man gapes at me, but I wear my most innocent grin as I scoop up Zara's hand and hopefully her drink.

"Now, lover, let's return to our booth and suck face."

She follows my tug, not even bothering with a good-bye to the guy.

Of course, we can't return to *our* booth since someone has already snagged it, but I find one farther in the back. More privacy, which is better anyway.

"Was that okay?" I ask the moment we sit down. "You looked like you wanted to get out of there."

Her wide eyes meet mine. "That was perfect. My goddess." She presses a hand against her chest as a giggle sneaks out. "I shouldn't laugh. Christian ... he's a good man. But I do *not* want to talk to him." She smirks my way. "Especially when I'm booked to suck face with you."

The heat in her eyes has me wanting to lean in and fulfill the promise I made. But some traitorous part of me is still hung up on the tense exchange.

"So, that was an ex-boyfriend?"

Zara's playful smile slips away, and she reaches for her beer. "Fiancé."

"What?"

"Ex-fiancé," she clarifies. "We were engaged."

"And you ..."

"I broke it off."

"Did things end badly?"

Zara twirls a strand of dark hair around her finger. "Not exactly. But they didn't end well either. He didn't want to have a baby with me."

Seemed like that guy was desperate to give Zara anything she wanted, but maybe that was just me amplifying things with —*It's okay. I can think it at least*—my magic.

"He's not into kids?"

"No, he was." She trails her fingers over the woodgrain of the table. "We talked about it a few times before getting engaged. How I wanted to have just one, and he was fine with that. How he looked forward to starting a family and being a father." Her hand curls into a fist. "But it wasn't until after we were engaged that I found out he didn't want to have that kid with *me*. A harpy. He told me we should use a surrogate and have a human baby. Or adopt."

My mouth gapes so wide that a bat could fly into the thing. I snap my jaw shut before stuttering the only words I can manage. "I ... why?"

Zara sighs with a grimace. "He said having a mythical child would be too stressful. Too much extra work. That humans were easier. That our lives would be better if we had a human child." She gazes at me, her eyes glassy. "All I could hear was him passing judgment on me. That *I* was somehow wrong. That our child would be wrong and too much work for him." She sits back hard against the booth, blinking the moisture from her eyes and sucking in a deep breath that squares her shoulders. "I don't need a harpy baby. Or a monster baby. If I can't get pregnant, then I would be open to a surrogate or adoption. But I do need a partner who will love our child, no matter what." She throws her hands up. "And humans are stressful too! What if we had a fussy kid? Or one with a mental or physical difference? Would he have just left us because our child wasn't some mild-mannered doll?" She scowls at the tabletop. "What if we went to an adoption agency and he only wanted to look at the white children? What if raising a child with skin like mine was *too stressful*?"

There's a strange mixture of emotions in my chest. One part of my heart breaks for Zara. Another part of me rages at the man who hurt her.

But another part of me is on the verge of laughing in disbelief.

That massive motherfucker was scared of a little harpy? And most mythics don't even display their magical side until puberty. Sure, a teenager with wings is an added stressor, but I'd be more concerned about raising a kid in the age of cell phones. There's a lot of creeps on the internet.

If I had a kid with Zara, there would be a strict internet policy. Child locks on all the devices. I would be the nosy dad, always asking who my kid was texting—

Wait. What the hell am I even imagining right now? Me, a dad?

Impossible.

Refocusing on the conversation, I ask the first question I can think of. "Did you say all this to him?"

Zara nods. "Didn't make a difference. Not really. He said he understood, but still only wanted a human child. It didn't feel like he *truly* understood. And it brought other things into perspective. Shone a light on the issues in our relationship I'd never looked too hard at. So, I ended things."

"Sounds like you made the right choice."

"Yeah." Zara sips her beer, quiet for a stretch as she stares at the table. When she speaks again, the words are so full of emotion that my body aches for her. "But it also felt like I was so close to getting the future I wanted—the little family I dreamed of—only to wind up at the beginning again. Starting from scratch. I don't need it—marriage, baby, all that—tomorrow, or a week from now, or even a month from now. Of course, if you ask Ba and Dada—my grandparents—the sooner the better. But they've been on my case for a decade. Me wanting a kid, it came about in the last few years, once I realized I was ready to take that road in life. And now, I have this longing in me." Her fingers dig into her chest, like she'll open a compartment and show me where that craving lives. "And the fear that it'll never happen."

"You're really set on that future, huh?"

Her expression softens into a wistful smile. "Maybe it's silly, but I was an only child, and I loved it. My mom and dad are great and have always made me feel special and loved. We would go on adventures together. Set up elaborate picnics in our backyard and play card games. My mom took me flying on dark moon nights, just the two of us. My dad raised me on cricket and would bowl me balls until his arm went numb just because he loved watching me perfect my form. We'd build blanket forts on rainy days. They still have my old tree house in their backyard." She sighs with a content smile. "We feel like a team. The Ironfeathers against the world."

What must that be like? Two loving, devoted parents.

My parents love each other—and *only* each other. The rest of the world are tools to be used. Objects to be experimented on.

"I'm sorry." Zara throws me a sheepish smile. "This is boring first-date talk. Especially when all this is temporary. No need to grill you about your long-term relationship goals." She pats my knee, then gives it a squeeze. "Thank you for listening though. And sending Christian off. I'm going to go use the restroom."

She slips out of the booth, and I watch her hips sway as she strolls across the room.

The image she painted of her childhood wasn't boring. Not it all. Just different from what I knew. But there were parts that overlapped. Growing up, I went on adventures, only they were with Broderick and we were usually escaping our parents.

As I watch Zara reappear and head to the bar to order more drinks, the werewolf bartender leans across the countertop, getting closer to her to hear over what is not particularly loud music. Then, he says something that has her laughing.

Jealousy swamps me.

Is he one of the werewolves on her list? Is he asking her out right now?

Breathing through my nose, I unclench my fists.

Zara is dating me for the next two months. She's mine.

For now.

10

ZARA

THE DATE WAS GOING WELL until Christian showed up.

I guess, in the grand scheme of things, it's good he saw me with Anthony. That he knows I'm moving on and it's time for him to do the same.

But what about Anthony's magic?

The last thing I want is for Christian's love for me to be further inflamed.

Because I do know, no matter how things ended between us, Christian did love me. Or part of me at least. He loved the small-town vet who would watch movies with him and cook dinner with him and go to the bars on nights off. He loved the idea of us getting married, living on the lake with his fishing boat parked at the dock, us having a dog or two or three together. He loved sitting on the back porch in a set of rocking chairs, watching the sun set as we shared some beers and I told him about my day and he told me about his. Christian loved the idea of us one day having a kid together.

But when we talked about that dream, truly dug into it a few months after he proposed, I realized the sickening truth.

There was a part of me—an internal, unchangeable part—that Christian did not love.

Still, he convinced himself that didn't matter. That he could love enough of me to make it work.

But I don't want someone who loves pieces of me. I want someone to love the whole of me.

Christian didn't want to accept that explanation when I gave him back the ring.

What if Anthony's magic makes Christian more persistent?

I suppress the concern by reminding myself that I have the final say of who I'm with, and if I don't want to be with Christian, then I won't be. As simple as that.

"I must be bad at this whole dating thing." Anthony's comment pulls me out of my wandering thoughts, and I glance toward the driver's side, only then realizing we're parked and we've made it back to my house.

"Gods, I'm sorry. I was in my head. Got caught there."

Anthony hits me with one of his lazy grins that sends flutters through my chest and straight down to the space between my legs. The man is a handsome demon, and he knows it.

"Exactly. If I were good at this, you'd only be thinking about me."

He unbuckles his seat belt and leans over to my side of the car. His face is inches from mine, and I breathe in his subtle—no doubt expensive—cologne and lick my lips in anticipation of his kiss.

But Anthony only unstraps my seat belt and returns to his side of the car. "Let's take a stroll to your dock. Show me this lake everyone in this town is so impressed by."

Anthony slips out of the car, and by the time I think to reach for my door handle, he's already around the hood and opening it for me, offering his hand like a true gentleman.

"Thank you," I murmur, still recovering from the almost-kissing moment. I find it more disconcerting, not getting to taste him when I thought I would. Now, I'm hungry for his mouth.

But he only slips his hand into mine and guides us toward the stone path that curves around to the back of my bungalow, connecting to the stepping stones that lead down to the lake and my floating dock.

The night is quiet, but not silent. There's the lap of small waves against the clay shoreline, interspersed with the squeak of bats and the occasional owl hoot. As we step onto the sun-bleached wood, I hear the slap of a fish tail in the water, and I wonder if it was some trout. Or maybe one of the merpeople have drifted into this cove.

Unlikely, as they tend to keep their other-form swimming to dark-moon nights when sightings are less likely to happen.

"All right. Maybe this is mildly enchanting." Anthony draws me with him to the edge of the dock, then pulls me into his arms, my back against his front.

A delighted shiver travels through my body, spurred on by the press of lips against my neck.

"You're not bad at this whole dating thing," I tell him, hoping he hears the honesty in my voice. "This is one of the best dates I've been on." Because this one had me laughing and excited and feeling both cherished and lusted after. What more could I want from a romantic outing?

"Well, it's not over yet." He tongues the pulse pounding in my neck.

"It's not?" My voice is a breathy tone I don't recognize.

"Of course not," he scoffs, regaining a touch of his arrogance, making me smile. "You haven't orgasmed yet."

That has my mind tripping, stumbling to a stop, then reversing to replay the words.

No, I'm pretty sure he said what I think he did.

"I ... what?"

"What's a date without an end-of-the-night orgasm?" Anthony asks, as if he's saying, *What's dinner without dessert?*

But these are not the same things.

"Well," I say, "I think it still qualifies as a date."

Anthony drags his hands up my sides, then back down again, the touch tantalizing. "No. Definitely not." The wicked man resumes kissing my neck, only to pause the torturous act to ask, "Do you want this to be a date, Zara?"

And I know what he's actually saying.

Do you want an orgasm, Zara?

Christian and I started going out in high school, and I've never been with anybody else. Maybe I should be easing into this.

But we only have a few months.

And ... I kind of want an orgasm.

"Yes," I say.

"Thank the gods," he mutters, his fingers finding my waistband.

"Here?"

I thought he was going to ask to go inside my house. But now that I think about it, I'm not sure when the last time I did a thorough cleaning was. Would like a chance to run a vacuum through the place before I have any guests over. Especially a guy who's used to five-star luxury accommodations.

"I like it here." Anthony's voice is smooth.

The opposite of my pounding pulse as his touch delves under my clothes, past the lace of my underwear to tangle in my intimate curls.

"And I like the idea of you remembering this every time you're down here," he says just as he slips a finger past my folds to graze my clit.

My hips jerk back, pressing my ass against his erection. The knowledge that he's hard for me makes me wet.

Which he immediately discovers.

"Do I do this to you, Zara?" One of his digits curls in my slickness, emphasizing the question.

I reach back to grip his hips, needing something to hold on to. "Yes," I gasp when I realize he's waiting for an answer.

Must have given the right one because he sinks inside me, two fingers, two knuckles, a delicious invasion. There's a skittering sensation over my skin, the ghost of feathers ruffling. I don't sprout any, having long ago controlled the urge. I know Christian found my other form off-putting.

Don't think of him. Think of Anthony.

Then, he thumbs my clit, and it's easy not to think at all.

"Oh! Oh ... oh ..." I moan the exclamations as he draws me closer to the soaring sensation I crave.

Anthony nips at the sensitive skin of my neck. "I'm yours, Zara. Use me."

I suck in a breath at that, the rush of excitement at potentially having power over this charismatic man.

"You want me to be in charge?" I ask, my voice tight with need.

"Yes." He licks my racing pulse. "Do whatever you want with me." He slips a third finger inside my heat as his thumb keeps rubbing my clit. "Make me beg. Make me crawl." He spreads me wide. "I'll kneel at your feet, wait for you to let me bury my head between your thighs." The fingers curl, stroking my inner walls, as his other hand cups my breast and pinches a nipple through two layers of fabric. "Anything, Zara. I'll do anything for you."

"Goddess," I gasp as the simple description of what he's willing to do sends my pleasure soaring. Then, I clap a hand over my mouth to stifle a scream. It would be horrible to thank Anthony for this mind-shattering orgasm by rupturing his eardrums.

One of the potential pitfalls of hooking up with a harpy.

My body shudders, then flies with the release. As I lose track of myself, brain sent whirling with pleasure, I don't know if I'll float off among the stars or topple into the lake.

When I come back to myself, Anthony has his arms banded tight around me, maintaining my balance for me.

"Wow." The single word is all I can manage.

Anthony nibbles on my earlobe. "*Now,* we can call it a date. And I very much look forward to dating you some more, Zara Ironfeather."

Then, the man slips his fingers—the ones that were just inside me—past his lips, tonguing my arousal, as if he can't get enough of the taste.

This is either an utterly amazing idea or an extremely terrible one.

11

ANTHONY

The morning after my date with Zara, I wake up to a full bed. But not a bed full of a beautiful woman.

Once again, there is a reptile lounging next to me.

"Snake! Fucking gods-damn snake!"

Just like the last time, I fumble and fall out of my bed before scrambling from the room, not giving the snake a chance to decide if it wants to munch on my leg rather than simply sprawl out next to me. In a familiar move, I take refuge on the top of my kitchen island, using the high vantage to glare around the space, searching for any way the creature could have broken in. I would feel a draft, wouldn't I?

The days are cool, and the snake's body is thick. If there were a hole large enough for it to squeeze through, I think it'd be pretty obvious.

It's not.

I have a teleporting snake.

At least I know who to call this time.

Despite my discomfort with waking up next to a scaly intruder, I am suddenly less annoyed, knowing I'll get to see my harpy sooner than expected.

My fingers are quick on my phone, finding Zara's name in my Contacts. Maybe she'll think I'm weird for calling immediately after our date, but at least I have a legitimate reason. And honestly, even if I didn't, I still would have called her this morning.

Or texted.

Or sent a picture of me shirtless.

I don't have a lot of time in this town with Zara, so I'm going to use every moment of it.

Maybe I can convince her to take a leave of absence from work, and we can spend all day in my bed.

As long as there's not a snake in it.

She picks up on the second ring. "Hey. I'm at work. Is this an emergency?"

"There's a snake in my bed."

Zara pauses, then says, "Are you talking about your dick?"

She can't see my grin.

"Remind me to introduce you to my brother. I think you two have a lot in common." Cautiously, I slide off the counter, feeling braver as I speak to her. "In that you often think I'm talking about my dick. Which, to be fair, I usually am. But not this time. There is a literal snake in my bed."

I can hear chuckling on the other end of the line, muffled, as if she has her hand over the mouthpiece. I find I don't mind it when Zara laughs at me. The situation is kind of funny.

"Will you come and save me again?" I press.

"Okay. Keith is here, so I can step out for a bit. And we're not too clogged up with appointments this morning. I'll be over soon, but I can't stay for long."

Damn. There goes my plan to replace the snake in my bed

with the beautiful harpy. But even getting a glimpse of her is worth it.

As I wait for Zara to arrive, I crack my front door. Luckily, today isn't as cold as it has been. Spring is finally here. Normally, I like the warmer months, but this time, I feel a sense of anxiety. The warmer it is, the closer to June we are. And June means I am leaving Folk Haven.

June means leaving Zara.

I've never felt this way about any of my partners before. Especially not after one date. I can't remember a time I used the title of boyfriend. If I did, I might have been drunk when I agreed to it. I don't drink as much as I used to, so I haven't been anyone's boyfriend in the last few years or else I would've recalled the momentous occasion.

But the moment that Zara brought it up, yes was my only answer. I want to claim her. I want to attach my name to hers. I want to wrap myself around her, both literally and figuratively.

This is not good.

But I can't stop myself.

By the time I hear the slight squeak of someone ascending the metal steps to my apartment, I still haven't made any headway on how I should feel or what I should do. All I know is that I have two months with a magnificent woman that I can't wait to taste again. And I want to drink directly from the source. Licking her off my fingers and watching her eyes widen during the act was satisfying, but only briefly.

I want more.

And now, I am half-hard in a pair of briefs, and the person who walks through my door is *not* the woman getting me aroused.

The new arrival is my baby sister.

Ame pauses in the doorway, looking over my scantily clad body.

"Did the snake steal your clothes?" she asks with a raised brow.

"Ame." I snatch a blanket off the couch and wrap it around my waist. "I called Zara."

As I watch my sister's face fall, I realize how harsh my comment sounded.

"I mean, come in." I gesture toward the interior of my rental. "You're here to help with the snake?"

Over my sister's shoulder, the face that I was expecting appears. Zara smiles at me, her eyes heating when she sees how few clothes I have on.

I love my sister, but I wouldn't mind if she decided to head out immediately.

"Well, look at you. Giving everyone a view. I brought Ame with me because I thought she might be able to have a chat with your snake buddy. Seems the little creature has developed a liking to you. Hopefully, Ame can convince it to give you some space."

My sister lingers by the door. "Do you mind that I'm here, Anthony?"

The humor on Zara's face fades at Ame's hesitant question. Which only drives home how much of a jerk I naturally am to my sister.

"Of course not. I was just surprised. And if you think you could get the snake to leave me alone, that would be fantastic." I give Ame the most generous smile I can manage even though my body clenches at the idea of her working magic in my apartment. "It's still in my bedroom. That's where my clothes are. And that is why I'm not wearing clothes. I swear I wasn't trying to put on a show."

I feel like I need to pretend I have some kind of boundaries when Ame is around.

"Okay. I'll go talk to them." Ame strides past me to the bedroom, leaving Zara and me alone in the kitchen.

The harpy meets my eyes, a huge smile returning to her face, even as her cheeks flush. Fuck, she's gorgeous. And I can practically hear her thinking about what we did last night. And if this continuous eye contact is any indication, she's not embarrassed in the slightest.

Zara knows what she wants.

And I figure she's the kind of woman who wants an up-front man.

So, why hold back?

"When can we go out again? Tonight?" I step in close to her, breathing in her scent of fresh air and spring flowers. "Let's go out tonight."

Zara chuckles and presses a flat palm to my chest, though she doesn't push me away. "You're that eager to lose at darts again?"

"You can beat me in any game you want as long as I get to give you the same prize at the end of the night."

The color in Zara's cheeks spreads down to her neck and over her chest, only to disappear into a set of aqua scrubs. I want to peel the medically approved material off her and map how far I can make that delicious color go.

"That is tempting." Her fingers tap on my bare chest. "But I can't tonight. I promised to watch a movie marathon with MJ. And tomorrow, I'm spending the day helping my mom and dad clean out their attic. How about Monday?"

Two days? Sounds like torture.

"Fine," I say while giving her my best brooding pout. The one that makes everyone change their mind and offer me whatever I want.

Zara only presses up on her toes and kisses my cheek. "Looking forward to it."

Guess I'm not as irresistible as I thought.

"Sorry to interrupt, but I don't think you're going to be able to get rid of the snake."

Both Zara and I glance at the doorway where Ame stands.

The black snake lies draped over her shoulders.

"What the fuck?!" I yelp, lunging forward to save my sister, but pausing halfway into the act, my arms outstretched and hovering in the air, worried if I make a grab for the animal, it might take a bite out of Ame.

She stares at me with wide green eyes. "It's okay. He won't hurt me."

"Ame"—I try to speak calmly—"whatever magic you're working, that's still a *wild* animal."

She's going to get herself mauled. And then not only will I lose my sister, but Jack will also disembowel me.

Ame's mouth quirks in a half-smile. "Maybe. But I think he's also your familiar."

"My ... what?"

That's impossible.

Ame reaches up to scratch the snake under its jaw. Like it's a pet. And the creature lets her, merely flicking out its tongue in response.

"His emotional grid is similar to Lucky's." She names her black cat familiar. "More complex than a normal snake. And the fact that he keeps approaching you makes the connect obvious." Ame offers me an encouraging smile. "He's your familiar. It's so nice to find them. Or have them find you, more like. I know Mor and Broderick are hoping theirs will come along soon." She moves to slide the snake from around her neck. "Do you want to hold him?"

"Hell no!" My feet reverse their course, and I stumble back across the room, hands held up in defense as panic cuts at my nerves. "I'm not a witch. I don't *want* a familiar. Don't need one. You're wrong." The volume of my voice rises with each declaration, as if that'll drive the points home.

Ame flinches, then ducks her chin. After a heavy pause, she murmurs, "I guess I could be."

Despite the inability to form facial expressions, the snake still manages to look dejected as he slips his long body off Ame's shoulders, drops to the ground with a thump, and slowly slinks out through the open front door.

"I'll make sure he gets back to the woods," my sister says, her focus on the floor as she follows after the slithering body.

"Anthony."

My stare connects with Zara's eyes, and my gut twists when I see the expression on her face.

Disappointment.

Please don't press me on this, I think to myself, wanting to say the words out loud.

This is the moment where Zara will try to tell me magic is a wonderful thing, only a tool to be wielded, and that I shouldn't dismiss it. The point Broderick is always trying to get me to consider.

I don't want to hear it from her. Don't want magic to poison our relationship.

"Listen—" I start, but Zara cuts me off.

"No. I need *you* to listen." She crosses her arms, gaze hardening to an unrelenting wall. "I know Ame is your sister and you have a family dynamic I don't know much about. But she is also *my* employee." Zara doesn't raise her voice, but every word is as unforgiving as iron. "I do not abide people shouting at my employees, whether they are related to them or not."

My mouth gapes in shock.

That's what she has a problem with?

Then, I think back on the last few minutes and how I talked to my sister. How she was trying to be helpful and I practically bit her head off.

If Jack were here, he'd already have his claws buried in my intestines for the disrespect.

"You're right. She didn't deserve that. I'll apologize to her."

Zara gives a short nod, then strolls out of my apartment without another word.

The space feels suddenly too big. Too empty.

And I wonder if I ruined things before they even started.

12

ANTHONY

THE HARPY who owns the apartment I'm renting also runs the dry cleaner situated underneath the living space. It occurs to me that as the owner of the building, she might want to know about—or better yet, be able to stop—the snake getting into my apartment.

Since my life is nothing but free time at the moment and I don't have a legitimate reason to bother Zara at her job, I gather up the pieces in my closet I've worn but can't go in a regular washing machine and head downstairs.

A little bell announces my arrival, and a white woman with golden hair and a welcoming smile sets down the pencil she was just sketching with.

"Anthony Shelly. How's everything working out for you upstairs?" Esme Sharpwing asks, every word she speaks so genuine and eager that I kind of feel bad I have to tell her about my unwelcome visitor.

"The apartment is grand. Everything I could need."

She wrinkles her nose with a smile. "I've seen your Instagram. I know it's more than a step down from what you're used to. Still, it's nice of you to be kind."

Kind? Me? Not likely.

And yet, when I open my mouth to tell her about the black snake, I instead say, "It's cozy. None of the places my agent sends me to are cozy."

Esme blinks wide eyes, and then her grin grows until it takes up a good portion of her face. "I guess Folk Haven does have that going for us. We're a cozy place." She tilts her chin toward my armful of material. "You have some business for me? I'm honored."

I saunter up to her counter and lay the bundle between us.

"Ooh. These pieces are so cool."

As she holds up each one, garments mainly gifted to me for walking in shows or posting for brands, my eyes skitter to the notepad she was writing in.

Correction: sketch pad.

On the sheet of paper is a detailed drawing of a gown. A fascinating design that seems to mimic scales.

"Did you draw this?" I tap a finger on the sheet.

Esme nods absentmindedly as she sorts my clothes. "That's the other half of my business. I make clothes. Most of the year, I'm working on gowns for the Halloween Ball. It's a big deal here."

"Really?" I didn't expect a small town to have a ball.

Esme smirks. "We might seem like a tiny place, but there's still power plays galore. And everyone needs the proper suit of armor." She waves toward the sketch, her expression turning playful as she mock whispers, "Consider me the local black-smith, getting all their chain mail ready."

I know more than most how clothing, or even lack thereof, is a powerful thing. What someone wears conveys a message or can act as a disguise, even cause a diversion.

"Clothing can be its own kind of magic," I murmur, more to myself than her, but Esme still responds.

"I think that too."

She rings me up, handing me a receipt that states my clothes will be ready in three days. But before I can turn to leave, she stops me with a question.

"Do you want to see my workshop? I have a few past the sketching stage." She throws a thumb over her shoulder toward the back of her shop. "Wouldn't mind the opinion of another fashion lover."

Unable to stifle my curiosity, I nod, and the harpy leads me deeper into Fresh Feathers.

Past the racks of clothes that are waiting to be cleaned, Esme shows me to a space that I realize is just below my bedroom. High windows let in afternoon light, illuminating an area filled with swatches of fabric, tall worktables, a high-end sewing machine, and multiple dress forms with gowns in all stages of construction.

A gold one draws me in, and as I stroll closer, I realize there's a thin gossamer lace over the top with a pattern that has me thinking of feathers.

"That's not for the ball." Esme comes to stand beside me, a dreamy smile on her face. "That's for my mating ceremony."

"Congratulations," I say and mean it. I'm conceited enough to admit that I was worried Esme might make a move on me. It's not the first time someone has used the pretense of showing me an interesting item to get me alone, only to flirt. "Who's the lucky ... one?"

She chuckles at my struggle to use a vague enough identifier that encompasses all genders as well as humans and mythics.

"He's a dragon. Sulien Blaythorn."

"Ah." I lean in to examine the expert stitching. "Monster baby," I murmur without thinking.

"What?" Esme chokes on a gasping laugh.

I try to cover my sudden embarrassment with a charming smile. "My apologies. Didn't mean to make an assumption that you would be having children."

"But if we did, they'd be a monster. That's what you're saying?"

Wow, it is suddenly hot back here. Obviously, not everyone talks about this subject as freely as Zara does. And that's when I realize how much I appreciate her candid nature. She doesn't put on a front or alter her behavior to try to please those around her.

I don't seem to either, but that's not the case. I do it all the time, but my accompanying smirk makes it appear as though I don't care what the world thinks of me.

"I didn't mean to offend you. Monsters are great. Monster babies are great. If Ame ever decides to have a kid ..." My stomach bottoms out at the thought. "Magic-wielding werewolves. Oh gods. They'll cause mayhem. And Jack won't hear a single word against them." I press a hand to my forehead. "It might be the end of the world as we know it." I meet the harpy's eyes, panic in my own. "They'll like me though, right? Because I'm their uncle, I have to get a pass."

Esme stares at me for a moment, then starts to chuckle, then to full-on belly laugh.

Rude. I'll tell my future demon nieces and nephews to go for her first.

"Oh goddess," she gasps, wiping tears from her eyes. "I guess that's one way to look at it." As her laughter subsides, she claps a hand on my shoulder. "A little bit of trepidation toward mythical babies is normal as far as I'm concerned. Parenting anything is scary. As long as you don't have monster prejudice, you're okay in my book."

She steps away from the golden dress and waves at a chart

hanging above a table that has a long list of names. "These are the orders I have so far for the fall."

There must be at least thirty.

"You make them all on your own?"

She nods and drags out one of the empty dress forms. "Luckily, I have a few special tools to help. Like this. Come here." She waves me over. "Put your hands on the shoulders"—I do—"close your eyes"—I do—"and think of someone you'd like to see in a gown."

Immediately, Zara comes to mind. In my fantasy, I dress her in that gold feathered masterpiece, the metallic color lying gorgeously against her tan skin, the mermaid shape hugging her ample breasts and wide hips.

Gods, I'd better not get hard in this shop.

"Open your eyes," Esme commands.

I blink my eyes open, then blink a few more times to make sure I'm seeing correctly.

The bust has changed. Before, it had the measurements a slim runway model might be required to match. But now, the silhouette is ... Zara's.

"How?" I ask in wonder, wanting to run my fingertips over the shape, but simultaneously not wanting to fondle an inanimate object in front of my landlord.

"I paid a transformation witch to spell them all. Makes it easy for me to adjust them to match the measurements of whoever my client is. Fewer alterations needed at the end."

For some reason, this magic doesn't cause the sticky fear to coat my insides. Maybe because my eyes were closed when it worked.

Or maybe because it's providing me with a hint of the woman I'm infatuated with.

"So, you model the clothes. Do you ever work on them? Ever make any?" As Esme asks, she shuffles through items on her workbench.

"I've made adjustments. When something didn't fit." I clear my throat and slip my hands into my pockets. "And I've made some suggestions to designers."

There was a man in Milan. He called me his muse. But in truth, I just told him what I wanted, and suddenly, he did too. I started to get … jealous. He was making the designs I wanted to. Using the fabrics I liked and the cuts I craved and hiring the models I admired.

It felt like he was stealing a piece of me.

But can anyone do that when I'm not even real?

Whatever the case, I left.

He still calls me, trying to convince me to come back to him. No matter the amount he offers, I told Julia it's always a no.

Never again.

Is Esme feeling the same draw? Does she want me to tell her what I like?

"Anthony?" When she says my name, I realize I've been quiet for a stretch. "Sorry if I touched on a tough subject."

Realizing then that I'm frowning, I let my face relax into my normal carefree smirk. "Not at all."

Her gaze narrows, and she snorts. "Fine. Anyway, all I wanted to say was that if you have any skill with a needle and you're looking for something to do while you're here, I'd be happy to have an extra hand. I can pay you. But, like, a normal amount of money. I'm not a high roller."

I don't need any money, I almost say. But instead, I consider her offer and that list of orders that will probably grow longer as Halloween grows closer. And how I'm bored, just waiting for when I can see my beautiful harpy again.

The thought of Zara pulls my eyes back to the dress form.

What if I hadn't told him my ideas? What if I had made them myself?

What if I made something so spectacular that even when I left this world, I'd still exist here somehow?

"I'll help you," I say, not letting myself talk me out of the idea. "But I don't want money."

"What do you want then?"

I sidle closer to the familiar form, this time allowing my finger to tease over the tantalizing shape. "I want to use this."

13

____

ZARA

THE THING about being a vet is that the job never truly ends. Even when I leave the office, peel off my scrubs, and shower away the animal smells, I still get calls and texts from family members, friends, and casual acquaintances, asking about their pet's ailments.

I have so many pictures of animal anuses on my phone that I'll never be able to wipe the memory clean. But I can't say no. Not when an animal might be suffering.

Which is why I spend the first part of my movie night with my best friend disinfecting cat scratches on the snout of her chocolate Lab, who is more interested in giving me kisses than sitting still.

"To be fair, I don't blame Lucky," MJ says as she sprinkles her own blend of spices on the popcorn she popped for us. "Crissy forgot how big she was again and bumbled into the poor kitty. Lucky swiped out of self-preservation."

I have to agree with MJ's assessment. Ame's cat is the witch's familiar, and the feline is pretty laid-back. Plus, Ame's mate is a werewolf, so Lucky is used to being around canines.

"They're not deep. Just keep them clean and make sure she doesn't paw or scratch at the area. Should heal fine." I leave the silly, panting dog in her plush bed and toss out the red-stained gauze.

Seeing Crissy—short for Croissant—makes me miss my old dog. He lived a long life, and it was time for him to go, but that doesn't do much to ease the ache.

Doesn't help that he passed soon after I broke things off with Christian. For the days afterward, I just wanted someone to hold me. Luckily, MJ is a good hugger, and so are my parents.

"Thanks for the after-hours surgery. I plan to pay you in snacks." My best friend holds up the bowl of popcorn with a grin I return.

"You spoil me. What will I do with my riches?"

As we tease each other, MJ and I settle on her couch. The forest nymph has a small house—even tinier than mine—but she's made every inch of the space cozy. Soft seats, warm blankets, and strategically placed lamps that let off a gentle glow. Even though we've stepped over the line into spring, this evening is chilly, and I appreciate the logs she's tossed into her wood-fire stove.

MJ doesn't live in a tiny home *exactly*. More like a tiny-and-a-half home. Up a set of steep steps is her loft bedroom, and the tall ceiling keeps the space from feeling claustrophobic. That, and the abundance of windows showing the surrounding forest. Unlike me, she didn't try for a space on the lake. As a mythic connected to nature, this is more of her vibe anyway.

Choosing where to live in Folk Haven is a delicate thing. Or more like a restricted thing. The town's founders set up boundaries based on mythical type—Of the Fin, Of the Claw, Of the Wing, witches, monsters, and a teeny section left for humans.

Based on your designation, you could buy a plot in an assigned area. My house sits in Of the Wing territory because harpies are considered Of the Wing. This organization might have made sense in the past. Might have been comforting for mythical creatures to know there was a safe place reserved for them in the world. But now, with so many of us mingling, the divides make less sense. Luckily, the town has no separations, and Mary Jo's house is technically in town limits.

But what about my future? If I mate with a non-winged mythic, will I have to give up my home? Move to monster territory because of our potential offspring?

When that future looks more like a reality, I'll talk to Moira MacNamara, Folk Haven's realtor. She's also a selkie on the town's Mythic Council, and I will petition that group if need be.

My child will already have to deal with enough subtle and outright racism as a person of color growing up in rural Georgia, I don't want them to be discriminated against for their mythic designation, too.

"What's on the marquee for tonight?" I ask to take my mind off the uncomfortable subject.

We tend to watch corny, old horror movies so we can laugh at the terrible effects and feel self-assured that neither of us would be so gullible as to fall for any of the villain's tricks. Then, I usually stay over, sleeping in MJ's bed, and we try not to scream at every random noise because we're actually a set of wimps.

"Oh! I heard of something I want to show you. It's short. I'll cast it on the screen, just a second." MJ fiddles with her phone and the remote. Despite being far out in the woods, she's made sure to have a good tech setup.

A second later, I'm wishing my friend had never even heard of the internet.

Because the image she brought up on her massive TV is of a

certain redhead looking handsomer than a man has any right to. And he's dressed in nothing but a towel.

"Oh my goddess," I groan, dragging one of the blankets over my head. I'm not sure if it's to hide from my friend's scrutiny or out of self-preservation because the hotness threatens to implode my brain.

"Exactly what I said. And then I drooled a little. And then I said to myself, 'MJ, only a bad friend would secretly salivate over her best friend's new boy toy. Do better. A good friend would bring up this picture and ask if the man can bang.' So, here I am, Zara, being a good friend and asking"—she rips the blanket off my head, and I see her evil grin—"can the man bang?"

"Where did you even get his picture?" I make a grab for the remote, but the nymph is tricky and shoves it under the couch cushion she sits on.

"From his social media. The guy's got loads more. I wanted to do a safety cyberstalk for you, and I found this!" She gestures at the screen, and my eyes can't keep away from the intimate view of Anthony's body.

Damn The Winged One's tricks. He looks like temptation just stepped out of the shower. His normally vibrant hair is a dark auburn because of the water soaking the strands. Anthony is lean, but his chest is chiseled, and all I can think is ...

Why the hell didn't I make him strip after our date?

"Zara?" MJ's voice is still light and teasing, but her tone has gentled a touch. "This guy is so hot that I'm concerned about him visiting my house because he might start a forest fire on the way here. Does the brain match the face? Is he monster-baby father material? You gonna put a ring on that?"

"I ..." An immediate answer eludes me. Those questions don't all pair up as well as MJ might think.

Because, yes, the brain does match the face. It surpasses the face. Anthony might pretend he's all surface, but I spent one evening with him and glimpsed beautiful depths I'd like to explore further.

Is he monster-baby father material? Well, not like I ever imagined. I had in mind a mythic who worked full-time in Folk Haven, who had a dad body and could most often be found in jeans and a T-shirt as opposed to whatever strange, fashionable outfit Anthony chose for the day. My plan includes minivans and responsibility. That's not really the vibe Anthony gives off.

But am I too rigid in what my idea of a father is? Did I just make my plan around a mythical version of Christian?

That's not what I want, is it?

However, when it comes to MJ's last question, the answer is clear.

There will be no ring on Anthony's finger.

He doesn't want one. This is a temporary arrangement.

And I don't see any reason to hide that from my friend. It'll keep her from building up her hopes and, in turn, keep me from muddling up mine.

"This is just a for-the-spring thing. He's taking a short break from work to visit his family. I ..." I realize I don't want to tell her about the covetous magic, suddenly feeling pathetic that I might need it to land future dates. "I need to get Christian out of my system."

"Well, damn. You found yourself a fine-ass man to help on that front. Sorry, but I need to go through a few more of these. For research's sake." MJ swipes and brings up an image of Anthony standing by a floor-to-ceiling window, gazing out at a city skyline, wearing an all-red suit, as if he were the devil, making a business deal.

"Oh, look," I mutter. "I'm pregnant. That did it."

Mary Jo cackles and scrolls through a few more brain-melting images of my temporary boyfriend. Part of me is giving myself a high five, part of me is considering feigning sick so I can leave and seek him out and jump his bones, and part of me is thinking ... *Why me?*

In middle school, I definitely went through a *hate the way I look* phase. Folk Haven has a lot of variety in its residents with mythics from all over the world looking for a safe place to live and raise their families. Probably more diversity than a small town in the South normally has. But that didn't stop the mind tricks hormones played on young girls when paired with what society labeled as beautiful. Even in this community, I noticed how the white girls my age were the ones getting sent flowers on Valentine's Day and asked as dates to the town's Halloween Ball and prom. That was one of the reasons Christian's interest meant so much to me. Possibly why I held onto our relationship for longer than I should have and forgave more than he deserved.

Now though, I love the curves of my body and the bronze notes of my skin and the fact that I can turn into a powerful avian mythic who can soar in the sky and rupture eardrums with my scream.

That's not why I'm wondering *why.*

The why has to do with Zara Ironfeather, small-town veterinarian who spends most of her time in scrubs and who hasn't traveled much and has no plans to. The woman who drinks cheap liquor on her nights off while watching bad movies with one of her few friends and dreams of adopting another dog one day and eventually starting a tiny family.

Why does Anthony—luxury social media influencer—want to spend even a few months with me? A night or two? Maybe. A quick hookup with a local? Sure.

But he's signed himself up for weeks.

I don't get it.

"Okay. I need a hot-guy cleanser. Let's watch some clueless college students get eaten by radioactive crocodiles." MJ switches over to a streaming service, resuming our normal routine.

"I'll make us drinks," I announce, filled with a jittery energy I want to dispel. Hopefully, some alcohol will do the trick.

While in MJ's compact kitchen, there's a buzz in my back pocket. I'm not on call, but I keep my phone on me just in case there's some massive emergency. But it's not Keith's name that lights up my screen.

Anthony: Are we still on for Monday? I am intrigued by these margaritas everyone raves about.

After the way we left things, me scolding him for the way he spoke to his sister, I can see why he might be unsure.

Me: I'm in if you are. And the margaritas get better, the more you drink.

Anthony: Ah, yes. So, like most alcohol.

Me: Exactly.

Three dots appear, then disappear, then appear again on the screen, and I like the idea that he's unsure of what to say to me. Anthony gives off an air of aloof confidence at all times. I want to unbalance him.

Anthony: If I tell you there's a snake in my bed, will you magically show up and tame it for me?

I turn my back on MJ, so she doesn't see my goofy smile.

Me: Is there really a snake?

Anthony: Depends on your definition of snake ...

Then, he sends a winky face, and I don't know why this terrible joke gets me, but I have to stifle a snort.

Me: I think you've had plenty of experience taming that anaconda yourself.

Anthony: Anaconda ... you flatter me.

Anthony: Do it again. I'm vain.

"Did you find the vodka?" MJ calls from the couch, which isn't that far away because, again, her place is miniscule. "It's in the freezer."

I try not to feel guilty that I was kind of sexting a guy when I'm hanging out with my friend. But also, not wanting to ignore him, I quickly send one more message.

Me: Monday.

As I grab the vodka from the fridge, I see the three dots pop up again. I hold my breath, and it bursts out in a laugh when I get his response.

Anthony: I'll bring my snake.

14

———————

ANTHONY

AME LOOKS surprised when I apologize to her, which makes me feel like an even bigger asshole.

"It's okay," she assures me as she sets her e-reader on the small table beside the overstuffed armchair she's settled in.

Despite the itching discomfort I feel around so many magical texts, I have to admit that Mor and Ame have done a great job at filling this library with the perfect *stay and read or study* furniture pieces.

If I did a photo shoot in here, would my followers suddenly want to educate themselves?

Or would they just make their homes into cozy hobbit holes?

Pushing away the thought, I refocus on my apology.

"It's not." I pace in front of her. "You were just trying to help. I shouldn't have shouted at you."

"You what?" The growl rumbles from the doorway, and I whirl to find Jack looming there. Other than being slightly taller than me, he's not technically a big guy, his body leaning more toward wiry than beefy muscle.

But the werewolf has an air about him that promises violence if you get on his bad side.

And anyone being even slightly discourteous to my sister earns themself a spot on his eternal shit list.

Wonder if I'll still have a job if he breaks my face.

"Jack"—Ame's voice catches her mate's attention—"I'm cold. Could you grab me a blanket?"

Indecision flits across his features for a moment, and then he stalks out of the room.

The moment he's gone, Ame turns wide eyes on me and mouths a single word. *Run.*

Don't need to be told twice.

I sprint in the opposite direction Jack went, feeling lucky when I reach the exit without encountering him. After slipping into my car and making my escape, I cruise toward town and consider what I should do for the rest of the day.

Bothering Broderick is always an option. He said he's at the university, grading papers in his office. Might be fun to go there and mix everything up.

I sigh and tap my thumbs on the steering wheel.

No, I don't want to bother my brother and make his life harder. What I want is to tease a pretty harpy until she blushes. But that's not an option until tomorrow night. Assuming Zara still finds me even mildly attractive after my childish display and the insensitive way I treated Ame.

Feeling entirely useless, I pull into an overlook that provides a sprawling view of Lake Galen.

"What am I doing here?" I ask my dashboard.

The thing is, I'm not entirely sure what the question is in reference to.

The overlook?

Folk Haven?

My existence in this world?

What purpose do I serve anywhere?

This isn't the first time I've pondered the question, and the answer is the same as always.

I serve no purpose.

But I suddenly have the urge to change that. To find something of worth, even just one thing, to make my footprint on this earth visible.

An idea, an uncomfortable one, comes to me. But I don't let myself reject it.

Even if I don't follow through with this plan, it'll fill some of this empty day. Pulling back out onto the road, I point my car toward an address I visited once before.

Violetta Radeva answers her door this time instead of having it creepily open for me. The witch stares up at me with a smile that makes me wonder if she just committed a crime. She's too satisfied with an aura of misbehavior floating around her.

Not that I'd know.

"So, the boy made of magic has returned. To what do I owe this pleasure, Anthony Shelly?"

My nerves itch at the description, no matter how accurate it is.

"I left our meeting abruptly last time. I thought you might be willing to talk again."

"Do you have anything interesting to say?"

"I ... no. Not really. Nothing new or intriguing. I'm a relatively boring person. I doubt people would find me so fascinating without my magic." I snap my mouth shut, shocked at the words that spilled out on their own.

Meanwhile, Violetta giggles. The lighthearted laughter makes her look younger.

"That was bad of me. But I wanted to see if this worked." The witch pulls a charm out from the neck of her blouse and slips the long chain it's attached to over her head. "Truth-telling. Not my specialty, but I managed it." Her thumb strokes the simple silver flower. "Took me three months to make, and the enchantment will wear out in two days." She tsks, then glances up, eyes narrowed, studying me. Then, Violetta sighs. "Here. Fair is fair. Give it a go."

She reaches up to slip the chain around my neck, and I feel the buzz of magic radiating off the silver piece.

Oddly, this sensation is almost pleasant. Like standing next to a friend. The charm doesn't seem to be trying to take anything from me.

Could I do it? Use a magical item?

All I need to do is ask a question. The one that comes to mind is ironic, in that I'm using magic in order to get the answer.

"Will you ever let my siblings in the Folk Haven coven without me declaring myself a witch?"

A satisfied smile curls her lips. "I will not."

Sighing, because I didn't expect anything different, I remove the charm from around my neck and hand it over to her. Violetta slips the item in her pocket and steps into her house, waving for me to follow.

"Let me show you my garden."

Garden. That explains the dirt under her nails.

Despite the open, airy layout of the house, I step carefully, feeling as though the calm interior is a mask for something more menacing. Like a trap could spring at any moment. But I make it to the back door without incident and breathe out a sigh of relief.

Violetta trots down a set of wooden stairs that lead directly into a gorgeous garden. The plants weave and tangle together, yet I get the sense there's an order to the disorder. That Violetta specifically wanted her plants to grow this way.

"Don't touch any of the leaves," she instructs. "Or the petals. Or the stems. Or the dirt." The witch tilts her head side to side, as if considering, then finishes, "Don't touch anything."

With those warnings ringing in my head, I tuck my hands into my pockets. Deep. As deep as they can possibly go.

And even with the ominous instructions, I still admire how gorgeous Violetta's garden is.

"Not exactly what you would expect from a sea witch, is it?" She arranges a floppy sun hat on her head. The accessory does nothing to ease her aura of intimidation.

Now that I consider it, she has a point. Sea witches bring to mind ... well, the sea.

A paved path stretches out just past the garden, and through the trees, I spy the sparkling waters of Lake Galen.

Even though Violetta now lives on a lake, surrounded by a forest, there are still ways she could bring the ocean to Folk Haven. But I don't see any signs of sand or shells or even simple designs that would indicate waves and beaches and sea creatures. Based off of what I view, if anyone had asked me, I would've identified Violetta as a wood witch.

"Is there a reason you've deviated so far from what one would expect? Are you perhaps hiding from someone?" I tease. "Should I treat you as an undercover agent?"

Violetta grins in the way that makes me wary of the expression.

"Not hiding. But there are certain people who would be glad to know where I am, and I find it entertaining to keep myself out of their view."

The witch walks through her garden, trailing fingers across the plants she warned me against. Maybe she was lying about the dangerous nature. Maybe there are safe plants interspersed among the threatening ones. Or maybe Violetta herself is one of the many threats in this garden, and like knows like. Whatever the answer, I won't be taking my hands out of my pockets until I reach my car.

"So, you're a sea witch who enjoys a beautiful garden."

"I was born by the sea. The salt water enhances my magic. And the magic that it enhances is *cleansing*."

The way that she says that last word has me pausing in my perusal. There's a hint of anger. Or disgust.

"You're not happy with your magical focus?"

"Cleansing. Bah. I have no interest in cleaning this world." Long, pale fingers pluck a bloom that she first cradles in her palm and then crushes to dust, letting the fragments of the flower scatter into the breeze. "There are so many more interesting things that one can do with magic. I have an aptitude for cleansing. If someone pays me enough money, then I will use that. But I'm not about to devote my life to something that holds no interest for me. And I have grown weary of the sea."

I'm intrigued despite myself. I've always thought of my relationship with magic as a sort of fight. Battling against a core part of myself that can't be changed.

But Violetta speaks about hers like a path she regularly decides to veer from.

But she's not made of magic, I remind myself. *Regular witches have more control.*

"Magic is natural to us," she continues. "All you have to do is make a choice to use it how you wish."

That's what Broderick is always going on about. How magic is a tool.

But I *am* magic, which only means I'm a tool too.

Broderick would probably agree with the label, though for different reasons.

"You make it sound easy," I say.

Violetta smirks at me, her eyes cold. "And you have made life hard for yourself, no matter that you attempt to exude a sense of not caring."

"My life is easy." I try to maintain my normal *don't give a shit* tone. "So easy that I'm not sure I even need to show up for it."

"Is that life?" Her voice is light, and innocent, and gutting. "Sounds more like dying to me."

My mouth opens to ask a clarifying question when I realize that I'm not sure I want the answer. So, instead, I force my own smirk, returning to what is easy for me. Not addressing what might be too heavy to bear.

Everyone else has muscles and bones and sinew, built to deal with the pressures of living.

But what do I have?

Are my bones real? Or are they full of holes that my mother's magic fills until she is tired of exerting the effort? Helena Shelly is an immensely powerful witch. I don't think it's out of the realm of possibility that she has been keeping me alive these past twenty-eight years and not even noticed the tug on her power. But a day might come where she does notice the slight itch in the back of her mind that is all that's tethering me to this world. And when she scratches, will my designer clothing fall to the floor, empty of the mockery of a body that once held them up?

"Look at you. So adept at lying with your face. I adore your mask." The witch purrs the words.

I wonder if I should be scared of Violetta. Maybe I am. But there's also something about the witch that I find comforting. Some touch of familiarity.

"Why, thank you." I grin wide. "I've worked so hard on it. Lovely when someone notices."

Violetta lets out a cackle and plucks a flower from her garden, extending the plant to me.

Is this the moment that I die? Can I be killed by this garden that is lethal to those who truly exist in this world?

There are times that I've considered if I have some type of immortality. If my lack of life means that this shadow of living will never truly end.

And still, I cling to the idea that death is a possibility. If only to feel more alive.

But I cannot find it in me to deny this small peace offering. I reach out and pluck the flower from her slim, callous fingers.

Nothing happens other than enjoying the soft brush of petals against my skin.

"Learn to control your magic," Violetta says. "You do not have to utilize it. But you must establish barriers."

My instinctual denial almost has me crushing the delicate bloom.

But Violetta isn't done.

"If you do, then your family will be accepted into the coven."

15

ANTHONY

When Zara opens the front door, her face is flushed and her eyes a tad wild.

"Sorry! I'm running a little late. There was a last-minute emergency at the office. A dog decided to eat an entire action figure. It was an interesting X-ray."

Ouch. Sounds painful.

I lean a shoulder on the doorway and give her a slow smile. "Don't worry about rushing for me. Take your time. I'll sit and watch you move." I'm just glad she didn't cancel after I was such an asshole to Ame.

Zara's nose wrinkles with her smile. "That sounded awfully suggestive."

"Good." Reaching out, I give a gentle tug on the end of one of her messy braids. "I meant it in a very suggestive way. Please be sure to do lots of jumping and wiggling and squatting while you're getting ready."

"You're terrible," she says, using a tone that makes me think she likes it. "And you look like a pirate. In a good way."

I glance down at the billowy black shirt I'm wearing, French-tucked into a tight pair of linen pants, the outfit rounded out with a set of thick-soled boots. She's right. I'm giving major pirate vibes, and I'm not mad about it.

"Will you be my booty?" I ask with a smirk.

Zara laughs as she waves me inside her house, and I try not to let on how eager I am to see where she lives. Despite my impressive fingering skills on the dock after our last date, I never got an invite into her abode.

Zara lives in a small house on the shores of Lake Galen. Broderick told me about the way lake property is partitioned off based on mythical type. I wonder what that means for Zara's future romantic plans. Will she and her partner of choice be able to live in this house? I guess if she chooses the dragon, that would work fine because he is a winged mythic. But what about the kappa? What about the merman?

What if she were to mate a witch?

And why would a thought like that pop into my brain? She doesn't have any witches on her list.

Shaking my head to get rid of the irrelevant notion, I let my eyes drift around the room she left me in. And damn if this isn't the coziest-looking spot I've ever seen. This is nothing like the loft that I had in London. I rented a place continuously because Broderick lived in the city, so it seemed like a good spot to have to come back to after I was done with jobs. Not that I was there too often. My agent had me traveling the world constantly. But it was nice to know that I had a claim on some small corner of the earth.

But was it mine, really?

Someone else decorated the rooms. Everything was modern and clean and completely lacking any kind of personality.

Not like Zara's house, which has a lived-in feel. The walls are covered in a sky-patterned wallpaper. The couch looks like I could sink into the cushions and take a long nap. There are blankets draped over the back, a pile of books on the coffee table, and an easel set up by the sliding glass door at the back of the room. In the fading evening light, the view of the lake peeking through the trees is gorgeous.

Between the easel and the couch, there's a plush dog bed.

Zara hurries back into the room, slinging a purse over her shoulder.

"You have a dog?" I nod toward the bed.

The excitement in her eyes dims as her attention lands on the cushion, and I immediately regret my question.

"I did. Marshmallow. He was this big, fluffy white malamute someone brought in a few years ago. They'd found him on the side of the road after a car nicked him. No sign of an owner, so eventually, I claimed him. He passed away a few months back. Old age." She throws a sad smile my way. "I keep telling myself I should get rid of his stuff or adopt a new dog, but I can't seem to do either. Not yet."

Zara sucks in a heavy breath, and I stroll across the room and wrap her in my arms. I've never been much of a hugger, but she brings the urge out in me. When she clutches my waist in return, I know I made the right choice.

Then, she releases her hold. "Come on. Time for you to experience Margarita Mondays at Marlin's Marina."

She grins up at me, and the shine in her warm brown eyes is so beautiful that I have to lean in for a kiss.

I make it quick, knowing if I go deeper, we'll never leave this house. "Do you want me to drive?" I ask against her lips.

I feel her smile.

"I'm going to drive. And we're not taking a car."

A few minutes later, we're at her dock, stepping onto a bobbing pontoon boat. I've been on Jet Skis, speed boats, and a few private yachts, but never a pontoon.

And yet this is the boat ride I'm most excited about.

"Best way to get to the marina is on the water," Zara tells me while untying the boat from the dock. "Life jackets are under the seat cushions. We don't need to wear them, but if we're pulled over, we want to be able to show them we have the proper amount."

"Pulled over in a boat?" I step onto the pontoon and cross to a bench seat, reaching for the little tab sticking out. "That would be a fir—fucking shit!" I leap back from the seat I just opened, my heart pounding frantically.

"What is it? Are you okay?" Zara drops the rope she was holding and hurries to my side, face creased in concern. "Is there something ..." Her question trails off, replaced by laughter as she leans over to look in the seat compartment.

"It's not funny," I mumble, which only makes Zara laugh harder.

"You *did* promise to bring your snake," she manages between snorts.

As the harpy takes great joy in my embarrassment, a familiar black rat snake uncurls from its life-jacket bed and slithers onto the bench seat.

"How did he even know we'd be here?" I grumble. "Are familiars psychic or something?"

The snake raises the upper half of its body, focused on me as its tongue flicks in the air.

Despite my annoyance at having the unwanted creature show up again, I have to admit, the thing is kind of cute with its triangular head and big eyes.

Oh no. It's getting to me.

And just when I'm about to put my unfeeling shields in place, Zara has to go and sit down in front of the snake and offer her hand to it.

"Lots of people are scared of snakes, but I think they're cool. And beautiful," she says.

The creature stretches its neck ... body—whatever—out until it can nose her knuckles. In a form of approval, it wraps around her arm, climbing the limb until the snake can drape itself over her shoulders. Zara's eyes shine with delight.

Seeing the two of them interact does something inside me. The way she easily accepts a beast that sends most others screaming.

This is the kind of woman who could love anything.

No. I grit my teeth. *Don't start thinking like that.*

Still, I don't have the willpower to dismiss the animal now that I know my harpy likes it. Especially after that Marshmallow story. With a world-weary sigh, I gingerly take a seat next to Zara and her new friend.

"I guess he needs a name. If he's going to keep showing up."

The grin Zara gives me is dangerous. "I've always thought guys with pets were extra attractive."

Fuck. Now, I can never get rid of him.

16

———

ANTHONY

THE MARINA SITS on the sloping banks of Lake Galen, and after Zara docks the pontoon, we have to climb a set of wooden steps on the shore to reach the restaurant. She said, normally, it's just a small place to grab food on the lake, but it transforms on Monday nights. The party going on inside is visible from the water, and the noise grows louder as we get closer.

"Are we crashing someone's birthday?" I ask as we approach the door.

Deterred by the ruckus, my new snake buddy opted to stay on the pontoon boat, curling up on a pile of rope like it was a cozy bed. Concerned about the chill in the air and having no idea how to take care of any living creature, I covered him with a dry towel and told him to find me if he needed me.

Seems he's good at that.

Zara offers me a beautiful grin over her shoulder. "This is a small town, and it's Margarita Mondays. Half the town is probably here."

Just outside the doorway, I pause.

Since I was a teenager and started sneaking into clubs, loud and outrageous parties have been a norm for me. This tiny marina shouldn't have me hesitating. But the thing about those places, those people, is that they were nameless faces that didn't mean anything to me. I would never see them again as I cycled to a new hangout each night.

But that's not how things are in Folk Haven. Everyone inside this marina likely knows who Zara is. At least the ones with pets do.

Everything I do tonight will reflect upon her. Will matter to her. If I'm a total asshole, which I often am, word will go around Folk Haven that Zara aligns herself with jerks.

"Hey. You okay?"

I blink and glance down to see that my harpy hasn't continued on without me. She's turned her back on the door to gaze into my face, a curious tilt to her brow.

I clear my throat and attempt an easy grin. "Just admiring the swing of your hips."

"I hope not. You had kind of a horrified look on your face."

"Oh. That." *What happened to my ability to be smooth?* "Just remembered I have to wait until the end of the night to peel those jeans off you. It's a terrifying concept."

Zara gives me a scrutinizing look, then slides her hand into mine. "Fine. Keep your secrets. But you look like a man who needs cheap tequila in a fun-shaped glass."

The warmth of her skin eases a touch of the panic in my chest. I can be a decent guy tonight. I won't embarrass her. "Right you are."

Only, when we step through the door, Zara is the one who comes to an abrupt halt this time.

"Oh. Shoot," she mutters.

"What?" I place a bracing hand on her lower back, worried what might have put that concerned look on her face.

She grimaces. "My parents are here."

Parents. Interesting.

I've never met the parents of someone I'm sleeping with before. For some reason, I'm excited by the prospect. I want to meet the people who molded Zara into the woman she is.

But the harpy doesn't seem overjoyed by the idea.

"Is that bad?"

"I don't know." She stares into my eyes. "It could be."

"You don't want them to know we're dating?" *Ouch. Why does that hurt so much?*

"That's not it. Not exactly." She pats my chest, and I find the gesture oddly soothing. "They can know. It's just ... I don't think they'll be happy about it. And I don't want them to say something that might hurt your feelings."

The concern she has *for me* twists in warm, pleasurable ways through my chest.

"That's okay," I say before pressing a reassuring kiss to her jaw. "My feelings aren't worth that much."

"Anthony. Look at me." Zara glares up at me, and the furious expression on her sweet face is entirely too tempting. "That's not true."

"It was a joke."

Some of the anger fades away, but she still gives me an intense stare. "I think, sometimes, you say things you think are true, but in a sarcastic voice so they sound like a joke."

Call me out, why don't you?

"Zara—"

"Your feelings matter." She presses, wrapping her arms around my waist as she speaks. "They matter a whole lot to me."

There's too much genuine concern in her voice for me to be flippant with my response.

"Okay," I mumble.

"But"—she frowns again—"my parents don't like witches."

My snarky, joking side comes back full force, as I'm desperate to shy away from heavy emotions.

"Cool. Me neither. We can shit-talk them together."

Zara's brows dip. "Your siblings are witches," she points out.

"True," I sigh. "And despite their personalities, I do love them."

"Right?" Zara offers a rueful smile. "And despite my parents' witch prejudice, I love them too."

We stand in a quiet moment of indecision, but I don't mind because her arms are still around me.

"Why don't they like witches?" I ask, not that I expect to be the one who changes their minds.

"It's a long story."

I have a sudden idea.

"Do they like to tell this story to strangers? You know, get all righteously furious and glare at the evil witch?"

Zara huffs a laugh. "Um ... yes actually. Why?"

Despite not wanting to end her embrace, I reach behind my back to find Zara's hand and twine our fingers together so I'm still holding on to her as I step out of her hug and toward the seating area of the marina.

"Let's go hear it from them. And rest assured, my feelings will not be hurt. Whatever witches did to your parents, I can almost guarantee, I've had it worse. So, I get it. And if your parents like telling the story, why not give them a rapt audience?" I can take some shit if it means I get on Zara's good side. "As long as you meant it. About not minding if they know we're dating?"

"Of course I meant it." Her brown eyes take a long, hard look at my face before the tension in her shoulders eases with a sigh. "Fine. But if things get brutal, we're leaving."

"Agreed."

Zara takes the lead, guiding me to a high-top table, where a middle-aged couple sits. The man resembles my harpy, with his midnight hair, thick lashes, and brown eyes, though his bronze skin is a shade or two darker than hers. The woman, well, she's all big blonde hair, vibrant blue eyes, and skin almost as pale as mine. But as I study her face, I see the resemblance in the heart shape of her cheeks. Plus, she seems to have as many ample curves as her daughter.

"Hey, Mama. Dad. Didn't know y'all were coming tonight." Zara's thumb rubs against my palm as she talks, and I'm not sure if it's to reassure me or comfort herself.

Either way, I have no plans to abandon her.

"Sweetie! So glad to see you out and about. Pull up some chairs. Who's this tall stick of butter you got with you?" Mrs. Ironfeather leans forward, her voice soft and sweet, her eyes sharp as a hawk's.

"Anthony, this is my mama, Eliza Ironfeather, and my dad, Sanjay Ironfeather. Mama, Dad, this is Anthony. Shelly." She tacks on my last name, as if an afterthought, but I see the recognition in both parents' expressions.

Eliza narrows her eyes further, and Sanjay, who had a welcoming smile on his cheerful face a moment ago, now looks carved out of granite.

Guess Zara was right.

"Shelly, as in the Shelly witches?" Mrs. Ironfeather asks, her voice so sweet that it's almost poisonous.

"Mama—" Zara starts off with a warning tone, but I step forward, ready to fall on the blade her mother's dagger eyes are waving at me.

"That's right, ma'am." Broderick told me when I'm in the South, I should tack on a *ma'am* or *sir* whenever talking to someone whose respect I'm trying to claim. "I come from a family of witches, and I've got to admit, I'm not a fan. Of the witch bit. Love my siblings. They're a good bunch. But Zara said you might have a tale to tell me about some witches that deserve an 'evil' before their designation. I'd love to hear that."

While I talk, I pull two chairs up to the table, guiding Zara into one and perching on the second.

Eliza blinks her wide blue eyes. "You want to hear about a bad witch?"

"You bet I do." Just then, a waitress pauses at the table. "And I'll grab the next round of margaritas." I hand over my credit card and watch smiles light up the Ironfeathers' faces.

"All right then. Get ready for an epic tale of love overcoming nefarious know-it-alls," Eliza declares, straightening in her chair.

And for the next half hour, Zara's mom relates exactly what she promised with the occasional interjection from Mr. Ironfeather. I get the sense he's not normally a talker, but that's fine because the harpy doesn't seem like she can stop.

The story starts with an eighteen-year-old Eliza attending Folk Haven High School and going on a senior class trip to New York City. The mythical parents were concerned about sending their magical children to a faraway city, even though everyone on the trip was legally an adult at that point, so they made sure a certain witch, Richard Pendear, was included as one of the chaperones.

One night, Eliza and a few friends went to a restaurant, and there, she met a quiet, handsome waiter she couldn't help flirting with. That server was eighteen-year-old Sanjay Patel. Eliza snuck out of her hotel room later that night and returned to the restaurant just as it was closing. She asked the waiter to go on a walk with her. He, mesmerized by her beauty and charm, said yes immediately. They wandered all through the city, talking and laughing and falling in love. Each night of the trip, Eliza slipped away to see Sanjay. They snuck into dance clubs, ate at his favorite Indian restaurants, and Sanjay took her to a theater to watch a Bollywood movie, hoping the romance on the screen would inspire a similar love for him. On the last night, he begged Eliza to stay, but she knew she had to go home.

This part of the story devolved into winks and nudges, but it's clear the two had a passionate farewell. One where Eliza revealed what she was and Sanjay didn't balk.

Not yet the time of cell phones—only a landline shared with two strict harpy parents who Eliza wasn't sure would approve of a human boy calling—Zara's mother promised to write and asked that he respond. Sanjay swore he would, and she vowed to return to New York once she graduated.

What Eliza didn't know was that her witch chaperone had followed the young harpy that final night, aware one of his charges was sneaking away. When the two lovers parted, Richard stayed behind. Catching Sanjay alone, he utilized an enchantment from his specialty—memory.

This witch was an integral part of Folk Haven because he could spell someone to forget almost anything. And that was what he did that night. Spelled Sanjay to forget the beautiful harpy girl he had met.

Eliza returned home, mourning the separation, but excited to write to the man she knew was her fated mate. But unbeknownst to her, Richard informed the Ironfeathers of their daughter's activities. Eliza's parents were glad for the witch's intervention, thinking the romance a flight of fancy that could ruin her life. They paid the witch to cast a simpler memory spell on their daughter. Merely to misremember the address Sanjay had given her.

Unaware of the manipulation, Eliza wrote to Sanjay for months, trying not to lose hope at the lack of response. Eventually though, she had to admit, the human boy she'd fallen in love with must not have wanted to speak to her or see her again.

Even though I know the ending of the story is happy, the pain in Eliza's voice as she tells this part of her history has my heart aching for the young lovers and furious with that Pendear asshole.

Witches do suck.

Unaware of my thoughts, Eliza continues, telling how, almost a year later, a knock sounded on her front door. She opened it to find Sanjay.

At first, she was overjoyed, then furious, then profoundly hurt and confused when he only stared at her and asked, "Do I know you?"

It took her a moment, but Eliza finally realized that he truly didn't know who she was. When she asked how Sanjay had found his way to her front door, he held up a scrap of paper with her address. The one she had written down for him. He claimed the address plagued him for a year. He'd dreamed about it. Tried to throw the paper away but couldn't. He'd held on to it like a talisman. When his parents started to talk of him getting married, he couldn't stand the idea of taking that step without first discovering what was waiting for him here.

Eliza confronted her parents, and when they confessed their hand in the deception, she packed her bags and left, in college then and preferring to live on her own rather than under their roof. She took Sanjay to the witch's house and demanded Richard return the human's memories. The witch had the audacity to quote an amount Eliza would need to pay for him to work the spell. Furious, Eliza covered the ears of the man she loved and let out her harpy screech. The magical scream shattered every window in the witch's house and obliterated all the glass items in the room.

"She was magnificent," Mr. Ironfeather announces at this point in the story, gazing at his wife with admiration as she blushes and preens.

Even without his memories, Sanjay knew he wanted to stay in Folk Haven with the gorgeous, powerful harpy. Much like Eliza's parents, the Patels did not approve. Eliza was a stranger, a white woman, and choosing her meant their son would live hundreds of miles away.

A shadow of sadness falls over Sanjay's face as this part of the story comes up.

Still, the two moved in together, officially mated—Sanjay taking on the female's surname, as is harpy custom—and a few years later had Zara. From the way they tell it, the arrival of a granddaughter helped to mend bridges with the Patels. But not Eliza's parents it seems. Their disapproval persists to this day. Meanwhile Eliza, Sanjay, and Zara visit New York at least once a year.

"And Ba and Dada like to make a surprise appearance in Folk Haven every few months. Usually when they think we haven't been calling enough," Zara explains with a smile and her parents chuckle in agreement.

They finish the story, telling how the memory witch kept a good distance from Eliza until the day he died, fifteen years after she destroyed his house. After Pendear's death, Mr. Ironfeather's recollections of that week in New York slowly began to return to him until, eventually, all that had been stolen was back.

"But we were so close to never finding each other again." Mrs. Ironfeather scowls out the dark window toward the lake, as if the witch who took her husband's memories lingers on the other side of the glass.

"I'm glad you did," I say with more feeling than I'm normally capable of mustering. But I think about the consequences of these two never making their way back to each other. "If you hadn't, there'd be no Zara." I turn my full attention to my harpy, who's in the middle of sucking up the last bit of her margarita, oblivious to my internal panic. "That witch was a pretentious asshole," I mutter. Then, I scoot my chair a few inches closer to my date and grasp her thigh under the table, just to remind myself she's real.

If anyone stole my memories of Zara and I found out, I'd gut them.

She swallows, smacks her lips, then glances down at my grip with a smile and color in her cheeks. "Told you it was a long story. I'm already done with my first drink of the night."

"We've got the next." The rumble of a voice has me glancing up to see Sanjay's focus on me.

I can't read his face, but I don't think he's hostile toward the fact that I'm getting overly clingy with his daughter.

"Anthony Shelly"—Eliza leans her elbows on the table and stares straight into my soul—"tell my mate your drink order, then tell me how you met my daughter."

Zara snorts, and I can't help a grin.

"The first meeting isn't the interesting one. Tell them about the second time." My date chortles, her delighted eyes flicking to her parents. "Get ready, Mama. This is a good story."

17

ZARA

THE MUSIC SWELLS through the marina, and suddenly, amid the lively music and laughing dancers and with Anthony at my side in his amazing pirate-y get up, this place doesn't seem so small and dingy.

Don't get me wrong; I've always liked the marina. But I knew what it was—a small-town dive that appealed to locals and locals only.

But here's Anthony Shelly, world traveler and luxury-life-style liver, with a glass of cheap margarita against his lips and his lithe body picking up the steps to a line dance immediately.

My shoulder brushes the person beside me, and I glance over to see Owen MacNamara close with a wide smile on his face.

"Hey, Zara. Haven't seen you around here lately," the hand-some selkie calls above the music.

He's right. With the crush of work, I've been staying later in the office. Plus, the lingering winter chill made traveling by boat uncomfortable, so I often skipped Monday nights to stay at home and sleep.

"You'd see me more if you adopted a dog," I call back to him.

Yes, I'm shameless when it comes to trying to get people to fill their homes with rescue animals. That's how MJ ended up with Croissant and why my parents are considering making a trip to the animal shelter in Toccoa.

Owen gives me a devilish grin, scoops up my hand, and twirls me. "You've convinced me. What pup should I get?"

I don't know if the seal shifter is serious or flirting. But the heated attention throws me off-balance enough to stumble into his chest.

Owen is a good-looking guy with his broad shoulders, shaved head, and warm brown eyes. He's funny, he owns the local recycling company, and his family is well-established in Folk Haven. The MacNamaras helped found this town. Plus, all three of his siblings have mated with a mythic different than their designation. Calder with a dragon, Seamus with a siren, and Moira with a monster. Not hard to believe Owen would be open to that type of relationship as well.

Another mark in his favor, I've seen him playing with his sister-in-law's dog, Gigabyte. The weird little creature is nervous around everyone, but I once watched Owen sit on a park bench and feed the pup treats until she fell asleep in his lap.

He is a top contender on my Monster Baby Plan.

So, why don't I want to lean more into his firm body? Why don't I want to give him a suggestive comment back? Why aren't his seductive lips seducing me?

"Unfortunately, you'll have to do without Dr. Ironfeather's assistance," a sardonic voice intones the moment before an arm slips around my hips and pulls me away from the flirtatious water mythic.

I glance back to find Anthony wearing a smirk, though his eyes have a hard quality to them.

"You see, I keep her quite busy nowadays." He still holds me to him, then scoops my hand up and presses a lingering kiss to my inner wrist.

And, holy goddess, it's like he licked my inner thigh. My whole body goes hot, and I feel my skin flushing dark with arousal.

Owen's eyes flick between us, expression still playful, but he tilts his chin. Gracious in the face of rejection, which makes him an even better candidate for Monster Baby Daddy.

"My loss." His brown eyes connect with mine. "I'll just have to wait until your schedule frees up." Then, he winks and disappears into the crowd, leaving a stiff Anthony at my back.

"Wow." I laugh, turning to face the redhead. "You weren't lying about your magic." I poke him in the stomach, wanting him back to his slouching smoothness and not this rigid posture.

Anthony's green gaze tears away from the retreating mythic to land on me. "You think he wanted you because of my magic?"

I shrug. "Owen hasn't ever asked me out before, and now, he's getting flirty? Yeah, seems like you're the reason."

Anthony frowns, then twines his fingers with mine and tugs me off the dance floor to a quieter corner. There, he boxes me against the wall with his arms, using his slim body to shield me from the room as he drops his head to speak directly into my ear.

When his words come, they make me shiver. "Have you considered these Neanderthals are drooling over you because your ass is edible in those tantalizing jeans? Or maybe they want to tug that neckline an inch lower to suck on those tight brown nipples of yours?"

"Anthony …" I breathe his name on a harsh exhale, trying to scold him, but only sounding needy in the end.

"None of them are good enough for you." His lips punctuate the words, skimming across my thrumming pulse.

"Because none of them are you?" I ask, figuring this is what he's getting at. That he's the only one that I should want.

He is. But that's a problem.

Anthony is leaving in a few weeks. I need to like someone else.

His nose traces the shell of my ear. "No. Not me. I'm the worst for you." His arms release from the wall, only to trail down mine until his grip reaches my wrists. Then, Anthony commands my hold, dragging my hands to his ass and silently directing me to clutch him close. Like he wants me to grab hold of him.

I do, pulling his front against mine and enjoying his low groan.

"Too bad," I tell him, feeling a sense of power come over me. "You're mine now."

And we don't talk about who deserves who. I don't think deserving even comes into it. What I need to ask is, who fits with me? Who works in the future I have for myself?

If I'm looking at the future as far as this spring goes, then that's Anthony, and I'm not about to give him up even if the perfect Monster Baby Plan candidate gets on his knee with a diamond ring.

A throat clears beside us, and I glance over to find my mom standing nearby, a single brow raised and a pinched smirk on her pink-painted lips.

"Y'all know this is a family establishment, right?"

The reality of the moment crashes back into me, and I drop my hold on Anthony's butt as if his ass cheeks transformed into the burners on a hot stove.

"Sorry, Mrs. Ironfeather," Anthony says in an over-the-top contrite voice. "I'll try to keep Zara in line. She's insatiable."

My mother snorts, then gives Anthony a genuine smile before sauntering away.

And I'm left wondering if that just happened. If my mother truly showed a hint of approval toward a witch.

He's not a witch, I remind myself.

At least, he refuses to admit he is. Anthony wants nothing to do with magic and never will.

That thought twists my stomach. But I ignore it as he laces his fingers with mine and tugs me back to the dance floor, keeping much closer this time.

And even though I see more smiles directed my way than normal, my date doesn't let anyone twirl me away from him for the rest of the night.

18

ZARA

As I sit on my dock—sketch pad in my lap, watercolors at my side—and watch Anthony saunter toward me, I consider if inviting him over was the best choice.

But my days off are so rare, and our time is limited. I find myself craving more moments with him.

"Hello there, my lovely." He strolls across the swaying dock and leans down to plant a hot kiss on my mouth that steals my breath and loosens my grip until the pencil I was holding clatters to the weather-worn wood.

"Oh," I gasp, worried my writing utensil will roll into the water.

But Anthony crouches down fast, snatches it up, and presents the pencil to me as if he were a knight offering his sword. "M'lady," he says, completing the picture.

And this is why this was a bad idea.

Because every time I'm around Anthony Shelly, I like him even more. Some part of my brain came to the conclusion that if we did this temporary dating, his shallow personality would wear away at his handsome face and cheeky charm.

But the man has depth. I've seen it.

And even when he's playful and lighthearted, it doesn't come across as vapid.

"Thank you, kind sir." I pluck the pencil from his hand and try to regain my composure. "I'm surprised you wanted to see me today."

Anthony tilts his head in a curious move as he settles in the chair across from mine. The sun plays off his red hair in a gorgeous ruby glow, but I worry about his pale skin.

I should've brought him sunscreen.

"Why wouldn't I want to see you?"

I shiver at his words. At the clear confusion, as if it should be obvious he'd always want to see me.

"After my parents' heart-melting, witch-hating love story, I thought you might want some distance to recover."

To reestablish that this is a casual dating situation, aimed at getting me a husband.

Thinking of that, I remember how, on the way to the restroom, I ran into Griffith. I was surprised to see the werewolf at a rival bar and told him so, but he chuckled, reminded me that Local Brew was closed on Mondays, and then leaned in close to whisper he'd hoped to run into some pretty ladies on his night off.

It took me a full count of five to realize he was talking about me. Not that I think I'm not a pretty lady. I've just never been so blatantly flirted with before. Especially not twice in one night. And definitely not while I was on a date with someone else.

Tilting me off my balance even further, Griffith offered me his phone number on a napkin, saying I should give him a call if—and I quote—"the redhead falls short in any categories."

I thanked him with a smile and tucked the number in my back

pocket, planning to toss it out when I got into the restroom. But as I held the piece of paper over the bin, I forced myself to remember that this was the goal. And Griffith was one of the names on the list I'd made of male mythics I might be open to starting a family with.

Taking the wolf's number wasn't cheating on Anthony. In fact, he would probably expect me to. As long as I waited until after our scheduled breakup to call the wolf, then this was exactly the plan.

So, why did keeping that string of digits feel like a betrayal?

And that, more than anything, is why me spending more time with Anthony like this, casually lounging on my dock like couples do, is a bad idea. I can't get too comfortable with him in my life. It'll hurt all the more when he walks out.

Anthony grins and reclines farther into his seat. "I liked your parents. They were funny. And sweet. And your mom is a touch terrifying, but in the best way."

As he speaks, I see movement in the corner of my eye. Glancing over, I realize Anthony's snake shadow is sliding his way onto my dock and toward the object of his adoration. Reaching his destination, the snake twines around the leg of the chair, climbing up and into Anthony's lap.

Unlike the previous freak-outs, Anthony simply sighs a long-suffering sound, pats the snake's head with a single finger, then goes back to staring at me.

"What did they think of me? Did they call you later and tell you to drop me like a hot stone?"

I snort and stare at my barely started piece, attempting to imagine the next line as I answer, "They bought you a margarita. And Dad invited you to play cricket. That's practically a proposal." When my dad found out Anthony lived in England for a few years, he brought up his favorite topic: cricket. He's always bemoaning the fact that Americans ignore the only thing he loves as much as me and Mama. The fact that Anthony not only knows about the sport, but understands the rules, and is willing to play in pick-up game Dad's trying to arrange, earned him major points with Sanjay Ironfeather. "And that you promised to bring Broderick, too? Smart move. You've won yourself two fans."

"Really?"

Glancing up, I find him with a wide grin that is too self-satisfied.

"Don't get cocky. My ex set the bar low. In the end anyway." A flush creeps up my neck, and I regret saying that.

"He was an asshole," Anthony says, his voice gentle now. "What are you working on?"

I shrug. "I wouldn't say I'm working. Just messing around with some pencils and paint. As a hobby."

I turn the sketch pad his way so Anthony can see the rough outline of a picturesque lake scene. He leans forward in his chair, studying my progress.

"That's gorgeous."

"It's just a sketch."

"Will you do me?"

"Do you?"

He smirks. "I meant, draw and paint. Will you *do* me?"

No one's ever asked me to do a portrait before, although sometimes, I'll make one of a pet who passed away and give the painting to the owners so they can have a special memory piece.

But a person? That would be new.

"Come on, Zara. Paint me like one of your French girls." Anthony sinks even lower into his seat, flinging out his long limbs and somehow landing in a pose that looks handsome, careless, and erotic.

It's on the tip of my tongue to ask if he'd like to try a nude when I recall that we're on a dock, visible to any boat that might pass by.

I doubt the local fishermen want to see Anthony's ... rod.

The thought has me snickering.

"You're beautiful," he murmurs, and when I glance up, his green eyes are locked on mine. "I wish I could paint just so I could capture that lovely smile of yours. The dot above your lip drives me to distraction."

The charmer.

I ignore the flutters in my stomach and the urge to touch my beauty mark as I flip to a new page in my sketchbook.

"Anyone can paint," I say.

He snorts, and I press on.

"They might not be very good, but they can still do it. I'll share my supplies if you want to try."

"I think I'd rather be your muse." Then, the tease reaches up and undoes the top three buttons on his shirt, leaving the material gaping. "There. Some more inspiration."

Yeah, inspiration for dirty thoughts. Face hot, I try to ignore my libido as I make a rough sketch of his pose. Anthony is all long, lithe limbs, and that vibrant hair of his has my fingers itching for my paints. But I want to make sure I get the details right too.

The sharp angle of his nose.

The plush, knowing curve of his lips.

The crease of the clothes hugging his body.

The lounging snake in his lap.

The actual *snake. Get your mind out of the gutter.*

"How did margaritas at the marina compare to your normal club-hopping?" I ask. "We must seem pretty tame. No VIP section." I toss him a quick smile before returning to my drawing.

"Clubbing is overrated," he murmurs, almost too low for me to hear. "Never had as much fun in a rave as I did line dancing."

When I glance up, I find Anthony wearing his trademark smirk. I silently wonder if he's being honest or trying to make me feel as though my small-town life can still compete with his normal luxurious lifestyle.

I know it can't. Not for him anyway. There are people who are comfortable on million-dollar yachts. And then there are people who would rather drive a secondhand pontoon.

Both are okay, but Anthony is only dipping his toe into my life. Soon, he'll realize this lake feels like a puddle, and he'll want to swim in more expansive, expensive waters.

That's why we have the two-month cutoff. Better for both of us.

Despite Anthony's propensity to tease, he stays quiet for a stretch of time while I work, and my concentration homes in on my page until I'd have trouble holding a conversation if I tried.

Eventually, once I start blinking too much to focus, I realize the sun has dropped low in the sky, shining directly into my eyes. I sit back, rolling my shoulders and cracking my neck.

"I'm sorry." I check my watch, shocked to realize two hours have passed. "Gods, you must be bored out of your mind."

But when I meet Anthony's eyes, he doesn't seem exasperated. And his subtle smirk is gone. The man simply stares at me, face relaxed, as one of his hands idly pets the black rat snake that's coiled in his lap.

"Watching you work is relaxing," he says, and I find I believe him. "Can I see?" He gestures toward the pad.

I stand, arching my spine and groaning when a few vertebrae crack.

"If you keep making noises like that, your joints aren't the only thing that's going to be stiff." There's his trademark teasing tone, and my muscles ease at the familiar sound.

"I'll try not to unintentionally arouse you," I murmur while picking up my pad and crossing to his side.

Anthony studies the drawing while I mentally critique my work.

"You made me too handsome," he announces.

I bark a laugh. "You look like you. The best I could do anyway."

Leaning down, I plant a kiss on his cheek, feeling the slight prick of his five-o'clock shadow, which has me wondering what he might look like with a beard. But Anthony is too clean-cut for that.

As if sensing the man wants to get up, the snake slips off his lap. Then—shocking both of us—he goes straight off the side of the dock, landing with a plop in the water.

Anthony's lazy air disappears as he lunges forward in time to see his new friend floating on the surface, smoothly gliding to the bank.

"The asshole can swim," he mutters, sitting back on his heels and clutching his chest. I think I can hear his heart pounding from here. He sucks in a deep breath and lets it go slowly before offering me a rueful smile. "I named him Sin, by the way."

Despite his scare, I find the reaction endearing. Knowing that the snarky man does care—at least about something.

Hopefully, when Anthony leaves, he'll find a way to take Sin with him. A little piece of Folk Haven to help him remember.

19

———————

ANTHONY

Zara invites me up to her house, and I'm all too eager to join her. An afternoon spent watching her concentrate on her canvas, nibbling her lip as she worked, had me wanting to crawl across the dock to replace her teeth with mine. Eventually, I had to stop looking. I didn't want her to paint me with a hard-on.

While she worked, I wondered if I wore the same look of intense concentration the times I'd gone to Esme's shop. This past week, I've been helping her out most days. Simple stitches, nothing intricate. But from the way the harpy smiles in relief at the end of each day, I know that my work is solid and I'm helping lighten her load.

She's even given me input on a design I'm working on. One for the gorgeous mythic waving me into her house.

When we first made this agreement, I thought my days would be full of Zara Ironfeather. That we'd rarely leave a bed and only then to eat food and find new places to give each other pleasure.

But unlike me, Zara has a more than full-time job and friends and a family she commits to spending time with. Her schedule is packed, and I'm not a priority.

And I don't like to pick at that painful reminder. Don't like to examine how much I want to be the top item on her to-do list in every way.

"Are you hungry?" She heads toward the kitchen.

"For your cunt," I reply.

Zara whirls on me, eyes wide, and I remember just how dirty that word is. I've spent a good amount of time in England, and they throw it around a lot more often than Americans do.

Still, it's accurate. I want her cunt.

There's a flush on her cheeks, but an eagerness in her eyes that has me hardening in my now-too-tight pants. Her gaze drops to the bulge, and I give in to the urge to rub myself. A slow massage that has me gritting my teeth to hold back a groan.

"Oh!" Zara snaps her fingers, as if just remembering something, and hurries out of the room, leaving me horny and confused.

"I thought you were going to feed me!" I call after her, sounding like the petulant man-child I am.

"Just give me a second!" she shouts in response, then returns a moment later with a thin chain and simple charm dangling from her finger. "I picked this up yesterday. I know most mythics opt for the tattoo, but I thought that was kind of risky since I want to have a kid someday." Her words come out a touch breathy, and excitement sparkles in her warm eyes.

If only I knew why.

"And that is?"

Zara blinks, eyes flicking from the necklace to me, the enthusiasm in her face dimming, and I curse myself for not knowing about whatever this is. A certain kind of jewelry? I thought I was well-versed in the biggest designers. But that's not what Zara would be showing off, right?

"Sorry." Her hand lowers. "I just realized this might not work for us. Or, I mean, it would probably work. But you might not want to use it."

I will do anything you want me to, I'm on the verge of saying, but stop myself before I come off too desperate. "Can you explain what it is?"

"A contraception charm." She winds the silver chain around her fingers. "Magical birth control. There's a witch in town who sells them. I just thought, since mythics don't have to worry about STIs, this would be more convenient than condoms. But it's a spell, so ..." She trails off with a shrug and turns, as if to retreat and take away the little object that I am suddenly, rabidly interested in.

Two long strides, and I'm in front of my harpy, my hands wrapping around her wrists to make her stay put so I can examine the little piece of magic.

"You're saying"—I speak slowly to make sure I'm not dreaming—"you got this little charm because you want me inside you. Skin to skin." The simple thought has my gut tightening in pleasure.

Zara put thought into this. She thinks about me when we're not together.

Likely not as much as I think about her, but still.

"It's magic," she repeats.

"True." And yet nothing about it scares me. Huh. Guess I just needed to have something mystical assist me in getting laid by the most gorgeous, winged woman in the universe to help me work past my discomfort. "But also true is, I'm still hard. It's a miracle. Let's not waste this opportunity."

Zara barks a sharp laugh that makes my eardrums wary.

But a part of me wishes she'd keep the sharp noise going.

Reveal her dangerous harpy scream to me even if it left me with a touch of hearing damage.

I once did a photo shoot with a deaf model, and the guy was hot as fuck and living his best life. Hearing is overrated.

I want the secret pieces of her. To know every bit of Zara Ironfeather. If she showed me her second form, I would bask in the discovery.

But Broderick warned me that asking questions about mythical designations is often seen as rude, and who am I to judge? I snapped at Zara the first time she called me a witch.

I don't deserve all of her.

But I'll take whatever she's willing to give. And it seems riding my cock bare is an option.

I pluck the charm from her fingers and slip the chain over her head, carefully tugging her braid through as well and settling her thick hair over her shoulder, the length resembling a certain snake I know.

"Since you prepared so well"—I lean down and trace my nose along the curve of her ear before nipping the lobe—"what do you want to do to me, Dr. Ironfeather?"

She makes a happy hum in the back of her throat. "I get to do things to you?"

"Oh, Zara. My lovely." I cup her head in my hands, tilting her so we gaze into each other's eyes. "I am at your service. I am your toy. Put me on my knees and make me crawl to you. I'll do it gladly."

She might think being submissive is something I get off on.

Normally, she'd be wrong. I don't give partners any more power over me than I have over them. Past sexual experiences have always been an equal exchange between me and whoever else was in the bed. Everything revolved around physical pleasure and eventual release.

Then, afterward, we'd part ways, and the experience would fade into the mass of hookups I've had throughout my life.

I don't want this to fade. I want every one of Zara's touches tattooed on my unmarked skin.

But the idea of demanding that from her lacks the appeal of having her demand it from me. If she leads, then every command will be proof she wants me. Any instruction she doles out will exist as evidence that she craves me.

And with her mental shields firmly in place, all of that will be without the influence of my magic.

"To be clear"—she trails a finger down the front of my shirt, and under the fabric, goose bumps follow the touch—"I'm in charge."

"My safe word is *Switzerland*."

That earns me another sharp laugh, then a set of strong hands giving me a shove backward. I stumble, my legs hitting something, and I land with a bounce on her couch.

"Shit! Sorry. I was trying to take charge." Zara reaches out, a worried frown on her face.

I grab her hand and kiss the silky skin of her inner wrist. "You're doing great." Then, I let her go and recline in a tempting sprawl. "What does my queen command of me?"

My harpy's eyes flit over me, as if checking for injury. When her tight shoulders relax, I know I've got her back. Her eyes drop to my crotch, and I bite my lip to keep from groaning.

"Take it out." Her voice has gone husky, and my cock twitches in eager response.

"Yes, Doctor," I purr, hands settling on my fly.

"Maybe I shouldn't like you calling me that, but honestly, I worked really hard for my doctorate, so it feels good to have it acknowledged. In any setting." She says all this with a little pleased smirk playing at the corner of her lips as her eyes stay adhered to my fingers while they drag down my pants zipper.

And I think I fall in love with Zara Ironfeather.

No. Ignore the big feelings. This is just sex with a smart, funny, beautiful, amazing woman.

"Doctor it is." And luckily, I can blame the strained note in my voice on arousal. Then, my hard length is in my grip, and my focus is on the harpy who is sinking her talons into my heart. "What now?"

"Show me what you would do if you were alone." Then, as if settling in for a class, Zara sits on the coffee table in front of me, her focus still trained on my very proud dick.

"Yes, Doctor," I murmur, dragging my fist to the base and giving a hard squeeze that forces a grunt from my throat.

With my other hand, I cup the head, rolling and massaging until my palm is coated with warm, slippery pre-cum. I use the lubrication to jack myself off. Hard and fast. My right hand slips back inside my pants to cradle and tug on my balls.

All this I do by muscle memory alone, my stare fixed on the harpy in front of me, who watches me work with fascination. When her tongue sneaks out to wet her bottom lip, I can't hold back a groan. Only then do her eyes flick up to meet mine, a sharp heat in her gaze.

"Stop."

I do as I was told, half in misery because I was close and half in ecstasy because maybe—just maybe—I'll be able to finish in her tight grip.

Zara stands and tugs her T-shirt off in a quick motion, revealing a glorious pair of breasts, cupped in a simple cotton bra. The contraception charm lays nestled in the valley between the two mounds of perfection. She tugs her leggings off just as fast, lacy underwear following immediately afterward.

At the sight of the dark curls in a perfect little triangle at the apex of her thighs, I lose track of time and reason.

"Give me," I beg.

Zara grins wide, no sign of play or teasing. Just joy.

"I've always thought"—she twists her arm behind her back —"that hooking up when someone was completely clothed"—

her bicep tenses, then her bra falls slack—"and the other person was completely naked"—she shrugs off the straps and lets the last bit covering her fall to the floor—"would be super hot."

"Correct," I choke out, having lost every ounce of suaveness at the sight of her peaked brown nipples. "One hundred percent correct."

Zara fiddles with the charm around her neck. "What am I going to do with you?" she murmurs, as if talking to herself.

"Anything," I rasp.

With a nod and a saunter that wrecks me, Zara comes to a stop in front of me, then spreads her lush thighs and straddles my lap, her knees pressing into the plush cushions. But the temptress doesn't immediately sink down.

My harpy leans in to kiss me slowly, like we have all the time we could ever need. I like that fantasy. The one where this never ends.

When our lips part, she gives me my next instruction. "Make me come with your fingers." Her fingers comb through my hair, and I could swear I feel the slight sting of claws. "Once you give me an orgasm, I'll fuck you. Is that what you want, Anthony? My hot cunt gripping your cock?"

"Fuck, Zara. Fuck," I pant and watch a dark flush spread up her chest and to her neck and face. Maybe the dirty words embarrass her, but she's not shying away from them. "I want that so bad."

And to prove I'm telling the truth, I suck my fingers into my mouth to get them slick before pressing through her intimate curls to find her throbbing clit. Gods, I can feel her pulse beat between her legs—she's so turned on.

Zara holds herself above my lap, arms braced on the back of the sofa, thighs quivering, as I ply her with pleasure. I pay homage to her naughty little clit while I fill her slick pussy with my other fingers.

"Oh goddess. Yes. Just like that," Zara moans the encouragement, her hips rocking.

But it's not until I give in to the urge to suck one of those teasing nipples that I feel her tighten around me. I glance up in time to see her bite into her wrist to stifle her tiny shriek as she comes. I keep the heel of my hand pressed to her pleasure spot, drawing the orgasm out.

Then, her fierce eyes meet mine, and she growls her next words. "Hold yourself straight."

I'm too wild from watching her lose herself to pleasure to immediately register her words. But they manage to penetrate my thick skull.

My cock is so hard when I grip it that I let out a hiss. But my touch is nothing compared to what comes next.

Zara relaxes her legs, the hot, drenched center of her seeking out my hardness. When she finds me, my harpy sinks fast, and I choke on a groan as her body claims mine.

"Anthony," she moans, leaning back to stare down at where are bodies are joined. "You feel so *good*." The word comes with a happy hum that threatens my sanity.

She was right about the dynamic of clothed and unclothed. This is dirty in the best way. My normally put-together harpy bare in my lap, flushed from her first orgasm of the day and fascinated with how my cock stretches the lips of her pussy.

"Are you going to fuck me?" The question is a desperate gasp.

Zara rocks her hips in answer, and I can't help but grab hold of her round ass to help each thrust.

"Goddess." She rides me harder, kneading my shoulders with her strong fingers before diving in to kiss me with a ravenous edge. "It's never—" She cuts off the statement by sucking on my neck.

"Never what?" I ask the question through gritted teeth, trying to hold back my release so this will never end. I want the rest of her statement, but I also want her to mark my neck with her teeth.

"Felt this good," she gasps a second before her body tenses, pulsing with another orgasm.

There's no fighting it after that. A spear of pleasure shoots from my root and straight up to my spine, blacking out my brain.

I am well and truly fucked.

20

ZARA

THE MAN in front of me looks like Anthony. Almost. There's a little bit of something off.

And then he speaks.

"I'm just not as free and easy with my nipples as you are." He uses the same dry note Anthony sometimes affects, but with less ease.

"We have the same set," a voice calls out from deeper in the apartment. "They're high-quality nipples."

What have I walked into?

Maybe I should have knocked before entering the apartment above the dry cleaner. But Anthony told me to come over after work and that he'd leave the door unlocked.

Did he know what would greet me?

My guess is, I'm looking at Anthony's twin in a mesh shirt that does in fact display his areolae. I grew up without siblings, so it's true that I don't have a firsthand experience on how they talk to each other. But I would've bet a good amount of money that nipples don't often come into those conversations.

Guess I would have lost some cash.

"I think I should announce my presence," I call out from the doorway so both men know I'm here. "Before this gets any more graphic."

"Zara!" Anthony strolls out of the bedroom, proving my guess that the man in the mesh is his twin.

When the siblings stand next to each other, their differences are even more striking. At least to me.

Anthony has a slouch to his shoulders that is artistic in a way. He has a swagger to him. A looseness. He gives the sense that he could flow in and out of a situation with ease.

His twin, however, has a rigid stance. Upright, shoulders square. Not a bad thing necessarily. He seems more present. But I also have a feeling that he's not a very good dancer.

Maybe we should invite him to the marina next Monday to test the theory.

"What's all this talk about nipples?" I set down my bag of bagels from Mary Jo's on the kitchen island and try not to stare at Broderick's chest.

Anthony strolls up to me and throws an arm around my shoulders, drawing my body into his side. "This is the perfect way to introduce you to my brother, Broderick. A man as handsome as the devil while somehow having zero game." He gestures at his now-scowling twin. "I'm trying to help him woo the mythic of his dreams. And he, for some reason, does not want to use his nipples."

"I hate you," Broderick mutters. Then, he clears the annoyance from his face and offers me a genuine smile. "Nice to officially meet you, Zara. I find it extremely impressive you've been able to put up with my brother for such a long stretch of time. You have a formidable will."

Now, Anthony is the one glaring. "You make it sound like dating me is a chore. I'm lovely." He turns his devastating gaze on me. "Isn't that right?"

"Of course." I pat his flat stomach. "You're an adorably snarky man." And I won't say anything more because then I might reveal how deeply my affection for him is rooting into my soul, transforming into something that could last far longer than a couple of months. "Now, tell me about Broderick trying to woo someone. Who is it?" In a town this small, I probably know them.

Anthony turns a wicked grin on his sibling. "She's a phoenix—"

"A firebird," Broderick corrects. Then, his cheeks turn ruddy as he no doubt realizes he as good as admitted he is trying to play Casanova.

"What's the difference?" Anthony asks, strolling over to his side and plucking at the shoulder of the see-through shirt, as if it just needs to lie correctly instead of finding half the missing fabric.

"A lot, apparently," Broderick grumbles under his breath, and I get the sense he made the misstep in front of his crush.

"Fine. My brother has it bad for a *firebird*." Anthony lets his arm drop and returns to hook me around the waist and fiddle with the belt loop on my jeans. "Ame might have told you. She was the rabbit rescued from a sorcerer last fall. When they broke the curse—boom!—she appeared." His snarky grin is back. "And—boom!—Broderick made an immediate fool of himself."

"How so?" I glance at the man who's now the color of a tomato.

He clears his throat more times than necessary before answering, "I might have told her ... she was a very cute bunny."

Goddess. I doubt a woman who was trapped in the form of a rabbit wants to hear that.

"Not the best pickup line," I say.

"I know. I knew immediately after I said it and tried to apologize. I think she's forgiven me. Or at least, she tolerates me now."

"When do you see her?"

"She works for Clean Haven." He names the local recycling company co-owned by the selkie Owen MacNamara and the human Finn Hammond. "She empties the bins at the university, and sometimes, I cross paths with her."

Anthony smirks. "Is that what you call working near a recycling bin on the day they get emptied?"

Broderick tugs at the collar of his mesh shirt.

"How do your interactions normally go?" I ask.

If the mythic doesn't want to talk to him, I'm about to give this man an *earth to Broderick* moment.

"That's the thing. I can't tell." The man looks hopeless. "If she seemed scared or uncomfortable around me, I wouldn't put myself in her space. Sometimes, I think she wants to talk to me. But other times, I'm not sure if she likes me at all."

I ignore the way Anthony's hands fiddle with the edges of my clothes as I try to help his brother.

"Walk me through a normal exchange."

The witch attempts to tuck his hands in his pockets, only to discover that he doesn't have any, and that's when I realize he's wearing leather pants.

What kind of seduction techniques is Anthony trying to teach him?

"Last Wednesday," he starts, "she came in to empty the bins. I said, 'Hello.' She said, 'Hello, Professor Shelly.' I said, 'It's raining outside.' She said, 'I know.' Then, I didn't know what to say, and she was leaving, but then she stopped at my table and put an apple on the corner and said, 'Here's an apple.' Then, she left." He holds his hands out, palms up, expression flabbergasted.

"That's fucking poetry." Anthony has on the biggest grin as he watches his brother squirm.

But a warm tingle of happiness alights in my chest, as I know I'm about to give this man hope.

"I think she likes you," I tell him.

The brothers stare at me—one eager, one incredulous.

"Really?" Broderick asks.

"How'd you land on that?" Anthony waves his hand at his brother. "I mean, I'm trying to help him seduce her, but it sounds like a lost cause to me."

Broderick scowls. "Thanks for the vote of confidence. Between that and my nipples, I've got this in the bag."

I snort, then say my piece before they start bickering. "From what I know of firebirds—which, admittedly, is not a lot—they like apples." When I was researching different monster histories, I came across a couple of firebird myths, and they tended to revolve around apple trees. "If she gave you one, that could be a good thing. *Could* be. I'm not guaranteeing anything."

Still, Broderick's eyes practically glow, and he turns back to the mirror. "I'll take it!" He frowns at the reflection. "Not this half-shirt though. I'd lose my job. Don't you have anything more professional I could seduce her with?"

"Picky." Anthony rolls his eyes as he releases me to stroll toward his bedroom, but he throws me a grin behind his brother's back.

"Thanks, Zara."

I turn to find Broderick's eyes on me in the mirror.

"Sure thing. I hope it works out."

He studies me, and I try not to squirm under the oddness of seeing Anthony's eyes, but them not being his.

"I hope it works out for you too." He speaks the words quietly, as if he doesn't want his brother to overhear.

As if he already knows his wish is in vain.

21

———————

ANTHONY

My phone has been buzzing all afternoon with my agent's name blaring bright and bold across the screen.

I don't want to talk to her. I don't want any reminders of my life outside of Folk Haven. She's going to want to talk about June. The month I'll be gone from here.

The time in the near future when my claim on Zara will run out.

The harpy will put her Monster Baby Plan into motion, and I'll be …

Fuck if I know. And I don't *want* to know.

I want to live in the bliss of this temporary relationship.

But I also don't want the persistent buzzing to interrupt my date. And knowing Julia, if she can't get through to me, she'll find Broderick's number and start pestering him. Or worse, she'll show up here and barrage me with work in person.

Get through this call, and then you can lose yourself in Zara.

It's been almost a week since we've spent any real time together. The life of a small-town vet is busy, and I'm lucky if she can get away long enough for a bagel lunch and a quick fingerbang in her car. Despite the standing invitation I extended to her to spend the night at my place, Zara hasn't taken me up on the offer yet. I get the feeling she's trying to keep distance between us, knowing that this will end in a few short weeks.

Maybe I should want to set up boundaries between us too.

But I don't.

The light is on in her house, and I can see a shadow moving around. *What is she doing?*

The sooner I get this chat over with, the sooner I can find out.

"Julia." I try to convey with the dead note of my voice how much I do not want to be on the phone with her.

"Anthony! How's my favorite guy?" my agent responds with enthusiasm.

Then, I remember I always use my dead-tone voice when talking to her and she always gives zero shits. I sigh, loud enough for her to hear.

"I'm on hiatus. Why are you calling me?"

"Right to business. I love that about you. So, hear me out. People are clamoring for you. Your fans. Companies. Seriously, they're offering top dollar."

Julia is a savvy businesswoman, but she still hasn't realized one important thing.

I don't care about the money.

I had plenty of it before my social media popularity exploded. The Shelly family is wealthy, and our parents left us each a trust fund. Even me, the magic puppet boy Mom made.

The reason I do this work is simpler. And more pathetic.

For the praise.

I've spent my whole life knowing I was nothing more than a tightly bundled being of magical energy that could disappear at any moment if my mother decided to reabsorb me. So, yeah, I got off on the idea of masses adoring me. Of mattering while I was here. Of enjoying the hedonistic delights of the world before I ceased to exist.

But all that doesn't tempt me so much anymore.

"Then, book it for June or later," I tell Julia, keeping my thoughts to myself. "Like I said, you have free rein from then on."

"That's the problem. They want you *now*. Or this weekend. But get this: I've made it so simple because I'm looking out for you."

You're looking out for you, Julia, just be honest about it.

"I got them to agree to Atlanta!" Her joy is palpable through the phone, and I bet she's staring at her commission figures. "You don't have to fly or anything. And they're going all in on it. Sending a limo to pick you up in that nowhere town, penthouse —of course—meals comped, liquor covered, anything you want. You've just got to be seen in their summer line. They want to get the hype going before it hits the market in two weeks. And you're their guy. Come on, Anthony. This is an easy gig. Practically a vacation."

Still sounds like work to me. The shadow behind the curtain moves again, and I spy generous curves I want to dig my fingers into. That I don't want to let go of.

"Can I bring a friend?"

"Of course! They'd probably double the offer if you could get that twin of yours to sign on."

I snort. Broderick would never.

"If I do this, Julia, then I need your word that you will not contact me again before June 1. Not for anything. I don't care how good the deal is. Understood?"

"Yes! Anthony, you are a star. My favorite. Seriously. I'll lose your number unless it's an emergency."

Fuck no. That is not a door I'm leaving open. Because her

emergencies are always money-related. As in, if we don't sign this contract, I might die.

"Julia," I growl, no dead tone this time. Now, I'm bordering on pissed. "Let me be extremely clear. I will do this *one* job. And if you contact me again before June 1 about anything—if I even see a thumbs-up emoji in a text from you—I will fire you. Do you understand?"

There's an uncertain laugh on the other end of the line. "Anthony—"

"Do you understand?" My voice is cold.

Silence for a stretch, then, "Yes. Of course. I respect your time off completely. No more jobs until June."

"Good. Email me the details." I end the call without a good-bye, knowing it's petulant. But she's the one who decided to disrespect the boundary I set.

Climbing from my car, I brainstorm how to present this idea to Zara.

What can I say to get her to agree to go with me?

Because the idea of spending the night at a club on my own sounds like hell.

But going to one with Zara sounds like another date, which is heaven.

"Can I come in?" I call out the question as I peek my head around the door.

Sin doesn't wait for an invitation, slipping between my feet and sliding over the hardwood toward the pillow Zara set down for him near the heating vent.

"Yes! I'm in the kitchen."

I could have guessed with the fragrant scent permeating the house. My stomach rumbles in appreciation. I find Zara standing by the stovetop, stirring a thick yellow sauce.

"What do we have here?" Slipping up behind her, I wrap my arms around my girlfriend's waist and settle my hands on her soft belly.

"How do you feel about Indian food?"

"Mmm. I feel good about it." Pressing my front against her back, I breathe in Zara's fresh-air-and-floral scent, melding with the strong spices. Not sure if I'm hungrier for the food or the woman. "I feel *really* good about it."

"The smell doesn't bother you?" She asks the question like someone has complained in the past. I wonder if that fucker Christian insulted her cooking.

His loss.

"It does." Her body stiffens in my arms, but I don't let her go. "It bothers me that it smells so delicious, but I can't start eating it immediately. Much like when I see you in public and want to immediately devour you, but our society scorns PDR."

"PDR?"

"Public displays of ravishment."

Tilting my head, I trace kisses up her bare neck as she shivers and chuckles.

"Even if everything I'm making is veg? No meat." Her words come a touch breathless, and I grin against her skin, proud of my effect on her.

"Is this where you tell me you're a vegetarian?"

That can't be right. I saw her eat turkey on her bagel.

Zara shakes her head. "My dad is. I grew up in a house full of compromise. Mom was a staunch meat eater before she met him. They would trade off cooking most nights." She grins at me over her shoulder. "Mom and I love when Dad cooks, but neither of us can give up burgers forever."

"Mmm. Well, I'm a man of many tastes. Tofu, burgers, your pussy. Love them all."

My harpy laughs and keeps stirring the dish.

"What's this called?" I tap the edge of the pot.

"Khichdi," she says, and I can't help noticing the careful way she pronounces the name. Hesitantly. "It has rice and onions and tomatoes and a few other things. If you don't like it, that's okay. But ... if you could at least try it." Zara keeps her focus entirely on the dish.

"Of course, I'm going to try it. Try it and love it." I rest my chin on her shoulder. "Can I help?"

Zara sucks in a small breath I might not have heard if I weren't so close.

"This is almost done." She points to a round metal container by the stove top. There are smaller containers inside it filled with colorful powders. "You can help with the spices in the bhinda nu shake—stir fried okra."

"I was born for this job," I declare. "I love getting spicy."

Zara snorts, and I welcome the sound of her humor. She's giving off vulnerable vibes, and I wonder if cooking this food means more than just making dinner to her.

Zara heats oil in a pan then directs me to spoon in certain spices, naming them as I do. Mustard seeds, cumin, carom seeds, asafetida, and turmeric powder. My arms are long enough that I can add seasonings while still bracketing her lush body in my hold. The air thickens with the savory aroma, and my mouth waters. Zara grabs a bowl of sliced okra and dumps the green veggies into the mixture we made.

Standing here, wrapped around her as we cook, feels awfully domestic.

My heart aches with how much I love this moment.

So, of course, when she places a cover over the pan, I have to go ruin it.

"My agent convinced me to do a job this Saturday," I tell her before burying my face in her loose braid as I continue to clutch her close.

"What does *do a job* mean?"

"Wearing specific clothes and going to a club, then posting pictures of myself living the high life."

"Hmm, sounds fancy." She rests her free hand over mine, stroking my knuckles with her thumb.

"I want you to come." Somehow, I manage to sound aloof rather than desperate.

"Come where?"

"To Atlanta." Without thought, my arms tighten around her, my body ready for her to refuse and pull away from me. "Just for the night. It can be like a vacation."

Zara turns her head, and I stop hiding in her hair so our eyes can meet. "So, hang out in your hotel room while you work?"

"Gods, no." Letting my arms drop, despite never wanting to let her go, I move to lean on the counter, fully facing her. Gone is my attempt at casualness. That was a bad choice. I want Zara to know how much I value her company. "I want you by my side all night. We'll go to the club together. Dance, eat, drink. Have a good time. It'll be a date on someone else's dime."

Zara studies me, a smile slowly unfurling on her plush lips. "That could be fun. I've never gone clubbing before."

She's saying yes. I can't fully believe it.

"You'll come?" *Is that my voice? Sounds too ragged to be mine.*

She nods. "Let me check with Keith. Make sure he'll be good at the clinic on his own."

I won't be alone.

Diving forward, I cup her round cheeks in my palms and press a hot, open-mouthed kiss to her lips.

And even though the food we made is tempting, all I want to consume is Zara.

22

———————

ZARA

EVER SINCE ONLINE shopping became a thing, I stopped bothering with retail stores. Why spend the whole day stripping down in a strange place with dressing rooms that have horrible lighting to only find one or two pieces to add to my wardrobe?

Plus, Folk Haven doesn't have many clothing shop options, which means I'd have to drive at least an hour to reach anything with enough variety for me to discover something I'd like and that fits me.

So, this, trying on a garment outside of the comfort of my home, feels weird to me now.

But I'm about to try a whole string of new things, so why not start here?

When Anthony asked me to meet him at Fresh Feathers, I thought he just meant so he could walk me up to his apartment. But he guided me into the dry cleaner and to the back room, where I discovered Esme's secret treasure trove of beauty. Spying some of the Halloween Ball designs months early was gift enough, but then Anthony plucked a hanger off of one of the racks and passed it to me, tilting his head toward a curtained area I belatedly realized was a dressing room.

"For this weekend," he explained.

Ah. The outing I'd agreed to. At the high-end club.

Maybe I should be offended that Anthony assumes I don't have clothes for the occasion. But examining this dress he picked for me, I can confidently say nothing in my closet would have worked. If I'm not in scrubs, I'm in jeans. If I'm not in jeans, I'm in cutoffs. If I'm not in cutoffs, I'm in a sundress.

This is a clubbing dress. A rich green silk that dips low in the front, but still has enough structure that I think my cleavage will stay in place. The skirt will cling to my hips, falling mid-thigh with a slit up the back so my legs can move.

The amazing thing about the garment is that when I step into it, the garment fits as if it were stitched for me.

What designer did he get this from? Did Anthony somehow eyeball my measurements and pass them on?

There's a zipper in the back I can't reach, so I step out of the curtained area with my hands pressed to my chest to keep the material from sagging.

"Zip me up?" I turn my back to him, and in the next moment, I feel a light touch on my lower back. The heat of his body plays against my skin as Anthony's fingers drag the zipper up, slower than necessary.

The man is teasing me.

"Where did you find this dress?" I ask, my question breathless.

"Do you like it?" His lips brush kisses on my bare shoulder as he asks. The thin strap of the dress leaves plenty of real estate for him to caress.

Goose bumps pebble over my skin, and I can't help leaning back into him. "It's gorgeous." My hands glide over where the material covers my thighs, loving the smooth texture. "It's like someone made it just for me."

Anthony's hands follow the path mine did, and he grows hard against me.

"I did."

"You ..." My brain is turning foggy with lust, so it takes me a moment to process his words. "You what?"

There's a lower, wicked chuckle. "I've worn enough of other designers' creations. I figured I'd try my hand at making one of my own. And you, my lovely harpy, are the perfect muse." His finger hooks under the slim strap on my shoulder and tugs it until it slips down. "Now, I need you to take it off."

I frown. "Why? I like it."

He lets out a rumble, deep in his throat. "Good. You can wear it Saturday. But now, I need it off you, so I don't rip the seams, trying to get at your pussy. After seeing you like this ..." His hands glide up to cup my breasts, the silk smoothing over my pebbled nipples. "I need you to fuck me."

My body shudders with need. "Then, unzip me. Now."

Anthony is faster this time, almost too fast, but there's no sound of tearing. I shimmy the glistening fabric off, careful to arrange it as I found it on the hanger, and then I turn to find the talented man eyeing me with devastating heat in his gaze.

"Where's Esme?" My voice is husky with need.

"Done for the day. Left me the key to the shop."

"Irresponsible of her." I tsk.

He gives me a wicked grin a moment before dropping to his knees in front of me.

"Give me a taste," he begs, hands on my thighs, face pressed against my belly, where he tongues my belly button in a teasing promise.

I never knew a man could want to go down as much as Anthony Shelly does. He acts like my vulva is a five-star restaurant and he's got a standing reservation. One that might get canceled if he doesn't eat every bite served to him.

Even though part of me wants to stay in constant contact with the man, I know my muscles will betray me the moment Anthony starts with that talented mouth of his, so I back away, out of his hold, until my shoulders find the cool press of the wall. Anthony stays kneeling in the middle of the workroom, stare locked on my mostly naked form. I took my bra off because the dress would have shown the straps, but I left on my lace panties.

Capturing his gaze, I pull on my commanding persona. The one I know makes him hot and hard.

"Crawl to me," I tell him. "Take these off." I tap the waistband of my underwear. "Then, make me come."

"Fuck," he groans, palming the bulge in his pants, as if he needs to release the ache slightly.

Then, he follows my directions perfectly.

23

ANTHONY

THE SUN IS warm on my skin. I only meant to lie on the library's dock for a few minutes, but as I blink my eyes open, I realize I must have dozed off.

There's a strange weight on my chest. Heavy, but not so much that I struggle to breathe.

Lifting my head, I glance toward my chest.

Sin is draped over me in twisting coils, using me as a rock to bake himself in the sun.

"Come on, man. Not cool."

Sin lifts his head, flicks his tongue at me, then slips off in a petulantly slow glide.

Which reveals my beautiful, new, snake-patterned suntan.

"What the hell?!" I sit up and rub my hand over my chest. Does absolutely nothing. Sin left his imprint. "You're lucky I don't have any shirtless photo shoots in the next few weeks."

Although some people would probably think a snake tan was badass.

They'd want one.

Everyone would start buying snakes just to lie out on the beach with.

Would they care about the snakes after that?

I grimace, thinking about Violetta's *elephant tusk* comment once again. The idea that I could post a funny picture of myself and that might result in the mistreatment of hundreds, maybe thousands, of animals has my gut twisting.

Sin curls up beside me, and I absentmindedly reach out to stroke a finger over his beaded skin.

"You finally made nice with your familiar. Have I been replaced? Is Sin your new best friend now?" Broderick appears at the edge of the dock, making the structure dip slightly as he steps onto the floating platform.

"Of course." I smirk. "Sin and I go way back."

Broderick snorts and settles on a lounge chair. He looks mopey.

"What's up?"

He sighs. "I had study meetings all day."

"And that's bad?"

"Today is Wednesday."

People often assume twins have telepathy, but half the time, when Broderick talks, I'm lost.

"Okay?"

He shifts, as if uncomfortable in his chair. "Wednesday is recycling day."

Ah. "No firebird sighting."

He drops his head back. "I could *feel* her. When she came into the lounge outside my office, I knew she was there. But I couldn't just kick my student out to awkwardly ogle a woman I doubt likes me."

"I would have," I claim with a shrug.

Broderick ignores my comment. "I'm a mess."

"Use your nipples." That's the extent of romantic advice I can provide. Not sure why he comes to me at all.

"It's getting to the point where I might," he mutters.

There's the sound of heavy footsteps on wood, and we both glance up to see Jack joining us. The werewolf gives my brother what could pass for a smile and a wave while I barely get a half-nod.

Guess he's still mad about the other day.

Doesn't the guy know siblings get into it sometimes? Though, truth be told, Ame's not the type to fight back. So, raising my voice to her feels a lot like yelling at an injured kitten.

Yeah, I'm a piece of shit.

"Hey, how's that bug in the grading system coming?" Broderick asks as Jack settles into one of the dock lounge chairs.

"All fixed."

Jack works in the technology department at the same university where Broderick teaches Literature and Creative Writing. I try not to let on how the shift to a topic I'm not a part of irks me.

If they wanted to chat academics, couldn't they have done it up at the house? Leave me and my snake to our sunbathing?

"Thank the gods. I cannot deal with another sobbing student pounding on my office door, demanding to know why they're failing." Broderick grimaces and rubs the bridge of his nose.

Jack shrugs. "Some might still be. Didn't give them all A's." The wolf leans forward in his seat, resting his elbows on his knees. His posture exudes an ominous air. "Ame's birthday is in four weeks."

The sudden change in subject has me blinking. But he's right. Baby sister is growing up.

"You planning something for her?" Broderick asks.

"Of course." Jack gives my brother a look, like he asked if the wolf showers regularly. Like the answer is obvious and he's offended anyone would even ask.

One thing is for sure—this wolf is gone over my sister.

That's the kind of love Ame deserves, and I'm glad she found it. Even with this scary asshole.

As if hearing the thought, Jack turns his intimidating stare on me. "You have until then to learn how to hug her properly."

I choke on my next breath. "W-what?"

Jack continues to hold my gaze, his stare unrelenting. "You hug her like it's an inconvenience. Like it hurts. You need to get over that shit. She's not about to magic you, so stop acting like it. You make her feel bad." The wolf rises to his feet, towering over the two of us, but I'm the one his shadow engulfs. "Ame will not feel bad on her birthday."

The pronouncement rings in the air, as if Jack is warning the universe that if his mate is unhappy, there will be hell to pay.

Before I can formulate an answer, the werewolf strides off the dock and back toward the house, leaving me with my mouth gaping.

Once I get over my initial shock, I glance Broderick's way, only to watch my brother grimace.

"He has a point," Broderick admits.

Fuck. My insides roil. I know I'm not great at connecting with my sisters, but I didn't realize I was making Ame feel bad about herself.

"I didn't know," I mutter.

My twin claps me on the shoulder.

"Now, you do. So, work on it." He smiles, but there's a touch of concern. "Or Jack might literally decapitate you. The guy's done it before."

24

ANTHONY

THE CLUB LIGHTS refract off the emerald shimmer of Zara's dress. The one I fashioned solely for her, and she wears it better than any runway model could manage. The play of light mesmerizes me. Or maybe it's the woman that has my mind focused on nothing else. All the times that I've gone to clubs to promote a new drink or a new fashion or any other product blend together into a mass of indecipherable nights.

This one stands out as a bright beacon in the haze.

I can't imagine being here without Zara. This packed club would seem empty without her tucked into my side. She stares around with wide eyes, and I guess Folk Haven doesn't tend to have gatherings like this. I'm not even sure the entire town could fill up this club.

There's a spike in my chest—something like pride because I could give her this new experience. I hope that she is dazzled by this night. I pray she'll be willing to go to future outings with me.

Could she go to every single one?

"Sir, please follow me." The club employee ushers Zara and me through the crowd toward the VIP section, where a brand representative waits with a wide smile. This is treatment I'm used to, but Zara seems surprised.

"Aren't we going on the dance floor?" she asks.

There is nothing more I want than to swing into that crowd, pull Zara into my arms, and feel the sway and press of her against me.

But I am here for work. At least for now.

"They just want to get a few shots of me in the exclusive section with the clothing line. Shots on the crowded dance floor would have trouble showing the outfit. I promise we'll be done with this part soon, and then we can dance the rest of the night away."

Zara smiles up at me and lets me lead her forward, seemingly up for anything that we do this night.

The VIP section is much like any other. Low couches and tables, roped off from the rest of the clubgoers, yet still completely visible by them. This is not a section that's meant to be fully obscured. It is supposed to be a coveted place. A throne set above the peasants. Something to aim for. Something to empty their wallets in order to achieve.

I settle in the middle of the couch, pulling Zara down next to me. The brand rep glances at my date with a small frown. I'm not sure what has her upset—Zara's lack of social media prestige, the fact that she's wearing a dress made by an unknown designer instead of the one I'm meant to be selling, or if she can tell that my date is a small-town girl and not a city seductress.

Whatever judgmental thought is going through her head, she'd better not let it come out of her mouth. If anyone in this club insults my harpy, I will leave immediately. I hold the assistant's gaze with hard, unrelenting eyes. She gets the message and pastes a wide smile on her face.

"We are so excited to have you here, Crimson Dread. Of

course, all drinks are comped, so feel free to order whatever you and your friend would like. I'll go grab the photographer now that you've arrived."

I give her a short nod, and she hurries away.

Zara, meanwhile, gazes around the club with fascination in her wide eyes. "How often did you go clubbing before you came to Folk Haven?"

I shrug. "Maybe three or four nights a week."

Zara blinks her wide, beautiful eyes at me. "How do you not have hearing damage? Or do you?"

That's not the observation I expected her to make. But now that Zara has pointed it out, the cacophonous music and the steady thrumming beat pounds against my eardrums in a way I never noticed before.

How have I not realized how loud it is in here?

Maybe it takes a set of new eyes to point out the layers of a place. Or a new set of ears.

"None that I'm aware of," I respond with a smirk. "But I've got many years ahead of me as an influencer. It might all go at some point."

Zara smiles and squeezes my knee with a comforting hand.

In that small gesture, I hear the words she doesn't say. *Don't do anything that will hurt yourself. Take care of yourself.*

This is a strange mixture of feelings I have toward Zara. One minute, I want to strip her dress off and kiss every inch of skin on her body. The next moment, I want to curl myself around her and bask in the comfort of her presence.

I have no trouble envisioning Zara with her little monster baby. That odd child will have a loving, devoted mother.

What would that be like?

Dammit, I'm jealous of a nonexistent kid.

Not that I see Zara in a motherly role for myself. That would be super weird and creepy. I simply wish that my mother had cared even half as much about her real children that Zara does about her yet-to-be-conceived offspring.

"What do you want to drink?" I ask over the music. "Like she said, it's all on the house."

"I don't know." The corner of her mouth quirks up in a teasing curve. "I'm tempted to buy a glass of that six-hundred-dollar tequila. A charmingly handsome man sold me on it."

I can't help my own devilish smirk as I wave a waitress over and ask for two glasses of the drink I advertised a few weeks ago. When she returns with our drinks, I make sure to leave her a generous tip. Just because the beverages are comped doesn't mean that the waitress's tips are.

"Cheers to new experiences." I tilt my drink toward Zara.

"Cheers to talented designers." Her eyes trace over my clothes at the same time she strokes her hand down the green silk of her dress. The one I designed for her.

Pride is an unfamiliar swell in my chest.

She clinks her glass against mine, then goes to take a sip.

And immediately grimaces.

Then, she stares around with guilty eyes. "Oh shoot. Do you think anyone saw me do that? They're not taking pictures of us now, are they?"

I grin at her adorable worry. "We're not trying to sell the tequila tonight, so you're good." Because I can't help myself, I lean over and press my lips against the corner of her jaw. "That rep for the brand will stop by and let me know when they're taking photos. She'll probably ask me to pose in a certain way. What do you want to drink instead of this overpriced lighter fluid?" I make sure to speak only loud enough for Zara to hear me. Even though I'm not shopping the tequila tonight, it wouldn't look good for me to bad-mouth it only a couple of months after selling it.

"It cost a lot." Zara frowns at the liquid in her glass. "I should drink it."

I rest my palm on her bare thigh, wanting to drag my hand up further. "You should drink what you want. Whatever tastes good."

She turns her head to meet my eyes. "I don't think this bar carries the kind of drinks I'm used to. What's good? What do you normally spend your nights drinking when you get to choose?"

That's the problem though. I can't choose. I let my handler for the night grab me whatever because if I show interest in a beverage, then that drink is gone by the second round, bought out by the covetous crowd. Still, I figure if I call for an entire bottle of something, we'll be set for the night. I don't think Zara is looking to black out. I raise my hand for the waitress, and she pops back into our section, takes my order, then returns a moment later with a chilled bottle.

"Champagne! Oh, that's perfect."

"Can't go wrong with sweet and bubbly."

"True. Though I have to say, I'm a fan of dry and sarcastic." Zara gives me a teasing grin over her glass flute, then closes her eyes and hums in appreciation at the taste.

Success.

Just when I'm about to lean in for a sample directly from her lips, a group of people appears at the entrance to the VIP section.

My job begins.

"Crimson Dread, we are so glad you were able to join us last minute! Silver Threadz is honored to have you as a brand ambassador." A woman with a stylized Mohawk grins at me as she clutches a tablet to her chest.

Gods, that sounds like I'm going to UN meetings on behalf of clothing.

"Of course," I intone, wishing this weren't a business outing and that I could spend the rest of the night watching Zara sample overpriced drinks before dragging her onto the dance floor.

"Here we have your partners for the evening." She waves a group of beautiful people into the low booth, and they crowd in beside Zara and me, all smiling, all eager.

All looking at my date like she's something to consume.

Damn it.

My magic.

Any one of these people who feels even the slightest attraction toward my harpy will now have an amplified lust because I can't keep my hands off her.

Violetta's warning sounds in the back of my mind. Maybe the witch had a point about exerting control. I'd really like to get that male model giving Zara a dazed-eyed grin to back off.

But I can't be confrontational on a job. That would blow up on social media in a bad—career-ending—way.

"I think I might check out the dance floor," Zara announces, standing and straightening her deliciously short skirt before throwing me an apologetic smile. "I don't want to be in any pictures. And I don't want to distract you. How about you come and find me when you're done?"

No. Gods fucking no.

"Okay," I manage, barely restraining the annoyed growl in my voice.

I'm not agitated with Zara. She makes complete sense.

I'm aggravated with this job and how I'll have to spend the next hour pretending all I want to do is lounge around an expensive club in designer clothes when, really, I'd rather be in a small-town marina, line dancing with people who have zero social media presence.

And I feel a tinge of sympathy for my brother. Turns out, I was too quick to judge Broderick for staying in his meeting when the object of his affection was within reach.

"She's gorgeous," the model at my side observes once Zara has slipped into the crowd of bodies.

"I know," I mutter, slouching back onto the couch and grabbing a shot of the gross tequila, throwing it back for real.

"That's a great shot." The rep gestures for a young man at her side, and the guy holds up a camera. "Keep doing what you're doing. Okay, everyone, grab some drinks and have a good time. Pretend I'm not here."

Easy enough. I only have eyes for the harpy I spy through the occasional shift in bodies.

Now, it's just a countdown until I can join her.

25

ZARA

Now, I know why they used to burn witches at the stake.

They're too hot to deal with.

After a stretch on my own, where I kindly turned down a handful of advances, Anthony finally appears at my side. The outfit he's wearing fascinates me. A set of fitted red dress pants makes a statement that's emphasized by a short-sleeved black button-up with jagged silver designs stitched into the fabric. The flashing club lights reflect off the metallic thread. The look is bold, but Anthony wears it like a second skin. And as he moves with me on the dance floor, I wonder if I could get pregnant just from the way he sways his hips.

If only. That would solve all my problems, right?

Wrong. That would only cause a waterfall of new ones.

There would be the brief joy of me having everything I wanted. A little baby to love and care for, plus a funny, sensual mythic as the father.

But Anthony is not the man to be my partner. This night, fun as it is, makes that fact achingly clear. Even if Anthony does suddenly decide he wants to try something long-term with me, there's no way I could raise a baby with a guy who goes out to clubs four nights a week, travels to different cities around the world, and constantly puts his life on display for others.

I'm a small-town vet who can transform into a mythical bird woman. Our lives might overlap for this temporary moment in time, but that's it. Our end date is necessary.

In the future, he'll roll through town to visit his siblings, and we'll bump into each other at Mary Jo's maybe, and we'll smile and laugh and reminisce about our fling.

But that's all this will ever be. A short, beautiful romance.

"I want you," Anthony whispers, but his lips are so close to my ear, hot breath brushing against my neck, that I hear him, even over the pounding music.

This reminder of how quickly our end is coming has my skin feeling tight and needy. Soon, we'll have our last kiss. Then, I'll never have this man again.

"I want you too," I shout over the beat. Do I sound desperate? That's how I feel.

Anthony meets my eyes, his green irises seeming to glow in the club lights. "Let's get out of here."

He tugs me through the crowd of people toward the exit, and I keep my fingers laced tight in his, imagining them teasing through the wetness that's already gathered at the center of me.

We only have to wait a moment at the valet stand before the limo provided by the fashion company pulls up and Anthony tucks me inside.

"Where to, sir?" the driver asks, and I expect him to name the hotel he mentioned having a room in.

"I'll double your tip if you just drive around."

"Anthony!" I gasp on a laugh.

He gives me a wicked grin that has my nipples going rock hard.

"Sure thing." The driver closes the privacy screen as he

accelerates, and before I realize what's happening, Anthony is off his seat, kneeling between my legs.

"I can't wait for the hotel. I need you now." He gazes up at me, eyes wild. "Say yes."

"Yes," I rasp, spreading my thighs wide.

He groans, leaning in to drag an open-mouthed kiss up my neck the same time his hand pushes under my skirt. Those devilish fingers of his wrench my underwear to the side and stroke through my arousal until I'm rocking against his hand, needy gasps escaping, and my talons threaten to sprout from my nail beds.

"I want in, Zara. Gods, let me into your tight pussy," he begs. "Please."

"Yes. Yes. Yes," I chant, feeling empty and achy, wanting to clench down on something hard as he teases me with light touches.

Thank goodness I wore the contraception charm. I made the choice only to tease Anthony, the simple jewelry around my neck letting him know I was ready whenever. But I didn't truly think we'd do anything before getting back to our room.

There's the clink of metal, and I realize Anthony has undone his belt buckle with one hand. He shoves his pants down, then stops stroking me.

I whimper a protest, but he digs his fingers into the meat of my ass and drags me to the edge of the seat. Watching in horny fascination, my eyes follow his hand as he jerks the length of himself, then uses the tip of his cock to stroke my clit. My whole body spasms, my skin prickling as my feathers try to force their way to the surface. But I hold my other form inside and concentrate on the erotic sight of Anthony slipping into my body.

"Fuck, Zara. What are you doing to me?" His hips meet mine, and his eyes seek mine out, still with that wild tinge to them. "I need you," he growls. "Fucking addicted to you."

That sounds heavy, but it's just the passion of the moment. Because right now, my heart is pounding so hard that I'm half-convinced I'll die if he doesn't give me an orgasm I crave.

"Then, take me," I demand, rocking my hips into his.

Anthony's eyes flutter shut as he groans, and next I know, his fingers have found their way to my clit.

"Oh gods. Yes, touch me."

Bracing my hands on the seat, I lean back enough to watch as the gorgeous man coveted by the world spends all his time and focus on my pleasure. The skin of Anthony's cock grows slick with our combined arousal, and he massages my bundle of nerves with such skill that I can't help thinking how he's had years of practice.

Plenty of partners before me.

He'll have plenty more after.

No. Don't think of that now. Be here with him while he's yours.

"Look at me, please," he purrs, and my gaze flies up to clash with his. "Let me see you come."

The erotic request has me choking and gasping, then coming. My inner walls flutter like wings, and in this single moment, I feel like I'm flying and falling at the same time.

26

———

ANTHONY

Zara is passed out in the bed beside me, her naked body covered in a tangle of sheets. The birth control necklace shimmers in the dim light from the bedside clock. There are a few stray black feathers scattered over the white bedding. I wonder if she realizes she sheds them sometimes during her orgasm.

I find the hints of her harpy nature fascinating, plucking one of the feathers up. The thing is downy soft. Could fill a mattress with them and sleep like a king.

With my queen at my side.

More like she's the queen and I'm her jester.

Whatever lets me stay with her forever.

I'm not the one for her. Can't give her what she needs. What she wants.

Tonight put into perspective just how bored I've become with my job. The only moments I enjoyed were when Zara was by my side. If I could take her on every future gig, I could probably keep up with this. But influencing isn't what Zara wants to do. Selling luxury products to the rich holds no appeal for her. She wants to help people. Heal animals.

But more than that, she wants her partner and a family.

She wants to stay in Folk Haven.

Even if my life and personality were different, if I were some reliable accountant with roots in Folk Haven, I'd still be me.

A magical replica.

Can a creature made purely of magic reproduce?

What if I convince Zara to take a chance on me, only to discover I'm sterile? She said she was open to adoption, but that doesn't solve every problem. She might build her hopes of a future—a life—on me, and then I could disappear one day because my mother ended the spell that had made me in the first place.

I might as well be a ghost. Living a half-life on this earth, about to pass on at any moment.

It's better that Zara and I keep this a casual arrangement, like we planned. That we go our separate ways at the end of May.

She'll find someone else to love.

The idea sends a white-hot bolt of rage through me. The idea of another man touching her, hearing his name in her husky voice, getting to look into her warm brown eyes as she falls apart because of his touch.

Not mine.

"Fuck him," I mutter to the future man who will fondle her feathers and give my harpy everything she wants. Everything I can't.

A selfish part of me, which—let's be honest—is most of me, wants to make him work fucking hard to push me out of Zara's memories.

If he's going to take my spot, he's going to have to work himself to the bone to give her more pleasure than I do.

Zara lets out a sleepy murmur as I kiss her bare shoulder. I slide lower, pressing my lips against the back of her arm, then her elbow. My harpy lets out a wistful sigh, her body turning into mine, the sheet slipping over the generous mound of her breast, revealing a peaked nipple.

The dusky tip is too much temptation for a weak man like me to ignore.

I encircle her with my mouth, sucking and licking and teasing until my harpy is squirming.

"Again?" she asks, her voice heavy with sleep.

I let her go with a pop. "I'm starving for you."

Zara tucks her chin, meeting my eyes with a set that sparks in humor. "You think I'm tasty?"

With a groan, I plunge beneath the sheets, seeking out the core of her. She's still slick from my earlier work, but I want her soaking all over again because of me.

No one else will love you this good. Can give you this the way I can.

Another man might give her a kid, but I'll tattoo the sensation of my mouth on her cunt until she can't have someone's face between her legs without thinking of mine.

Though I want to plunder and claim, I hold myself back, seeking to draw this out. Bring Zara to the edge and hold her there before sending her flying. My tongue traces along her intimate folds, dipping inside her heat and enjoying the way her thighs tense and hips rock with each of my strokes.

"Anthony." She moans my name. Pleading for more. Needing me.

How am I supposed to give you up?

Shoving the thought away, I concentrate on the heady taste of her on my lips, the soft press of her skin against my fingertips, where I grasp her thighs and hold them open for my ministrations. The sting of her talons in my hair as she reaches under the sheet and cradles my skull, pulling me closer as she tries to seek out her pleasure.

"You want it?" I ask against her pussy. "You want to come on my mouth?"

"Yes!" she gasps. "Now!"

"Mmm." I purr the sound as I lave the gentlest lick over her clit.

Her body jerks, but I back off and earn a frustrated growl.

The sound only has me chuckling.

"Not yet. I want to play."

"You've been playing all night—" she starts grumbling, then cuts off with a gasp when I slip three fingers inside her.

"There we go. You took that so nice," I praise her, my mouth against the smooth skin of her inner thigh.

Concentrating on the feel of her inner walls, I bend my knuckles, making a *come to me* motion, while reaching my free hand up to spread flat over her lower belly, applying pressure. Imagining my fingers meeting my palm, I seek out that special sensation in her body. The fuse for the fireworks.

"What are—oh—oh-oh goddess—Anthony!"

Found it.

"Do you like it when I tug?" I demonstrate by pulling the hand inside her toward me, keeping my fingers hooked in her the whole time. "Or when I stroke?" This time, I still my palm and bend my fingers, as if beckoning her toward me. Calling her orgasm to follow my lead.

"Uh ... both. Both are ... I can't ... the first makes me—" Zara cuts off on a throaty gasp when I tug again. "Yes! Wh-what ..." She trails off into whimpers as her body writhes, and I threaten to give myself tennis elbow, working her G-spot, all the while grinding my hard cock into the mattress for an ounce of relief.

I might come just from watching her break apart.

"Gods, I love watching you like this," I whisper between placing open-mouthed kisses on her stomach, drunk on the sight of my hand working her soaking wet pussy. "You gonna come for me? Gonna scream my name?"

As if scared of doing exactly that, Zara grabs a pillow and presses it over her face just as slickness coats my fingers and her entire body convulses with a rolling orgasm.

Even through the pillow, I hear a high-pitched shriek that sets my ears to ringing. Over my shoulder, there's a crack, and I glance back to see a spiderweb of shattered glass in the mirror.

Whoops. Forgot that other neat harpy trick.

But I find I'm not too remorseful. More like gleeful.

This is the type of orgasm a woman doesn't forget, even when she finds the perfect cookie-cutter man of her dreams.

Suddenly furious at the reminder of my future replacement, I slip my fingers out of her channel, rear up on my knees, and drag her hips onto my thighs. When I sink inside Zara, her pussy is still twitching from the aftershocks of the orgasm, and I revel in the clenching on my cock.

"Fuck, you feel amazing." I hold her steady, working myself in and out, memorizing every bit of her.

"Goddess," she gasps, still panting, her chest flushed as she gazes up at me with lust-glazed eyes.

I did this to you. No one else can do what I do to you.

Desperate to bury myself as deep in my harpy as I can, I guide her legs up, ankles on my shoulders, and I lean forward until she can't look anywhere but into my eyes. Then, I pound in hard and fast and unforgiving.

Furious that she'll walk away from me eventually.

And that I'll let her.

"Anthony." This time, when she says my name, it's all soft and dreamy with a smile that breaks my heart.

Even though I'm fucking her hard, she finishes in a gentle way that is almost a continuation of the first, her inner walls embracing me.

"Zara. Fuck—" I'm not gentle or elegant. I grunt as my balls draw up and spill, filling her with my magical cum that can't do what I want it to.

I empty myself inside Zara as her legs slip from my shoulders. She cradles me against her body as pleasure and agony tangle inside me.

All I want is for this to last. For this to be real.

All I want is for *me* to be real.

But I'm not, and this fleeting joy is all I have.

27

———————

ANTHONY

THERE'S a golden-orange radiance on my eyelids. A pleasant color that's soothing and distracts me from the fact that my lids are so hard to open. But eventually, I crack them, realizing the glow is from a shade above my head, blocking out the strong light of the sun.

Did I fall asleep outside again?

My sluggish brain attempts to work through what happened before I took my extremely heavy nap.

Zara and I arrived back from Atlanta yesterday. We got in late after exploring the city together, and she invited me to stay the night at her house. In thanks, I tongue-fucked her until she tied me to her bed to get me to stop. Then, my harpy rode me hard, leaving me breathless.

I remember waking up this morning to a bed empty, except for a handful of feathers and a note from Zara, saying she left for work. I pocketed one of the feathers, went back to my place to shower and change, walked down Main Street to Coffee & Claws, where I bought breakfast and coffee for myself, plus a

183

cup of medium roast for Zara. I drove to Folk Tails and dropped the caffeine off for my overworked vet, who only had a moment to press a quick thank-you kiss to my cheek.

Then, I ... decided to visit Violetta.

Yes, that's what I did.

I arrived at the sea witch's house, and she poured me a glass of sweet tea before we walked out to her garden. Tilting my head to the side, I spy a riot of vibrant blooms.

Did I really take a nap in Violetta's garden?

I'm friendly with the witch, but I wouldn't say I trust her. Not enough to be unconscious in her presence.

But here I am, waking up from a nap, trying to ignore the start of a headache.

"Oh good. You're alive." The witch's voice sounds mildly curious.

I can't tell if she's joking.

With a groan, I push myself up into a seated position, realizing I'm on an outdoor lounge chair underneath an awning in the very center of the garden.

"Is there a reason I should be dead?" I ask in a light tone. Violetta did give me that ominous warning the first day. "Did I accidentally touch one of the plants I shouldn't have?"

The witch straightens from where she was examining a bush, then grabs a shovel and starts spreading mulch.

"No. No accident." She pats the fragrant wood chips in an even layer across the roots. "I intentionally fed you a magic killer. In that glass of sweet tea I gave you."

The sentence makes no sense. Or maybe my brain is still functioning on a sleepy lag.

"You ... what?"

"A magic killer." Violetta repeats the descriptor as if something with *killer* in the name is nothing to be concerned about. "Mixture of herbs meant to rip out all your magic." She sends me a triumphant grin from under the brim of her floppy hat. "It worked. Not that I doubted myself. I'm extremely powerful. Besides, it's a type of cleansing. My specialty."

"That's a joke." I don't say it as a question because believing she's telling the truth is absurd.

Still, I probe around inside my brain. My body. My soul.

No buzzing. No tingly force threatening to spill out and do something it shouldn't.

"I tell better jokes than *that*," she huffs.

I can't find a single trace of my magic.

The witch is telling the truth.

Fear and fury war in my chest.

"What in all the fucking hell dimensions were you thinking?" I shout and shove off the chair, running my hands over every inch of my body, desperate to make sure there are no pieces missing. That I haven't started to fester and rot and disintegrate.

Violetta frowns, pausing in her gardening. "You're being extremely ungrateful."

I laugh, a crazed, high-pitched noise that has no true humor in it.

"You poisoned me!"

The witch rolls her eyes. "I gave you what you wanted."

"I didn't want *poison*!"

"Poison," she sneers. "Such a vulgar word. You should save it for my *truly* terrible acts. This one was quite kind, don't you think? Now, we know for sure you are not purely magic." Violetta smiles sweetly at me. "You're welcome."

Now, we know? So, she wasn't sure beforehand?

"And if I were?" I grind out through clenched teeth.

She shrugs. "Then, you'd be dead. And I doubt pure magic can return as a ghost, so I wouldn't have had to bother with you again." Her voice holds zero concern about my possible demise. "But you're not dead, are you? Just a boring old human." Violetta waves her hand, encased in a dirty gardening glove, at my unharmed form. "*This* is what you wanted. Proof you are more than a spell. Maybe your mother used magic to divide an embryo. But she did *not* form one from magic. She is not a goddess, though she might proclaim to be one. You are a blood-and-bone being, who also has magical powers. You're a witch." Violetta shrugs again. "Or you were. Now, your magic is gone."

Gone. My magic is completely gone?

The idea is unfathomable to me. As much as I hated my magic, it felt like hating my bones. A necessary evil to survival.

"Forever?" I rasp the question.

"Unlikely." Violetta returns to spreading mulch. "My guess is, the power should return in a day or so. I think. Honestly, this was the first time I've used this. So, maybe your magic is gone forever. Wouldn't you love that, Mr. Mopey? But chances are, it'll reappear. Then, you can go back to hating yourself. But for now, you have nothing left in you to loathe. Go frolic about in a meadow or whatever you wish." She tosses her shovel into a wheelbarrow, grabs the handles, and leaves me on my own.

My emotions tangle in turmoil. Part of me is livid that Violetta would make this decision for me. Have me drink something that could have killed me, if the witch is to be believed.

But there is another part of me that is so elated that I'm ready to do as she directed and dance.

I have no magic. None.

And every piece of me is still holding together. No important threads have unraveled. I haven't collapsed on the ground, like a lifeless puppet.

I exist. I am real.

And I want to run through the world in my mortal body and feel everything again, knowing that a real hand touches every surface. That the sensations are mine and I get to keep them all.

I want my harpy.

The craving for Zara is sudden and overwhelming.

I lurch forward, wobbling as the world around me feels heavy. *Does magic come with a side of weightlessness?* No matter. The drag against my limbs will remind me that I'm grounded in reality.

That everything I do and everything I am is real.

I leave, making sure not to brush a single plant as I weave my way out of the garden.

My mind is far ahead of me. Down the road and into Of the Wing Territory.

When Zara gets off work, a human man will be waiting for her.

28

———

ANTHONY

WHEN ZARA WALKS up the steps of her front porch, it's all I can do not to start kissing the hell out of her.

"Hey, I didn't know you were coming over." She tilts her head curiously, but the smile on her lips keeps me from thinking I'm an ass for showing up, unannounced.

"Sorry. I should have texted."

Zara slips her key in the front door, throwing me a sultry look over her shoulder as she presses it open. "I don't mind. But I'm going to need a minute to clean up. Had multiple animals pee on me today."

I try to affect my normal casual air, slouching against her doorframe. "If you insist. But no amount of urine could make you less attractive. You elevate the scent."

She snorts and waves me inside after her.

I wonder if Zara notices anything different about me. If I seem more present. More solid.

I bet I at least seem jumpier. I can't dispel this energy thrumming through me. Pure excitement.

I want to use it. Channel it.

Directly into her.

"I'll be out in a minute," she says, heading toward the bedroom.

"Are you going to take a shower?" I call after her.

"Yeah."

"Do you want some company?" Gods, please say yes. I don't know what I'll do if I have to sit on the couch and wait, hearing that running water, knowing it'll be making trails over her bare body, and not being able to see the magnificent sight.

"Come on back."

Hell yes.

I jog through the small house, finding Zara topless in her bathroom, turning the knob to get the shower going. The contraception charm dangles around her neck.

"I need at least one round of soaping before you touch me," she warns, holding a hand up when I would lunge forward to snatch her into my arms. "Why don't you take your time undressing?"

I smirk. "Sounds like you're looking for a show."

My harpy shrugs with a grin, then shucks off her scrub pants, and tugs off her sports bra and panties.

"I've had a long day," she says as I stare in rapture at her gorgeous curves. "Could do with some high-quality entertainment."

"I'm here to please," I murmur.

Zara steps under the falling water and slides the glass door closed, still able to see me clearly. The evil temptress covers a loofah in body wash and starts dragging the sudsy foam all over her curves. I want to press my face against the glass like a kid at the window of a candy shop.

But I promised a show.

I hook my thumbs in my shirt and drag the material over my head, forcing my muscles to slow instead of tearing off every stitch I'm wearing just so I can dive into the shower with her.

When my eyes latch on to her soft brown gaze, I see longing and hunger in her expression, making the subdued movement worth it.

With lazy fingers, I leisurely unbuckle my belt, slowly sliding it from my belt loops, only to jerk it at the last second, sending a harsh snap sounding through the bathroom and earning a gasp from my harpy. Her loofah is all but forgotten as she gapes at me, her nipples hard.

"I think you got that spot already." My eyes drop to her hand, where she's been distractedly rubbing her rib cage for the last minute.

Zara jerks in surprise, and I watch a delicious flush spread over her chest. I want to kiss that heated flesh.

She returns to soaping herself, and I slip my thumb into the waistband of my pants, sliding the button undone and dragging the zipper down until the fly gapes open. My cock was half-hard the moment Zara stepped out of her car, but now, my guy stands at attention, unable to do anything else when the woman I want above anyone else stands feet from me, soaking wet and wanting.

The heat of the shower begins to fog the glass, creeping between us, blurring her image.

The loss of sight sends an irrational spike of panic through me.

I can't lose her.

"You'd better finish up that first round because I'm coming in," I growl, no more patience for playing.

She invited me in here, and now, I'm ready to take her.

Without magic. Just me and my body.

The thought and the need to see every inch of Zara has me ripping off my pants and briefs, kicking the two across the room and stalking to the shower. I open the door enough to slip inside and find her under the cascade of water, fragrant suds dripping down her bare body.

"Gods, you bring me to my knees," I groan, ready to drop this moment and bury my face in her warm center, tonguing her until she cries my name.

But Zara's hands on my shoulders keep me upright.

"The tiles will hurt your knees," she scolds as laughter dances in her eyes. "Stay up here." She presses her back to the wall and pulls my front against hers. "With me."

Then, my sensual harpy claims my mouth, kissing me long and deep as the warm water pounds against my back, and I'm sure I'll melt here, seep directly into her, where I'll never want to leave.

My hands land on her hips, and then I drag one up to tease her eager nipple and let the other drop to grip her muscular thigh. With a guiding touch, I encourage Zara to sling her one leg around my hip, and she's the perfect height for me to nestle my cock in her folds.

I don't slip inside yet, only thrust against her slick inner lips, coating myself in her pleasure and angling to massage her clit.

"Goddess." Her head drops back against the wall of the shower, and I kiss up her exposed neck, my hips moving at a more frantic pace.

I need her to come now. With me, like this. Without an ounce of magic making her want me. This is me and Zara. Honestly lusting after each other.

But it's more than lust.

I know it is for me, and now, I'll prove how good we can be together. I'll make this so good that Zara won't be able to fathom an end to us.

"Come on. You want to come on my cock, don't you?"

Her chest heaves, her breathing ragged, and there's a wild look in her eyes.

"Anthony." She moans my name, and the sound is so fucking good on her lips.

I pinch her nipple, then slip my hand down to angle myself upward so I can sink in deep. Zara's eyes flutter as little whimpers escape her throat.

"Come on," I tell her. Beg her.

Come for me like this. Come for just me.

My fingers find her clit, and I stay buried deep as I work her and press hot, open-mouthed kisses against her neck.

Finally, she yelps, and the glorious, pulsing clenches I wanted seize her body, shuddering through her in a rolling release. Gripping hold of my cock.

"That's it. Gods, you did so good."

As she rides the ecstasy, I thrust in her. The wet sounds of her orgasm, coating me with each penetration, mix with the pounding of the shower water.

"You're everything, Zara. Gods, I can't get enough. I'll never get enough." I groan the words against her hot neck as I pound into her, my balls heavy, wanting to spill. Every part of me is weighted, more present than I've ever been. I'm alive and between the thighs of my harpy, and the happiness filling me is a certain kind of terrifying.

But I don't retreat. I lean into it. I dive into her.

"Do you feel me?" I groan. "All I can feel is you."

"So good," she whimpers. "Keep going."

One of her hands clutches my back; the other digs into the meat of my ass, encouraging every thrust I make.

"Better than any time before. Can't get enough," I pant, never wanting this to end, but also craving that brain-melting spike that I know will be a high I've never experienced.

"I need you," Zara moans, pulling me hard against her and grinding her hips into mine.

That does it. My pelvis practically shatters from the force of my orgasm. The sound that leaves my throat isn't human, but more like an animal.

I feel wild and proud as I realize Zara is coming around me a second time. She bites into my shoulder to stifle a sharp scream. Her inner muscles milk every last drop out of me, until I'm barely able to stay standing.

"Hells." She huffs the curse against my skin, a sense of wonder in her voice. "That was ..."

Her inability to find a description has me grinning. I don't want her to be able to describe it. I want the way I make her feel to be so mind-boggling that she can never find the words. All she can do is crave more.

I lean back enough to meet her big brown eyes.

She gazes up at me with an almost-sleepy smile. A full day of work and mind-altering shower sex must have worn her out. But I'm not ready to let her go yet. I'll hold her up. Like I want to do forever.

"Guess what." I lean in to tease my nose over hers, and Zara chuckles.

"What?"

"You just got a dose of pure, unadulterated Anthony."

Her brows wrinkle in confusion, her lips twisting in a small smile. "What do you mean?"

"I mean"—I dip down to whisper the words against her neck, loving the way she shivers in response to the heat of my breath—"my magic is gone."

Her body jerks, which sends a surprising streak of pleasure through what I thought was a spent dick. Seems like my body wants to go again.

"What do you mean, it's gone?" she asks.

I chuckle, tracing my tongue over her neck. "Violetta fed me a potion. Didn't realize it at the time, but it eradicated my magic."

Raising my head, I hit her with a grin I can't get rid of, wanting Zara to know I'm not really mad at the meddling witch. My harpy is protective, and the frown she wears now is adorable. But there's no reason for her to go off and scold the woman on my behalf.

"It's okay. I'm glad she did it. Gods, it's amazing, knowing what I'm like without it. Freeing." My cock is half-hard already, and I rock my hips, loving the feel of Zara's body gripping me. "Could you feel the difference? This was ... fuck, I just felt so real this time."

"You were certainly ... enthusiastic." Her voice sounds strained, and I meet her concerned eyes. "Are you okay?"

Gods, she's perfection.

"I'm amazing. I never imagined I could exist like this. Not a single ounce of magic left." I twine a wet strand of her hair around my finger. "But Violetta said it likely wouldn't last forever. Probably not more than a day or two." I'm not looking forward to the magic returning, but it means a lot, knowing I can live without it. "She didn't permanently change me without my permission."

"Oh. Okay." Zara still looks off-balance, and I suddenly worry this revelation, on top of a long day, is too much for her to absorb.

Time for me to take care of my woman.

Gently, I slip myself out of her hold, swooping in for another quick kiss.

"Why don't you finish your shower, and I'll get some food going?" When I cup her cheeks in my palms, she's all soft warmth.

"Yeah, okay," she replies after a pause. "Thank you. I am hungry."

Zara offers me a subdued smile, and my heart aches to see her so worn out.

I want to take care of her. Be here for her. And not just tonight.

Knowing I'm permanent changes everything.

I can plan a future.

A future with a harpy I love.

29

ZARA

THE NIGHT IS DARK, devoid of the moon. The empty sky is a reflection of the sensation in my chest.

Last night should've been wonderful. I've never seen Anthony express that level of unbridled joy.

But the reason guts me.

I spread my wings and launch from the tree branch I've been perched on for the last half hour as I contemplated the reason for Anthony's excitement. Hoping that taking wing will calm the turmoil in my mind, I glide over the calm waters of Lake Galen. Many mythics take advantage of the dark-moon night to assume our magical forms and spread limbs that would otherwise terrify our human neighbors.

But it's not only humans that are discomforted by us.

Anthony told me of his temporary lack of magic with so much eagerness that it was visibly radiating off him. That he could find such happiness in the lack of powers is what won't let my mind settle.

I understood his dislike of magic, but I didn't realize his disgust for it ran so deep. So many things are coming together in my mind now, and the conclusion makes me want to cry. I falter in my flight and look for another sturdy branch to land upon. When I find one, the landing is smooth and easy. Instinctual. I let my clawed feet dig into the bark as I clasp the trunk with my taloned hands.

I know I'm not beautiful in my harpy form. Some mythics are gorgeous in their other states. Sirens maintain the look of a human, only with glorious, sprawling wings. Merpeople simply replace their legs with glittering fish tails.

But my skin disappears, covered with soft feathers. My face sharpens, my eyes alter, and my wings, as broad as a siren's, meld cleanly into the birdlike body that I take on.

I know I'm not beautiful. But I love this part of myself.

I found out the hard way that Christian didn't.

And now, I can guess the reaction that Anthony will have if I ever reveal myself to him.

I am the embodiment of magic. And he loathes magic.

Would he want me to take that potion?

Would he prefer if we were both simply human?

This ache in my chest is my own doing. Our arrangement was only ever meant to be temporary. It shouldn't matter how Anthony feels about my mythical form. And yet my heart—without my consent—started to make plans. Ones that involved a handsome redhead who made me smile and laugh and feel loved.

Anthony doesn't love me.

He's never said it, and even if he did, I could only trust that he would love half of me.

But the truth that hurts even more, which I refuse to turn away from, is that Anthony could never love a monster.

This is like Christian all over again. Only worse somehow.

"Why did I do this to myself?" My voice comes out in a husky murmur, agony nailed into every syllable.

I fooled myself into thinking Anthony knew and understood all of me.

When the charming man sank deep inside my body, I felt my wings as if they were sprawling from my back, and I convinced myself that he could see them. I imagined that when Anthony smiled down at me and whispered those endearing words, he was looking at all of me. I didn't feel like I was hiding a part of myself from him.

But maybe I was.

Maybe there was a shadow in my consciousness that understood this fragile relationship would come crashing down if he got even a glimpse of the magic that was inseparable from my soul. I've never offered to show Anthony this side of myself. He has never asked. We've been playing pretend, and now, I've fallen outside of the game, and I'm forced to remember it was all just temporary.

And I can't play anymore.

Anthony might be here for another few weeks, but last night has to be our final night together.

The feathers around my eyes suddenly feel cold, and I realize that tears are streaming from the corners. I don't want to say good-bye to him. I don't want to give him up. But how can I stay with someone who hates a part of me? How can I be with someone who celebrates the lack of this half of me that brings so much joy?

I can't stay with Anthony even for one more night, knowing he would look at this side of me with disgust.

We were never going to work. I shouldn't have let myself forget.

I give myself over to the wind again, flying high in the night to remind myself that I am powerful and I am worth more than one man's opinion. I will not be ashamed of the magnificence of me.

Anthony can keep his magic hatred to himself. He can drink his own poison.

I will not sip from that cup.

30

____

ANTHONY

MY MAGIC RETURNS after roughly twenty-four hours. I feel the
hum and buzz of it in my veins, though I don't find the sensation irritating. Not now, when I know it might live in me, but it
is not *me*.

And with some help from Violetta, I can always get rid of
the power again. At the moment, I don't feel the need.

What I do need is my harpy.

If I'm not a body formed by magic, then that means I'm real.
And if I'm real, then I've got swimmers with DNA.

*I could give Zara her monster baby. She doesn't need to go to
some other man and fall in love with him.*

Not when I'm already in love with her.

My fingers tap an excited rhythm on my steering wheel as I
drive the forested roads of Folk Haven toward her home. I
wanted to stay over at her place last night, but she told me the
night of the dark moon meant she was going out. So, I left
despite wanting to stay.

Next month, I'll convince her there's no reason for me to go. I can keep the bed warm until she returns in the morning.

As I pull into Zara's drive and spy her car parked out front, I'm glad for the dark moon. Zara said she always takes work off the day after to recover from being out until the early hours. Which means she's here, hopefully well rested because I plan on wearing her out again.

I bound up her front steps and barely hold myself back from pounding on her door. I'm that excited to see her lovely, sleep-mussed face. Instead, I press the doorbell and hear a small chime. After a moment of waiting, there's the muffled sound of shuffling feet, and my heart pounds harder in anticipation.

This day will change everything.

When Zara opens the door, my breath leaves me. She's wrapped in a cotton robe that stretches over her curves. Her hair sits in a messy bun high on her head, and her eyelids blink in surprise at the sight of me.

She's gorgeous.

"Good morning, my lovely," I croon to her through the screened door.

"Anthony. What are you doing here?" Zara pushes the door open, but instead of inviting me inside, she joins me on the porch.

It is a nice morning. The air warming in the spring sun.

"I wanted to see you. To talk to you." Dipping at the waist, I kiss the corner of her jaw and breathe in a lungful of her fresh, flowery scent. "Yesterday was amazing."

To be with her when I was completely and only myself. Not an ounce of magic. I'd never been more present. Surer.

Zara and I are meant for each other.

"About that." The press of her palm on my chest forces me to take a step back.

When I see the frown in the dipped corners of her mouth, my throat tightens.

Something is wrong.

"What's up?" I ask, trying to keep my tone light and teasing but hearing the desperate rasp as I force the question out.

She crosses her arms over her chest. "I know we still have a couple of weeks left in our arrangement. But I think we should break things off now. This is beginning to feel too serious for me."

Someone must have chopped a tree down, shoved it over, and let the massive trunk fall straight onto my oblivious head because, in this moment, I am demolished.

She's done with me.

The woman I love doesn't want to see me anymore.

Just as I'm about to commit fully to the spiral of despair, her words pierce through the uproar in my brain.

This is getting too serious for her.

But that's what Zara wants. She wants to be serious.

She thinks that *I* don't want serious.

A grin crashes across my face. She jerks her head back, the frown deepening on her mouth.

"I love you, Zara Ironfeather," I say, making sure not an ounce of my normal flippant sarcasm is present so she knows to trust every word. "I love you, and I want to be with you. No end date. Let's be serious. Together."

There. No reason for her to worry we're on different life tracks. I'm traveling down the same road she is.

Why is she shaking her head?

Instead of flinging herself into my arms, smiling ear to ear with joy, my harpy takes another step away from me, hand held up, as if to ward me off. "I wasn't asking for you to say that."

Don't panic. Stay calm.

"I know. But I am. I mean it."

"Right now."

I can feel my brow furrow. "What's that supposed to mean?"

Zara halts her retreat, no longer resembling prey to be hunted. Now, my harpy straightens her shoulders and meets my eyes.

In them, I see defiance, sadness, and a touch of pity.

"You're scared of magic."

I flinch at the baldly stated truth.

"I don't like it," I admit. "But what does that have to do with us?"

Hurt washes through Zara's eyes, and I know I said the wrong thing.

"I *am* magic." She spreads her arms wide. "It is part of me. Inseparable. If a witch gave me the potion you took, I would be half of myself. The only half you could accept."

Panic claws at my chest—and not in the pleasurable way her little talons sometimes did.

"That's not true."

"It is." Zara holds my eyes. "You let your fear and hatred of magic seep into every interaction you have with mythics. I've seen the way you treat Ame. The way you shy from her and her powers. Do you know what that would do to me? If I let myself love you, then had to hide all my magic? Constantly afraid of your scorn?"

"I wouldn't—"

"You *did*. Just yesterday. You were like a man released from death row. You celebrated your brief freedom from the evil clutches of magic. That's when I knew, even if you were falling for me the way I was falling for you, we would never have a future."

No. This can't be how it goes. I fucking love her with everything that I am. How could she ever think I'd hate even the tiniest part of her?

"Zara, please," I beg, my voice a desperate rasp. "Give me a chance."

"No." She cuts the air between us with a sharp hand. "I won't do this again. I won't give you the chance to hurt me when all signs point to you doing exactly that. I can't trust you, Anthony. I certainly can't have a magical *child* with you. This is the same exact issue I had with Christian."

"I am not him!" The words are a growl as I pace away from her, then turn with my arms open wide. "You want to have a monster baby? Let's do it. Let's start right now."

I want our life together to start right *now*.

Zara shakes her head. "What kind of mother would that make me? Having a child with a man who will hate part of it? You talk a big game, but when it comes down to it, you cringe from magic. You make everyone who loves you walk on tiptoes or risk losing you. I'm not going to do it. I deserve someone who loves all of me."

"I do." Can't she see? The strength of it practically radiates off me. My love is so intense that it could burn her.

But the risk of her getting hurt is what this is all about.

"That's what you say. It's not what I see." Zara sighs and rubs both her hands over her cheeks, which I realize are wet.

Zara is crying because of me.

"You shouldn't push for this," she says, her voice weary. "We live different lives, even without magic. We don't match. You don't belong here. There are men that do, but you're not one of them."

Fear of losing her allows a spark of jealous resentment to sneak out of my mouth. "You have someone else in mind? Someone better suited?"

Zara looks at me now, her eyes sad. "That was always the plan. You can't be mad that it worked."

The thought of her going out with someone else ... kissing them—gods, *sleeping* with them—has me wanting to break open my rib cage and tear out my own heart.

"Of course I can be mad." I glare, all signs of my *give no shit* attitude gone in the face of losing the woman I love. "I'm fucking furious."

Emotions tangle and battle in my chest. Part of me wants to find something to say that will make her hurt as badly as I do. Another bit wants me to fall to my knees and swear to be everything she needs and more.

But the last part—the strongest, mainly because it's the persona I've affected my whole life—demands I put my mask back in place.

Pretend not to care until I'm not pretending anymore.

I shove my hands in my pockets and forcefully ease the tight muscles in my jaw.

"But if you want me gone, fine. Seems you have this all figured out." I step down from her porch, my gait unhurried, hopefully looking as though I couldn't care less and not like I'm holding myself back in case she changes her mind and calls out to me.

"Anthony."

At the sound of my name on her lips, I whirl around, barely managing to keep the desperate hope off my face.

I raise one insolent eyebrow.

Zara stands at the top of her porch steps, arms hugging her middle, looking radiant with the morning sun setting her bronze skin to glowing.

"Thank you," she says softly. "For your help."

Then, she turns and disappears inside, leaving me to bleed out on her front lawn from the gaping wound in my heart.

31

———

ANTHONY

IT HAS NEVER BEEN SO easy to pretend I don't give a shit.

Because I don't.

The club music pounds, but I barely hear it. The lights pulse and flash, and I silently wish they would burn out my retinas so I wouldn't have to stare at this crowd of people who mean absolutely nothing to me.

It's been two weeks since Zara broke things off with me. Since I offered her my heart and she sliced it to ribbons with her talons.

I wince at the thought and not at the painful imagery, no matter how accurate it feels.

Because I'm not being fair to Zara.

She was nothing but honest with me, and her points were valid. When have I shown her she could trust me with her magical side? All I've ever done is shy away from mine. She's right to hold herself back from me.

Zara deserves someone who won't flinch away from the mythical even if I want to eviscerate the blood and bones of anyone else who ever touches her.

"Crimson Dread! We're so happy to have you here tonight. Honored, seriously."

A grinning woman in a fitted, bedazzled business suit stands in front of me. I didn't realize she'd approached until she said my social media name.

Unable to come up with a response, I offer a nod.

She seems to think that's enough. "Tonight, we'll have you showing off our latest innovation, sure to be the drink of the summer"—she gestures to the waitress, who strolls into the VIP section with a chilling bucket containing no less than five bottles of the same liquor—"margarita vodka."

Gods, no.

One, margaritas are a tequila drink. Why would anyone mess with that?

Two, margaritas have me thinking of Monday nights at Marlin's Marina and the taste of salt and lime on Zara's lips.

Kill me now.

"And here, we have your boy toy for the evening." The vodka representative waves toward a dark-haired, dark-eyed man with a strong jaw, golden skin, and a devastating grin.

A few months ago, I'd have been happy to have a guy like him plastered over me all night. Now, the thought just has me feeling ... tired.

I don't want to do this.

"Abdul is a travel influencer and a rising star himself. We really think you two can start a buzz."

Great, they don't just want ad shots. They want a full gossip blowup. Couple of C-list celebrities combining forces to get A-list coverage.

"Feel free to get hot and heavy. We want people to know we support the LGBTQIA+ community," she says with an encouraging grin.

Annoyance sparks in my gut.

"Maybe instead of paying two male strangers to make out for a marketing campaign, you could donate some profits to an LGBTQIA+ charity. Support the community by, you know, actually supporting the community." My voice is deadpan.

The rep's smile falters, but then she pins it back in place, though I can see the move takes some effort.

"That's a great thought. I'll make a note of it. Now, how about you two get acquainted, and I'll get the photographer?" She hurries away.

Abdul settles on the couch beside me, still smiling.

"I'm okay with not getting 'hot and heavy,' as she so charmingly put it," he says, pitching his voice so it's only loud enough for me to hear. "My partner and I are in an open relationship, but they wouldn't be happy, knowing I'm making out with someone who isn't into it."

The unexpected comment has me offering Abdul a genuine look of relief. I know he's just doing a job, too, but I'm glad he's not pissed off.

"Good to know. I ... just got out of something serious. Not really ready to do anything with anyone. Even for work."

Especially for work. Now that I know what it's like to share those intimate moments with someone I love, that's all I want to do.

"Cheers to new friends who support the LGBTQIA+ community then." Abdul holds up his glass with a smirk, and I bark out a laugh.

"Cheers." I tap my drink against his, then take a swallow.

Disgusting, but I manage not to grimace. Then, I remember how Zara couldn't hide her reaction when she tried the pricey tequila, and I almost smile before my heart breaks all over again.

"Let's hear some travel stories then," I prompt my companion for the evening. "The messier, the better."

Abdul grins and launches into the time he got stranded on

an island in Alaska because the ferry workers went on strike. He's a good storyteller, and I can see why people are eager for his content. I barely notice when the photographer arrives and starts taking shots of us, more focused on keeping my mind off a certain harpy for a record amount of time—five minutes or more.

But listening to Abdul is one more glaring billboard on the pointless road of my life.

It has a simple message ... *what am I doing here?*

This guy obviously loves traveling, and the influencer gig is just a way to fund his trips and share his explorations with the world.

I can't say the same.

Sure, at one point, I found a certain high in taking advantage of all these luxurious offerings and having a million random people adore me simply for the way I smirked.

But other than the few genuine words I exchange with Abdul, this night seems pointless.

And I have hundreds more on my schedule. Stretching into the future will be nights like this until I lose my looks and my swagger, and then I'll be empty and alone, without even the comfort of nostalgia, looking back on a life I never fully lived.

When I'm in my final years, I know what my mind will hold on to for comfort.

A too-short spring in a small town with the woman I loved.

The woman I *love*. Still do. Always will.

"Anthony?" The publicist calls my name, and I jerk my head her way, having forgotten where I was. "We love your normal smoldering disinterest, but now, you're kind of sliding into dejected frowning territory. Maybe try a smirk?" She gives me an enthusiastic brow raise.

"Sure." I do as she asked, forming my mouth into the familiar position, and earn myself a thumbs-up.

What am I doing here?

Violetta's comment from all those weeks ago plays through my mind.

"Sounds more like dying to me."

Dying. This is dying. Slowly but surely slipping downward. Not reaching for anything or trying or taking a true risk. I'm not growing. I'm withering.

Fuck that.

This passive approach has brought me nothing but misery.

It's time to put in an effort.

Time to hold on to what I want.

Time to stay instead of run.

Time to fight.

First step, get out of this fucking nightmare of a nightclub.

I shove up from the couch. "It was great to meet you, Abdul."

I reach out to shake the man's hand, and he returns the gesture.

"You too."

"Wait!" The vodka representative makes to grab my arm, but I dodge her unwelcome touch. "We still have you for another half hour."

Her wording makes me shudder. Have me. Like they own me. I'm their doll to move around and position as they please.

I thought magic was what made me a puppet. That the mystical unknown was the thing to fear. But this is what I should have been worried about. Losing control of my own life.

"I'm going. Take it out of my commission."

Ignoring her protests, I stride out of the VIP section and disappear among the dancers, weaving through the mass toward the front door.

With each step, I feel a growing sense of purpose fill my body. Lending me weight. Making me solid.

Finally, I start to feel as though I truly exist.

32

____

ANTHONY

MY PHONE STARTS VIBRATING INSISTENTLY before I'm even out of
Atlanta.

Always hopeful the caller will be Zara, I glance at the name
showing on my dashboard display.

Julia.

"Gods, seriously?"

When I had my revelation about the misery my job caused
me and walked out of the club, I thought I'd have at least
twenty-four hours before I had to break the news to my agent,
but the rep must have called her.

Sin raises his head from the tight coil he's made of himself
on the passenger seat when I press to accept the call.

"Anthony! My best guy! Already seeing great numbers for
the posts that went out tonight. You are killing it."

"Julia—"

"But what's this notice I got about you checking out early?
Did you find another bed to sleep in for the night?" There's a
suggestive note in her tone I do not like. "Don't worry. I'm not

here to scold you. But check your calendar for flight info. I have you on a plane tomorrow afternoon and on your way to New York. Do not oversleep and miss it."

Suddenly, I'm not feeling an ounce of guilt about the news I plan to share with her. Not when she didn't even pause to listen to the reason I walked out. Not checking to see if I was okay or if something went wrong or made me uncomfortable.

I'm not a person to her. I'm a pretty paycheck.

"Julia!" I bark her name, shoving my voice into the middle of her string of instructions. "I quit. Cancel all future appearances. I'll personally cover any deposits made to hold spots on my calendar."

There's the sound of high-pitched laughter on the other end of the line, and I swear I hear music and chatter in the background. Julia can't even give herself a break.

"That's a good one, Anthony."

"It's not a joke. You're great at your job, but I'm getting out of this work before it bleeds my soul dry. Focus on your other clients. You'll be fine."

I know I'm her top earner, but she's not about to go bankrupt without me.

"Wait."

The ambient background sounds fade, and I imagine her stepping away from whatever gathering she's attending in order to concentrate on soothing her high-maintenance client.

"Okay, I know this has been a full schedule, diving back in. We should have eased your entry. How about I clear your calendar for next week, and then we'll only accept offers from tropical locations for the next few months? Sipping cocktails on the beach. Showing off some surfboards. Easy money." Julia keeps her tone soothing, but I can detect a small, desperate note underneath.

When I say no, she'll keep negotiating.

But the thing is, she doesn't have anything I want.

I want a lake, not a beach.

I want a small town, not a buzzing metropolis.

I want margaritas with well tequila, not a six-hundred-dollar bottle of liquor.

I want my family, not hired actor friends.

And more than anything, I want a strong, intelligent, gorgeous harpy who is way out of my league.

"I quit, Julia. I quit."

Then, I hang up and turn off my phone. I doubt that'll be the last plea she makes, but those can be handled tomorrow, once I've had a good night's sleep, surrounded by people who care about me.

The drive to Folk Haven takes close to two hours despite the lighter traffic in the middle of the night. Unlike the constant glowing high-rises of Atlanta, the town looks asleep other than the handful of street lanterns. I drive through the quiet town, passing Fresh Feathers by. The apartment above the dry cleaner isn't mine anymore. As far as I know, Esme has already found a new renter.

I keep driving, heading toward the house I used to avoid, but still probably has a room for me.

As I approach the library, I shut off my headlights, not wanting to wake anyone. Mor showed me where the spare key was, saying the house was open to me anytime. Not sure if that applies to three-in-the-morning arrivals, but here I am.

After pulling in beside Mor's truck, I cut the engine and climb out, making sure to circle around the passenger side and hold the door open for Sin. He slinks out of the passenger seat and disappears into the surrounding woods. Growing used to him coming and going as he pleases, I don't worry about his choice to spend the night in the wild.

Before mounting the front steps, I find the flowerpot that the spare key hides beneath. After brushing off the stray pieces of dirt, I twist it in the lock and push the door open slowly to avoid making a noise that might wake someone.

The moment I step inside the house, something whispers a harsh word in my head.

Wrong.

33

ANTHONY

THE FEELING of wrongness is stronger than the normal hum of magic from the books tugging at me. In fact, the pull is less prominent than before. Muted. As if a blanket was thrown over the shelves, blocking their greedy thrum.

But when I peer into the room on my right, I see the neatly arranged spines sitting in their normal space with no barrier between us.

Odd.

Then, I hear the crash and a curse in a deep voice.

There're three men living in this house. I would know Broderick's voice anywhere, the kappa Niko's voice has a higher pitch, and something in my gut tells me that wasn't Jack. Maybe because the werewolf is too smooth to knock anything over, or maybe because he'd never curse out loud in the middle of the night and risk waking up my sister.

Whatever Jack would do, I know it's not him.

Does Mor have a guest over?

Maybe. But the out-of-place sound and the muffled feel to the air have me worried.

There's no harm in checking, right? If I'm wrong, the worst thing that could happen is I accidentally wake someone up, need to apologize, and that's that.

If I'm right ...

Broderick's, Ame's, and Mor's faces flash through my mind.

If I'm right, the worst thing that could happen is unacceptable.

On light feet, I jog up the stairs. There aren't any lights on when I reach the second floor, but I sense movement through the cracked door at the end of the hallway.

Ame and Jack's bedroom.

I doubt they would sleep with the door open. They're a newly mated couple.

So, why is it open now?

If this is just Jack moving around, please don't let him kill me. I silently send the prayer up to the gods.

Creeping closer, I brace myself for the wolf to stick his head out of the doorway after having scented my approach and to give me one of his *I'll murder you* growls before sending me on my way.

But he doesn't. I make it to the open doorway in time to see a large figure bump into a dresser against the wall. The hit was hard, sending most of the items falling to the floor.

"When did it get so fucking dark?" the stranger mutters between curses.

Nothing about this makes sense. First of all, the almost-full moon shines in through the parted curtains, casting a decent amount of light into the bedroom. The guy should be able to see fine.

Which leads to the next confusing thing.

"Who the hell are you, and why are you in my sister's bedroom?"

Better yet, why are Ame and Jack still fast asleep in their big bed? The two are cuddled up together under the covers, dead to the world.

Terror rips cold claws through me.

No. She can't be.

"Who said that?" The stranger whips his body around, flinging his arms out, as if to grab me, but I'm too busy sprinting to the bed and tearing the blankets off so I can press my fingers against Ame's neck.

There, slow and steady, is a pulse.

I'm so relieved that I don't even care that Jack is butt-ass naked. To be sure, I check his neck too, half-hoping he doesn't wake up so I can keep my fingers, but a stronger half-wanting him to because what in all the hell dimensions is going on?

"Where are you?" the stranger growls, and I return my attention to him. He still isn't looking directly at me, and he has his chin tilted up, nostrils flaring, as if he might be able to scent me.

Even a nearsighted human should be able to see me in this room. It's as though the interloper has gone blind, but only recently. He doesn't appear used to his lack of sight.

"What did you do to them?" I demand, stalking around the bed, then lunging toward the man, meaning to grab him around the neck.

Shouldn't have let my fury drive though because I forgot I have zero fighting skill.

Somehow sensing my attack, the man throws a wild fist, catching me in the side of the head. The intruder hits like a sledgehammer, and I slam into the bedroom wall. Groaning, I collapse to the floor.

"No one else was supposed to be here."

The words come on a delay with the way my left ear rings. With a grunt, I shove myself up to my knees.

"The doors were locked. How did you get in?" As the

stranger speaks, his grasping hand lands on my neck. Before I can swat it away, he has a painful hold on my hair, dragging me to my feet. "What did you do to my eyes?" he hisses, his breath hot in my face, smelling of salt and sea. "Why can't I see?"

He shakes me, and my head pounds with the violent movement. I scratch at his hand and drive my knee toward his groin, but only hit the inside of his thigh.

Still, he lets out a pained howl and drops me. Belatedly, I realize my attacks didn't do the job. Sin digging his fangs into the man's ankle did.

The snake releases his hold and slithers across the room to avoid flailing kicks.

"What was that?" he screeches. "It bit me!"

The guy is howling loud enough to wake the dead, and there's still no movement on the bed.

How deeply are Ame and Jack sleeping?

What if they never wake up?

I try to shove away from the flailing man, aware that even without his sight, he's more than a match for me. There's a smooth stroke along the back of my hand, and I realize Sin has returned to my side. I move to gather him close to my chest, protect him from the intruder, when I catch sight of a strange discoloring on his scales, which transfers to my skin.

A red powder.

Glancing across the room, I realize one of the items the man knocked over was Ame's little wooden box, full of the magic amplifier my family created to hone their powers. A mound of the red powder spilled onto the floor, disturbed only by the familiar that recently slid through it.

Sin brought the powder to me. He knows what it's for.

If I tried, I could get out of this situation without magic. Stay quiet and sneak away from the enraged man who can't see. Run out of the house and call for help.

But that would leave my sisters and my brother alone in this place with him for who knows how long. He put them to sleep. Wanted them passive.

What is he planning to do to them?

Whatever it is, I'm not about to let it happen.

I've never used my powers intentionally before, but I understand the gist of them. What I want, other people want.

I rub the grainy red powder between my hands, imagining the clinging grains burrowing into my skin and feeding the mythical force I've always tried to make lie dormant.

My magic responds, coming alive, thrumming through my skin until I glow crimson. Not that my attacker can see.

What I want, everyone else wants.

I want him gone.

I drag in a deep breath. "I want you—"

The man's leg flies out, landing with a crunch against my ribs, and I know from the sound and the jagged slice of agony that the impact snapped a few of the bones. My breath wheezes out of me, the spell unfinished.

Keep going. If you're alive, you can work magic. You can save them.

But when I try to fill my lungs, a sharp pain keeps me from pulling the air in properly.

"I ..." The word wheezes, barely more than a whisper. "I ..."

"By The Finned One! Shut up." The stranger draws his foot back again, and my arms reflexively cover my chest and my familiar.

Don't let me die here. I want to see her one more time. Just once more.

The wishing gets cut off by a horrible rending noise, like rusty nails being pulled from dry wood. The grating groan has both me and the intruder turning to face a wall that's suddenly bulging, as if alive, not that my attacker can see.

Which he proves by whimpering, "What's happening?"

Even if I could speak, I wouldn't have an answer.

I watch in fascinated horror as the wallpaper tears and wooden boards bend and split, extending like arms.

The wall reaches out and grabs the man.

He screams and struggles, but there are too many wooden arms clasping him, dragging him into their ominous embrace.

"Let me go! Gods, what is this? What did you do?!" He jerks and fights, but nothing frees him.

What did I do? Nothing.

Only my palms tingle with a strange pulse of power and pleasure.

That couldn't mean ... I couldn't have ...

"I want you," I said before his kick cut off the rest.

Did I make the house *want him?*

The creepy arms have stopped moving, but in their newly rigid state, they seem to be hugging the man. Holding him close. He is now the house's possession, captured and claimed, unable to move from where the wooden limbs hold him flush against a mangled wall.

"Wild," I rasp. The one word is all I can manage with the pain in my chest.

I really wish I were a healing witch at this moment. With slow movements, I carefully slide my hand under my shirt and press a palm against my aching ribs.

"Want ... to ... heal."

I wait. And wait. And wait some more ...

Nothing.

"Fuck," I wheeze.

Yeah, well, I guess magic doesn't fix everything. Or if it can, I'd probably have to have been training with it for decades rather than making a split-second decision I was cool with the tool.

Speaking of well-trained witches, I need backup fast and have an idea that might be terrible. But I don't have a lot of options.

With shaking fingers, I work my phone out of my pocket and leave red streaks on the screen as I navigate to a familiar number and hit the Call button.

After the third ring, she answers.

"I will murder you."

"Violetta." I speak her name with the little breath I have.

"Anthony. Give me one reason why I shouldn't hex you for waking me up at this hour."

"My family ... is asleep."

"As I should be."

With the phone pressed against my ear, I lean against the bottom of the doorframe of Ame's room just as another one of the intruder's terrified wails sounds.

"What was that?" Violetta purrs, sounding more awake and mildly intrigued.

"Man ... broke in ... library."

"You sound strange."

"Ribs ... broken."

There's quiet on the other end, then an eerie croon. "The man hurt you? Tell me his name, Anthony."

"Don't know." Black dots speckle the sides of my vision. "Got him." Maybe I shouldn't have said that. Maybe I should've given her some more urgency to help, if she's even willing. But my reasoning is fading into a blur of pain. "Ame won't ... wake up."

Everyone else must be stuck in the strange sleep too.

If they aren't already dead.

Please, Dark One, don't let them be dead.

I need them to wake up. I barely hold back the desperate whimper.

"Fascinating."

"Please." I don't care if she hears weakness in my voice and exploits it later. In this moment, I am weak. I have no way to save the ones I love. "Need help."

"Fine, fine. I'm on my way. And I suppose …" She sighs, as if this next part is a burden she doesn't want to bear. "I'll call Madeline."

That's not what I expected her to say. In the haze of pain, I struggle to place the name.

"Witch?" I manage to ask.

The more magic to wake everyone up, the better.

"Yes. A healing one. Sounds like you need a gentle touch, and I'm not the babying type. Try not to die before we arrive."

Violetta hangs up before I can find the strength to ask her to hurry. My hand falls to my lap, screen still lit and showing a list of contact names. Just below Violetta is another I want to press.

Zara Ironfeather.

What if these are my last moments?

As I struggle to breathe, the possibility of an end feels close. I don't know that I've ever felt more mortal than in this moment.

I let my thumb drop.

Onto her name.

It rings. And rings. And rings again.

I'm about to be satisfied with a recorded version of her husky voice when the phone call clicks.

"Anthony?"

She's awake. My harpy sounds sleepy, woken up by my call. But the fact that she can wake up while everyone else is stuck in this magical sleep gives me comfort.

"Sorry," I wheeze.

"What's wrong with your voice?" My lovely harpy is more alert now, and I can envision the spark in her brown eyes. Can see her as clearly as if she were crouching in front of me.

Sin curls in my lap. A comforting weight to offset the pain in my chest.

"Thank you," I tell her, wishing I could say more.

Thank you for giving me those beautiful weeks.
Thank you for being honest and true.
Thank you for not letting me ruin your dreams with my fear.
"What's going on? Where are you?"
"Love you." The words are a murmur before I end the call, and the blackness swamps my eyes and eases my pain.

34

SEV

SITTING HIGH IN A TREE, I watch as the mermaid police chief escorts Hamish out of the library, the selkie's hands cuffed behind his back.

"Can't find good minions these days," I mutter, disgusted with the seal shifter who couldn't complete a simple errand.

I drag my hands through the golden strands I've let grow long. I find I've been in a whimsical mood lately. Enjoying the way the golden locks make me resemble some fairy-tale prince.

Beneath my beautiful face lies the terrible darkness. A twisted monster I bring out when it suits me.

I'd coax the beast to the surface now if it would do me any good. If I could use the world-rending power of my other form to get what I want. But there are limits to even my magnificence.

Hence, the requirement for minions.

How I wish I could complete the task myself. Any other place, I'd force my way in and leisurely stroll through until discovering my treasure.

Only this house doesn't like me.

The old dragon who lived in it, Dimitri Novac, knew who I was and the items I collected. Before I thought to take from him, he spelled the place against me. I even tried getting on his good side by commissioning him to craft wildly expensive pieces for me. He took the business while still protecting his hoard. The magic he dug into the bones of his home was so strong that it remained after his death. Even when his daughter sold the house to those book-wielding witches who opened their home to the public, I still couldn't cross the threshold.

But Dimitri couldn't keep everyone out.

And Hamish isn't the first to fail me.

"Dead, but still winning. This round goes to you, Dimitri." I direct my comments at the star-filled sky. "Another day then."

Slipping from my perch, I make sure to keep a good distance from the house. The witches have a werewolf, and his nose might give me away. If he knows what to scent for, that is. I likely smell like terror.

And gingersnap cookies.

Love a good gingersnap.

Weaving through the dark forest with ease, I come upon a garden of metal statues—the proof of Dimitri Novac's genius before the grief of his lost mate twisted his mind.

"When I find you, mate"—I trail a claw over the extended wing of a Pegasus in flight while speaking to the mysterious mythic I've yet to stumble upon in my century of life—"I will never lose you."

From others, that might be an empty promise.

But they don't have the power I do. When something is mine, I keep it.

My mate will be my most precious treasure.

All the metal figures seem weightless despite the heavy material of their creation. Dimitri imbued life into each piece.

But there is one that stands in contrast to the rest.

It's downright monstrous.

"You're looking as hideous as ever," I tell the statue as I tweak his nose.

There's no response from the beast. Not that I expected one.

"Don't give me that look," I chide the snarling figure. "Trust me when I say, you're better off where you are. Not that I planned this." Circling slowly, I recall the lovely violet shade his pebbled skin used to be. "Would have preferred you to complete the task I assigned to you. But don't feel bad. You're not the only failure." I face him again and wonder if he can hear me. "Hopefully, you've taken some time to think about your actions. You were making poor life decisions. Trusting the wrong people." I lean in close, mouth inches from his pointed ear. "And I'm not talking about me. *I* never betrayed you. Not to say I wouldn't, if the occasion called for it. But I *haven't*. Yet."

I pat the statue's shoulder and saunter around the towering form once more. He really is quite monstrous.

With a sigh, I settle on the ground by the figure's feet, mind back on the impenetrable house.

"I've tried flattery, force, and subterfuge. What else is there?"

All I want is a tiny—immensely powerful—trinket no one is currently using. *I* don't even plan to use it. Just add it to the rest of my collection.

"Look at me, lecturing you about poor choices when I'm the one who trusted a selkie to follow through. Should have known a seal would bumble around enough to get caught."

But Hamish Barclay owed me, so I figured, why not? Use my ample power over the mythic to finally discover the treasure I know Dimitri hoarded away underneath his piles of useless, non-magical metal.

I'm not worried about Hamish sharing my name. He can't. I made sure of that. He might try to lay blame at my doorstep, but the selkie won't be able to get the words out.

See? Don't trust anyone, and you never have to worry about getting betrayed.

"Do you think they'll torture him, old fellow?" I tap a fist on the monster's foot as I continue to speak to myself. "I hope they do. He's annoying. And likes to grab things that aren't his."

Likely not though. The mythics in this town are so tame.

So boring.

With a sigh, I thrust myself to my feet and face the water glittering through a break in the trees.

"I'm off. Things to steal. Plots to make. A mate to find."

I offer the statue a charming smile before striding away.

"Till we meet again," I call over my shoulder. "Try to remember not to anger me when the day comes. I'd hate to kill you."

My imagination conjures a terrible roar in response, but in truth, the woods are silent. Not forever though.

One day, he'll wake.

And what fun that day will be.

35

———

ANTHONY

WHEN I COME TO, there's a warm, humid breeze on my face and low voices murmuring around me and a pounding pain in my chest.

I groan.

"Hush. I'm almost done."

The commanding voice isn't familiar, and I blink my eyes open to see a woman with onyx skin and gray braids bent over me with a frown of concentration.

"What—"

There's a snap inside my chest, and I scream, back arching off the ground. Or at least trying to. An iron band holds me down, and I roll my head to the side to see Jack has me in a firm grip.

Another snap, and I bite back the screech, only letting out an animalistic moan this time.

"She's healing you," the werewolf explains. "Let her work."

"She's torturing me, and you love it," I gasp. Then realize I *can* gasp. And talk. There's no longer a dagger digging into my lungs.

Huh. Maybe Jack wasn't lying his ass off after all.

There's a thump, and the ground quivers, and then I hear the most beautiful sound in the world.

Zara's voice.

"What's going on? What are you doing to him?"

The unyielding restraint of Jack's arm loosens, and I hope that means all my ribs are popped back into place. Suddenly, my vision is full not of the stranger working magic on me, but of a beautiful avian face, covered in delicate black feathers.

"Zara," I sigh, smiling for what feels like the first time in years. "My lovely."

And she is, by all the gods, the loveliest being I've ever seen. This is the form all those little feathers teased me with. Why did Zara never show me this part of herself? I could cry in joy that I finally know all of her.

The lips beneath her sharpened nose dip in a frown. "Someone needs to explain to me what's going on right now." Her voice rises in pitch as she speaks, the sharpness pressing in on my eardrums in a combination of pain and ecstasy. I don't think anyone else feels that way because when I tilt my head to the side, they're all wincing.

"I'll explain." Ame stands from where she was sitting on the front porch step, wrapped in a blanket. "Hamish broke into the library. He put us all under a sleeping spell somehow. We don't know what he was planning to do, but I think Anthony arrived and interrupted him." Her wide green eyes meet mine. "Not sure exactly what happened. I think Hamish hurt you, right? But what's all that weirdness with the wall?"

Oh, right. The greedy house.

Now that my chest isn't on fire, I sit up and gaze around the gathered group. Mor and Broderick stand side by side, their focus on me. Jack moves to Ame's side, wrapping an arm around her shoulders. Niko, the kappa renting a room in the library and Jack's best friend, perches on the step my sister vacated. Over Zara's feathered shoulder, I spy Violetta. She stands with her arms crossed, curious gaze focused on the house rather than me.

"Well," I start, "here's the thing ..." And I try to organize my mind and explain the events of the night in as sequential of an order as I can manage. I think I do a good job despite having been in excruciating pain for part of it. And for having the woman I love crouching over me, looking like a feathered goddess.

I want to forget everything around us and pull Zara in close. Caress the silky wings that extend from her back and slip my fingers under the feathers that cover her intimate places.

She doesn't want you, I remind myself.

But then I stop that toxic thought and reevaluate it.

Zara doesn't want the version of me she thinks I want to be. The *don't give a shit* playboy persona I wear for my job.

Well, I don't want to play that role anymore either.

And her point about me hating magic?

A valid one. But tonight, I embraced that part of myself to protect the ones I love. I can do it again.

And again. And again, until I'm not afraid anymore.

Until I can prove to my harpy that I love every mythical bit of her.

When I'm done with my tale, I face Zara, deciding to start proving myself to her now.

"You're beautiful," I say.

Her eyes widen, feathers ruffling, and the sight reminds me of the piece of her I keep tucked in my pocket. A talisman of love.

"He's tipsy on healing magic," the witch who was working on me says to the group. "He'll need to rest."

"Please don't tell everyone I'm drunk the second after I tell the woman I love she's beautiful," I complain. "Sounds like I don't mean it." Reaching out, I scoop up Zara's taloned hand and press a kiss to her smooth palm.

"Anthony." She sighs my name, but not in a good way. She reaches out to tuck a strand of my hair behind my ear. "Just because I came when you called doesn't change things. I care about you. But we're not together."

Ouch. Did I scream in agony again? 'Cause that hurt worse than a kick to the ribs.

But I don't wall myself up. Don't hide away from the pain.

Zara needs more than words.

"You don't believe me now, but I'm the mate for you. You'll see." With a grunt, I heave myself to my feet.

Zara stands in a much more graceful manner.

"You need to move on, Anthony." She speaks quietly, trying to make her rebuke private among this group of onlookers. "You'll just make this more painful if you don't." She steps back. "I'm glad you're okay."

With that, she launches into the sky, and I watch in awe as she soars away.

Magnificent.

When I lower my eyes, I find my entire family—at least the ones I care about—watching me.

My eyes meet Ame's, and I recall the image of her curled in her bed, unaware of the danger looming over her, even her formidable mate unable to protect her. The fear I had in that moment resurges, and I stumble forward to scoop her into my arms.

"Anthony?" Her voice is muffled against my shoulder.

"If he'd hurt you ... I'd like to say I'd have killed him, but I'm not very skilled at violence. I would have tried though." Placing my hands on her shoulders, I move Ame far enough away to meet her gaze again. "I love you. Magic and all. I'm sorry for hurting you in the past. I'm kind of fucked up."

A throat clears off to the side, and I glance over to see Broderick with glassy eyes.

"Eh ... well ... we're all kind of fucked up, right? That's what makes us Shellys." He steps forward and wraps an arm around my shoulders and one around Ame's.

"Thank you for coming back," Ame says, her wide green eyes holding mine. "We always miss you when you're gone."

Great. Now, she's going to make me cry.

"I plan to stick around this time. Think I like it here."

Ame grins wide and pulls me in for another hug, my twin part of it this time too.

"Get over here, Mor."

I pretend to scowl at my older sister, and she pretends to be exasperated with a dramatic eye roll.

"Fine," she mutters, adding her arms to the huddle.

Over my little sister's head, my stare clashes with a dark set of eyes belonging to a surly werewolf.

For the first time, Jack gives me a smile.

36

AME

THE WARPED WOOD stretching out from my bedroom wall is hard under my touch. Not even slightly pliable. No indication of it having taken on a life of its own to grab an intruder.

The police came up here and pried Hamish out of the strange restraints.

"He thinks his magic did this?" Jack stands in the middle of our bedroom, arms crossed, frown digging deep lines into his handsome face. "Has the house ever moved for you?"

"Not that I know of." If it did, the adjustment was so subtle that I never noticed. "Maybe it wasn't Anthony. Maybe it was the hoard protections."

One of the reasons Mor wanted to start her library in a house previously owned by a dragon is that they instinctively imbue their homes with protective magic. Natural defenses against someone trying to steal their hoard.

"He said Hamish couldn't see," Jack reminds me. "Like he was blindfolded. I think the house did that. Maybe this was the house and Anthony." My mate taps a finger on an extended piece of the wall.

"I'm not sure how I feel about the house being a living entity." I meet Jack's eyes. "If it is, it's seen you do a lot of dirty things to me."

Jack offers a wolfish grin, crossing the room to wrap his arms around me.

"Don't care if a pervert house was watching. I'd do them all again. Tonight, if you want."

I bite my lip to keep the silly smile from overtaking my face, but can't stop the eager shiver that goes through my body.

Still, I shake my head. "I can't sleep in this room. Not with the wall looking all creepy and Anthony's blood on the floor."

My mate's arms tighten around me, and from that small gesture, I know what he's thinking. How we both were lying vulnerable in this room while someone with ill intent loomed over us.

"Why was he here?" I whisper, partly to Jack and partly to myself.

"Revenge," Jack growls.

I'm not surprised his mind went there. When my werewolf was wronged in the past—through no fault of his own—all he wanted was to exact vengeance on the man who had hurt him.

And sure, Hamish has reason to dislike me and my mate. When he got handsy with me at last year's Halloween Ball, Jack punched him in the gut, and The Council put a restraining order on the selkie. But was that really worth enchanting an entire house and almost killing my brother?

Was he here to kill me? To kill Jack?

Either way, The Council won't be lenient this time. I'm not sure what Hamish's punishment will be, but I doubt I'll see him for a very long time, if ever again.

As I turn in Jack's arms, a flash catches my attention. Just then, my cat sneaks around our legs and leaps for a hole in the wall left by one of the reaching boards.

"No! Lucky!"

But it's too late. My familiar disappears inside the wall.

"Shit," Jack mutters, letting me go and stalking to the opening. He tries reaching his arm inside, but his bicep stops him from getting too far.

I crouch on the floor, peering through more cracks to see if I can spy my naughty feline and entice her out the way she came.

There's a flash of black fur, but I'm distracted by the golden glow reflecting off the glossy strands.

Where's that light coming from?

With my smaller arm, I reach into another hole, skittering my fingers through cobwebs.

"Lucky," I call. "Here, sweet girl. I'll give you tuna if you come out."

No dice.

"Jack will let you sit in his lap," I singsong.

If she doesn't come for that, there's no hope.

My werewolf grumbles above me, but doesn't retract my offer.

Still no response from my familiar, but I pause when my fingers brush smooth wood. The sensation is odd. At least, finding it in a wall is. I explore further and make out an almost-box-like shape. There are a few irregular bumps, but for the most part, it seems to be a container.

Or a compartment.

"I think there's something in the wall," I say as I pull my arm out.

"Yeah, your cat," Jack mutters.

"Our cat," I correct him as I study the wall that butts up against what I just felt.

There are scratch marks on the wood, and I recall how Lucky has a bad habit of sharpening her claws on this spot.

What if she wasn't using this as a nail file?

What if she knew there was something back there?

I press my palms flat against the wood and feel along the grain, leaning in close to examine the spot.

Then, I see it.

A circle, only slightly darker of a shade than the surrounding wall, the circumference no bigger than a dime. With a careful pressure, I push the spot.

A square section of the wall swings out on hidden hinges.

"What the fuck?" My werewolf crouches beside me.

"It's a secret door," I tell him, although *door* is generous. It's not large enough to walk through. Barely the size of a shoebox lid.

I swing it open all the way to reveal a compartment, the one I felt the outside of. What once seemed to be a neatly shaped box now has a few warped edges that reveal small breaks, no doubt caused by my brother's magic and the house's reaction. A furry black cat leg comes through one of the ruptures, swiping, as if to grab the contents of the compartment.

"Lucky," I scold, "stop trying to steal things and get out of the wall."

My familiar lets out a mournful yowl, and her leg retracts. Which only leaves the original contents.

A golden apple.

Jack and I stare at the strange piece of fruit, and I wonder if he feels the same wave of power radiating off it that I do.

"Is that yours?" he asks.

"No. I didn't know this was here."

But it seems Lucky knew.

"Then, it's Delta's?" He names the dragon who sold us this house.

"Or her father's maybe."

Dimitri Novac was a powerful dragon by all accounts with a

hoarding hermit's personality. He sounded like a man who would have secret compartments in his walls.

"What are you two staring at?"

Mor's voice has me jumping, and I realize I was half-mesmerized by the shimmering golden apple.

"Ame found something." Jack places his hand on my waist and guides me back, under the pretense of giving my sister a better look, but I get the feeling he wants me far away from the unknown item.

Morgana crouches down, and her eyes widen. "Goddess. I can feel the magic from here." She stands up and shakes her hands, as if they tingle. "Don't touch it. I'll get a safe container."

We both nod, and she strolls out of the room.

Jack guides me to my feet and settles on the bed, pulling me into his lap. As I let him hold me, I ponder our odd discovery.

And wonder if maybe Hamish was after something other than revenge.

37

ANTHONY

Working in a garden is fucking hard.

"Is this the first time you've touched dirt?" Violetta looms over me.

"Of course not."

I sit back on my heels and swipe sweat off my forehead with the back of my arm, careful not to let my gloves brush my face. The witch claimed this bush wasn't dangerous, but she had an evil smile when she pointed me toward it.

"I once mud-wrestled a rugby player for charity." Despite the fact that I'm dying of heatstroke, I manage a smirk. "Things got real dirty."

Violetta scoffs, even as her lips twitch in amusement. "I expect you to apply that same gusto to those weeds. They aren't going to pull themselves."

"Yes, ma'am." I dive back into my task with renewed vigor, eager to show the witch she's not wasting her time on me.

On my drive back to Folk Haven after leaving that night-club, I came to a few conclusions.

First, even though I'm rich, I still need a job. People in this town won't respect me if I sit on my ass all day. What's more, I want to contribute. I like Folk Haven and want to do my part to make it prosper.

Second, I need to learn how to handle my magic. I don't want it spilling out of me anymore, making people covet something just because I've expressed interest in it. And learning to control my magic is the biggest step in getting over my fear of it.

Third, it's no use pursuing Zara until I fulfill task one and two. When I've established myself as a member of the community, who has a healthy relationship with his mythical nature, she might finally believe that I'm someone to trust her future with.

That I won't hurt her like that asshole human did.

So, say hello to the new and improved Anthony Shelly—part-time design assistant at Fresh Feathers and part-time weeder in this beautiful, lethal garden that might murder me.

Is this what being a responsible adult feels like?

After another hour of work that sets the muscles in my back and shoulders on fire, Violetta reappears with a jug of sweet tea and gestures toward the shaded lounge chairs, telling me to take a break.

An involuntary groan escapes as I sink onto the cushioned seat. "I'm weak."

"You are." She slides a glass toward me. "But we'll get some calluses on those hands and bulk up that willowy frame of yours."

I grunt, reaching for my glass, only to pause. "This one isn't poisoned, is it?"

"What?" The question sounds in a deep voice, and we both turn to see a tall, dark-haired, golden-skinned man strolling toward us. "What did he say?"

"Levi!" Violetta stands from her seat and opens welcoming arms. "I didn't know you were coming by today."

"Hello, Mama." He leans down to press a kiss to her cheek, even as he keeps his eyes on me. "Did you poison someone?"

Now, I recognize the man. Levi Abadi. Violetta's son and a monster.

Maybe Zara would like to chat with Violetta about raising a monster baby. I tuck the thought away for another time.

"Of course not. Look at him." Violetta strolls over to pat my sweaty head. "He's fine. Anthony enjoys dramatics."

Levi's eyes narrow as he studies me. "Anthony Shelly, right? I know your sister. I was with them for the Lucian Smite issue." He names the sorcerer that used to have Jack imprisoned before the werewolf escaped. A group of mythics took care of the evil asshole last year.

Let's just say, Lucian Smite is no more.

"Which no one invited me to," Violetta interjects. "I am still holding a grudge about that."

"I'll add it to the list," Levi murmurs, his stare remaining on me. "How do you two know each other?"

I'm about to explain about the job she offered me, working in her garden in exchange for magic lessons, when her decisive voice cuts me off.

"He's my lover," Violetta says.

I choke on air as Levi blanches.

"I—no—we aren't—not that—I mean—" I stumble over my denial as Violetta raises an eyebrow. "I love Zara Ironfeather. I'm not sleeping with your mom," I finish.

The sea witch rolls her eyes. "You couldn't play along for even a moment? Did you see his face?" She pinches the monster's cheek. "He was adorably horrified."

"Sorry. Trying to stay on The Council's good side." I nod Levi's way, and he returns the gesture, albeit stiffly. "I'm working for your mom. I'm her weeding wench." I gesture at my dirt-streaked clothes.

"I see," Levi murmurs, then finally focuses on his mother.

I breathe a sigh of relief. There's an aura of power emanating off the man. Not ominous necessarily, but I get the sense he could crush me if he felt like it.

"The poor boy was desperate for work," Violetta says. "And he has the most delightful magic. Doesn't have a clue how to use it though." She affects a stage whisper. "I might steal it. For fun, you know?"

"Mama." Levi uses a warning tone, but I see the twitch at the corner of his mouth.

Oh good. She was joking.

I think.

Either way, it's nice to see their back-and-forth. Violetta can be prickly, but clearly, her son has affection for her.

I do too, I realize.

Then, a glaring connection snaps into place in my mind.

"Oh gods," I groan.

Violetta smiles my way. "What has you mourning the way the world is this time?"

"I just realized you remind me of my mother."

The witch's jovial nature evaporates. "No, I don't."

"You do," I insist. "But a *good* version of her."

"I'm not good," she screeches. "I'm terrible! I'm terrifying! I poisoned you!" Her eyes flick to her son, and she visibly reins in her temper. "Allegedly."

"That's my point." I rise from the lounge chair. "That's exactly the kind of thing my mother would have done. But she would have poisoned me to find out something she was curious about, and she never would have bothered to make sure the poison tasted good. You dosed me with spelled sweet tea to prove something to *me*. You poisoned me to help me."

"I have to stop visiting here so often," Levi mutters.

I stride up to the scowling witch and scoop her into a hug.

"Oh hell. Please don't kill him," Levi says.

"You're the mother I would have had if she'd loved me," I

tell Violetta as I set her back on her feet. "I'm not saying you're the paragon of motherhood. But you love your son. And I think you like me." I grin wide when she stares up at me with a pout. "And you're still terrible. And you're still terrifying."

Violetta's lips curve with a deceptive sweetness as she reaches up to pat my cheeks.

"You say such lovely things." Then, she cups my chin, and something dark flickers in the back of her eyes. "What is your mother's name again?"

That's not a good look.

"Why?"

"I'm merely curious. She lives by the sea, doesn't she?"

We grew up in a town in Maine with a view of the Atlantic Ocean from our house.

"How do you know that?"

The dark shadow infuses her entire smiling face.

"The water. It tells me things. Only after I feed it, of course."

"Mama"—Levi breaks in with a stern tone—"you can't kill another witch."

She frowns and lets my chin go. A weight I didn't realize had been bearing down on my shoulders lifts suddenly.

"Why not?" Violetta asks, voice tinged with frustration. "She doesn't live in Folk Haven. And she sounds like a bitch."

Violetta would murder my mother for me? I must be messed up because her willingness to commit violence on my behalf is touching.

"Thank you for looking out." I lean down to press a kiss to her cheek.

"Oh, stop." She bats me away. "Get back to weeding. And don't forget to practice your mental shields as you work."

"Yes, ma'am." I do as I was told, offering Levi a parting nod.

The guy gives me a smile, and I have the sense he approves of me in some way.

One more mythic on my side.

38

———————

GRIFFITH HAS A VERY NICE SMILE.

The curve of his mouth acts as the perfect hint to his hidden animal. Wolfish. When he smiles, the man conveys a simple message with the tilt of his lips.

I want to eat you up.

The problem is, I don't think I want to be consumed.

Not by him anyway.

Don't think about anyone else. This date is about Griffith. Griffith and me and if we're compatible.

"So, that's the last time I let gnomes host a karaoke night at the bar."

He offers me another wolfish smile across the picnic table, and I chuckle at the story.

The laughter isn't forced. Griffith is funny. He's pleasant to be around, and his face is nice to look at.

But there aren't any flutters in my stomach. No ache in my shoulder blades because my wings threaten to stretch wide if he looks at me the right way.

The werewolf is attractive, but I'm not attracted to him.

This puts a big bummer on the date. I should be enjoying this delicious bagel Mary Jo made me and soaking in the deep rumble of Griffith's laughter as I think about how far I want to go with him later.

Instead, I'm mentally planning the *it's not you, it's me* letdown and how not to use clichéd words to tell him my heart and downstairs aren't interested in what he has to offer.

By no fault of his.

"You've got a bit of cream cheese. Right here." He points to the right side of my mouth.

"Goddess, I'm always a messy eater." I swipe my hand over my cheek, but my fingers come away clean.

"Missed it. Here." Griffith extends his long arm across the table toward me, his T-shirt tightening over corded muscles.

Why don't I want to lick all those dips and ridges? They're very lickable.

Still nothing. Not even when he cradles my chin and swipes his thumb over the corner of my mouth, then pulls his hand back and licks the drop of cream cheese off his thumb.

Damn. That's a good move.

Just in case, I check in with my vagina ...

Nope. Not a twitch. She might as well be curled up in a cozy blanket, reading a sci-fi novel.

"You're not feeling this, are you?"

At Griffith's question, I jerk my chin up, staring at him with wide eyes.

"Excuse me?"

His grin has gone from wolfish to rueful, and I find the alteration easier to look at because I don't feel like he's trying to seduce me anymore.

"My top-notch flirting game." He picks up the remaining half of his third bagel. The guy can eat, and Mary Jo gave me a huge grin after he placed his order, happy I brought her a big spender.

But I push thoughts of my friend's business to the side as I refocus on my date's words.

"Something you might not know about wolves"—he taps his nose—"we can tell when someone is turned on. And you, lovely Zara, might as well be talking to your grandpa."

"Hey!" I can't help laughing as I try to sound affronted. "Both my grandfathers are devilishly handsome." Even if one is a major asshole I still don't talk to. But Dada is more charming than a siren's song when he wants to be, and I've seen women of all ages sigh over his grin when he's working the dining room of his restaurant. Still, my grandfather only has eyes for his wife, the two of them proof an arranged marriage can mean decades of devoted love.

Griffith smirks. "Fine. But admit it—our chemistry isn't crackling. It's cool. I'm not gonna get fussy about it." He leans his elbows on the table, dipping his head closer to mine. "My fault really. I scented your arousal at the bar and fooled myself into thinking some might be toward me. But it was all that pretty witch fellow, huh?"

My humor deflates, and I stare down at my food, hoping my date doesn't see the pain in my eyes.

It's been a week since I left a still-healing Anthony in his front yard, three weeks since I ended things, and the amount my body and heart crave him hasn't lessened by even an ounce. I thought beginning my Monster Baby Plan again might help. Looking toward the future. Finding a love that could work.

Maybe that would ease the ache of turning down the man I love.

I still believe I made the right choice. Anthony has shown multiple times in multiple ways that fear of magic will rule his life. Our relationship would be doomed from the beginning.

"Hey, sorry. That was a shitty thing for me to do. Bring up an ex." Griffith reaches across the table to cover my hand with one of his.

The touch doesn't feel suggestive or romantic, which is why I allow it. Why I can find comfort in it.

"No, I'm sorry. I thought I might be ready to date again." After sucking in a deep breath, I manage a genuine smile, and he returns it. "I might need some more time."

"That's cool. But I think we can both tell when that time comes, I'm not going to be the one you're calling up." Griffith gives my hand a squeeze.

"Sorry. I really wish I ... smelled better?"

His mouth falls open in a grin, and he booms out a laugh, the sound so genuine that I feel the tension leaving my body as I chuckle along with him.

Maybe Griffith and I aren't meant to be romantic, but I like the idea of being friends with him. He's got an easy way about him that is relaxing to be around.

"You smell just fine," he says after his laughter finally trails off. "Got the scent of a good friend coming off you." He grins. "Want to share a cookie before you have to go back to work?"

"That sounds perfect."

The werewolf pops up from his seat, and I watch him stride toward the truck with a smile on my face. I like Griffith. But he's right; the affection isn't romantic. Still, I wish I could help him out. As I observe him chatting with Mary Jo, I wonder if my friend might get on with the werewolf. She's been single for a while now. Not that she needs to date, but I think she might want to. Or at least, her obsession with binge-watching rom-coms would indicate she has a mild interest in love.

And maybe having a partner would get her to give up her unspoken feud with the town's baking bear shifter.

I make a note to ask Mary Jo about her romantic life next time we hang out.

"A werewolf bartender?"

The question comes in a snarky tone the moment before the speaker slides onto the bench across from me. Every dormant nerve in my body thrums to life.

"Anthony."

How did I not realize he was here?

"You can do so much better." His eyes follow Griffith.

I sigh, hoping to exhale the hurt of having him so close, but not close enough. Which is my decision. Like choosing not to eat cookies and having a plate set before me, and now, I'm wondering why I would ever eschew cookies in the first place.

But cookies are too weak a metaphor. The man is a drug, and I'm addicted.

"You're not better for me," I tell him while simultaneously reminding myself.

Anthony frowns. "You were supposed to say, *What, like a self-centered social media influencer?*" He affects a high-pitched voice for that last bit.

I press my lips together to hide my amusement. "Was that supposed to be an impression of me?"

"And then," he continues on, ignoring my question, "I could triumphantly say, *I'm* not *a social media influencer anymore. I quit.*"

I gape at him. "You what?"

"I quit," he repeats. "A week ago, although I think my agent is finally finished begging me to come back."

When Anthony first sat down, my goal was to get him gone. But now, I'm curious and anxious, and I don't want him to leave until he sets my mind at ease.

"Why would you quit your job?"

He shrugs. "I never needed it. I'm exceedingly rich—which I would like noted is a fantastic bullet point on a husband résumé. Specifically for the father of a monster baby." Anthony rests his elbows on the table and leans toward me. "I could bribe a lot of people into looking the other way if our offspring went on a rampage."

As he speaks, a teasing note in his voice the entire time, I shake my head. Getting rid of the hope his words are trying to inspire.

"You shouldn't have quit your job for me."

"Let's be clear." Anthony reaches out to trace a gentle finger along the back of my hand, following the line of one of my veins. "I quit my job *because* of you. Because you showed me a life that would make me happier than anything I'd been doing up to that point. But I didn't quit *for* you. I quit for me."

My cheeks heat, and my clothes feel entirely too tight. "Okay. Fine. But your job was only a smaller issue."

"Yes. The magic." He's reached my nail, and he fondles the dull tip. My talons tingle, wanting to extend for him. "You said you are magic." The corner of his mouth curves in the most tempting smirk. But the expression is more sad than teasing. "That's what I thought I was too. For the longest time." Anthony's eyes meet and hold mine. "My mother does not think of my siblings and me as her children. To her, we are experiments. My father feels the same. She told me I was made, not in the biblical sense. But that I was only the result of a spell she performed while pregnant with Broderick."

I gape at him and the horrible reality of his family life.

Despite my obvious dismay, Anthony continues. "I've lived every day thinking I might disappear at any moment. When she'd decided her experiment was done. I never believed ..." He trails off, confidence gone in the wake of this vulnerable expression. But then Anthony firms his shoulders. "I never believed that I was real. Not until Violetta dosed me. When my magic was gone, I was blood and bone and still alive. That day I discovered my mother lied to me about what I was. Who I was."

"Anthony ..." My words disappear as my mind replays that

day he came to me. The eagerness and joy. Now I understand why he held so tightly to that hatred. He had good reason to.

But still, knowing this, does it change anything?

Even having a valid reason doesn't mean the results would be any less damaging to me and my future offspring.

A throat clearing beside us cuts off my whirling, confused thoughts.

Griffith is back.

How long has he been standing there?

Still, I'm grateful for his return. At least until I see the flash of pain on Anthony's face.

I never wanted to hurt him.

But he clears it away fast and stands with a flourish. "I must be in your seat."

"Yeah." Griffith glances between us as he drags out the word, and awkwardness solidifies in the air around the three of us.

"You two have fun Lady-and-Tramping your cookie or whatever you had planned. I'll just go grab a bagel and be on my way. To my new job. Which is in this town." Anthony offers a bow that should look weird, but the smooth man manages to make it appear charming. He moves to leave, then turns back for a final word. "Also, I love you, Zara Ironfeather. And if anyone hurts you"—his eyes flick to Griffith, then back to my face—"I'll find the darkest spell book in my sisters' library and have a hexing party."

He winks and saunters away.

Griffith chuckles, but his eyes are serious as he watches Anthony's departure.

I should be furious that Anthony just threatened my date, especially since we've basically agreed this is *not* a date but instead a friendly outing.

But one thing pricks at the back of my mind until I realize what the truly amazing thing was about Anthony's warning.

He threatened Griffith with *magic*.

39

———————

ZARA

"This is your fault."

At my mother's words, I send her an exasperated look. "You've got to be kidding me."

"It is. Your father and I were perfectly fine, living in our empty nest. But you had to keep sending those cute images of shelter dogs, and now, we're here."

"I sent you one link months ago. And I don't see how me suggesting you adopt a dog directly resulted in said dog getting a face full of porcupine quills."

While my mom scolds me, I carefully remove the handful of spikes from the German shepherd's snout. Luckily, the adolescent is a sweetie and only whines instead of snapping at me while I work. My father's constant string of baby talk helps soothe the pup. From the way Mom tells it, he bonded with the girl within seconds of seeing her at the shelter. Now, she sleeps in the bed with them, eats organic dog food, and goes with Dad on all his errands. Which included his weekly hike through the

Chattahoochee National Forest and is why they are here today. Samosa pissed off the wrong woodland creature.

"You should've heard your father when he brought her home. Wailing. I thought the dog was dead. He's too attached. He loves her more than you."

"Hmm," I murmur, focusing on the last quill that's lodged particularly deep. "Does he love her more than you, Mama?"

My mother scoffs. Then, she glares at my father when he continues to murmur to Samosa how she's his favorite girl.

I dislodge the spike, and the pup gives a pathetic whimper.

Mom's face softens, and she reaches out to scratch the shepherd behind her ears. "That's a tough girl. So brave."

I don't think my dad is the only one with a massive soft spot for their newest family member.

"All done." I dab the punctures with disinfectant and examine her face to make sure I didn't miss anything.

"We thought you were coming to Marlin's last night." Dad doesn't look at me as he talks, still checking every inch of Samosa, no doubt looking for any other things that might need fixing before I send them out of here on their unpaying asses.

More of that friends and family discount.

"I wasn't up for it." More like I couldn't be in a room with happy, drunk people when I would either be a sad, sober person or a sad, drunk person.

And the prospect of getting asked out on another date? No thank you. After Griffith, I decided to take a break. Maybe wait a few months until I dip my toes into the dating pool again.

The hesitation is annoying. After Christian, I was ready to get out into the romantic world almost immediately.

But after Anthony ... I can't fathom even holding hands with someone who isn't him with his beautiful, long fingers.

"How is that witch?" Mom asks, as if she doesn't know his name.

"I don't know," I mutter, focusing on typing info about

Samosa into her digital chart. Ame set the system up for us, and having all our files on the computer is extremely helpful.

"Why don't you know?" Dad asks, and I glance to the side to find them both watching me.

"Because we're not together anymore," I remind them.

Though they like to pretend I never speak to them, I make it a point to keep my parents updated on my life. A few days after I ended things with Anthony, I had dinner at their house and let them know. Luckily, no one had mentioned Anthony to Ba and Dada or else I would've had to get on a conference call with my dad's side of the family to explain why I'm suddenly single again.

"Why not, dear? He's in town, and he's signed a year lease on that apartment above the dry cleaner. Seems like a solid young man."

My fingers pause on the keyboard, and I turn to face them fully. "He's what?"

"A solid young man." My father repeats my mom's words. "Do you not like him anymore?" He grimaces at my mother. "Should we have turned down his margaritas?"

"What?" I yelp.

My mother waves a hand at me but aims her words at my father. "The drinks were a gift. Not a bribe, I'm sure. Besides, we didn't tell him anything about Zara. We're fine."

"You are *not* fine." I circle the examination table to properly glare at the two of them. "What's this about Anthony buying you margaritas?"

"Well, you didn't come last night. And we had an extra glass. And we saw that witch boy staring around the room."

"He looked pathetic," Dad adds with a triumphant grin, as if Anthony's misery is something to celebrate.

"Exactly. Like an abandoned puppy. Then, he spotted us, and—oh, it was so funny—he tried to do that swagger thing he does." My mom does a decent impression of Anthony's slouchy walk. "And he came to our table and asked if we expected you to show up."

"We said no," Dad adds.

"Exactly. We said no. And my goodness, I thought the man might sink to the floor—he was so disappointed. We had to give him your margarita. Then, he bought us a round. Maybe two."

"Definitely no more than three," Dad assures me.

"Of course." My mother nods sagely. "No more than four. Then he asked your dad about when they'd get a cricket game together. And did you know he makes clothes? He's working with Esme. Promised to get me on her list for a gown for the Halloween Ball. Plus, he's so charming, you know, dear?"

I know better than most. I can't believe this. Anthony Shelly is wooing my parents.

I don't know what to do with this information, so I simply gape at them.

They exchange a look I can't interpret, and just when I'm about to interrogate them further, a raised voice from the front lobby sounds through the door.

My spine goes rigid, and I hurry around my parents, thoughts of them getting drunk with my handsome ex set to the side as I worry about Ame facing off with a man who doesn't sound happy.

A man who is here for me.

40

ANTHONY

AME FORGOT HER LUNCH, and I have to practically arm-wrestle Jack for the privilege to bring it to her. Luckily, the werewolf has an early meeting at the university, and I tell Mor if she sides with me, I'll pick her up a latte from Coffee & Claws on my return trip.

Two against one means I'm headed off to Folk Tails with a surly shifter glaring at my back.

It's okay though. He's stopped growling at me, which Ame claims is progress.

When I park in front of the veterinarian office, I pray to the gods that Zara is working today and that she happens to be out by the desk when I go in. All I want is to see her. A quick glimpse.

And make sure that bartender hasn't put a ring on her finger yet. Yeah, it's only been a week since I stumbled upon that date, but if he knows what's good for him, he'll lock her down as fast as possible.

Like I should have done.

She doesn't hate my guts, so there's still a chance.

I smooth my hands over my white linen shirt and check my hair in the mirror, then grab the brown paper bag that a werewolf lovingly packed for my sister.

The guy is a pushover. And, man, do I envy him.

What I wouldn't give for the privilege to pack Zara a lunch every morning.

Maybe one day, she'll let me.

A bell chimes when I step in the front door, and I hear Ame's voice, but I can't see her because there's a wall of a person in between the two of us. The massive back looks familiar.

"Sir, if you don't have an animal, I can't make you an appointment." Ame speaks in her calm, no-nonsense voice, but I pick up a line of tension.

Good thing I'm here and not Jack. The werewolf probably would've tossed the man through a window already.

"It's a consultation about *getting* an animal. I want Zara's professional opinion."

The voice and the back of his blond head click a memory into place.

Christian Trader. Zara's ex.

What the hell is he doing here?

"Christian." The husky voice with a touch of scolding isn't my sister's. "What are you doing here?" I hear the squeak of sneakers on tiles, but don't see anything because of the fucker's billboard-sized shoulders.

"I'm thinking of adopting a dog," he says. "But I can't decide between a few. Could you help me?"

You underhanded son of a bitch. Using a dog to woo the gorgeous vet?

Why didn't I think of that?

"You don't need my opinion. If you do adopt a dog, I hope it's because you want them. That you're not using them."

Oh yeah. That's why. Because my harpy is as intelligent as she is gorgeous and doesn't put up with bullshit.

"Zara"—her ex leans forward, over the counter, crowding my sister as he does—"let's just talk. I miss you. You gave up on us too fast."

Her loud, exasperated sigh comforts me. "I did not. We want different things. And you can't ambush me at my job."

"Couples talk things through and compromise." Christian sounds angry now, and I see his fist curl at his side. "You blew everything out of proportion without giving me a chance." The man sounds like he believes his words, but that doesn't mean he's right. And his continued berating of Zara—when she freely offered him *everything* I wish I could have with her—sets off a poisonous fury in my chest. "You never understood what I was saying. I want—"

"You know what I want?" I cut him off, and the bus-sized man turns to see who's speaking, revealing a wide-eyed Zara and a curious Ame.

Magic stirs beneath my skin, and I dip my hand in my pocket, fiddling with a container full of red powder. The amplifier I carry with me at all times now. When the assist touches my bare skin, there's a surge of power, and I draw it to me like Violetta showed me, letting the magic filter into my words.

"I want you to realize how giant of an ass you are not only because you no longer have the most perfect woman in the world in your life, but also because you hurt her while you had her. I want that knowledge to live in your brain and fester. Know that any child of Zara's, even one that could have been made with your lackluster genes, would be a gift to the world. One you don't—and will never—deserve. I want you to know that. And I want you to leave her the fuck alone."

I can see in his human eyes the brief struggle against my might. This is new. Normally, I coax people to act upon wants they already have.

But this time, I'm changing his nature.

Is it wrong? Is this my villain origin story?

I really don't care. He hurt Zara, so I give zero fucks about his free will. I never claimed to be a moral man.

Finally, Christian's aggressive stance fades, his shoulders relaxing, and he strides out of the office without a look back.

Silence falls between the three of us.

"You just magicked him," Ame observes, no judgment in her voice.

"Yes, well ..." I don't have an apology in me, so I plop the brown paper bag on the counter. "You forgot your lunch. Please eat it so your mate doesn't skin me alive tonight."

Even though I know I should turn and leave, I can't help one heart-wrenching look at the woman I love. "Hello, Zara. You're looking"—*don't say anything too desperate or else she'll be uncomfortable*—"like a goddess in scrubs."

Nailed it.

"Anthony ..." She doesn't say anything else, merely stares at me.

"Anthony Shelly." A voice thick with a sassy Southern drawl draws my attention to the other side of the counter, where Eliza Ironfeather stares me down with her fists on her hips.

Sanjay stands a step behind her, their new dog's leash in his hand.

Great. I thought I was getting on their good side. After that display, I'm probably back to being the Wicked Witch of the West.

"Good to see you both." I dip my head in their direction. "I apologize if that was ... disconcerting." Knowing their history with manipulative magic, I probably just triggered bad memories.

"Too right. Shook me all up." The woman's lips tilt up in a smile. "You can set my nerves at ease with a round of margaritas next Monday."

A tiny ball of tightness eases in my chest. Maybe I don't get the love of their daughter, but it's nice to know the Ironfeathers still like me. At least enough to accept free drinks from me.

Trying for my trademark smirk, I offer Eliza a nod. Attempting not to look like a brokenhearted mess, I glance at Zara a final time, then make an abrupt turn before I start begging or bribing her to give me another chance.

The heat of the day seeps into my skin, a sticky weight that makes my longing a discomfort that exists both inside and outside my body.

"Anthony!"

My feet trip to a stop, and I turn at the shout, certain I imagined it.

But there she is, French braids bouncing, face flushed, as she jogs after me.

My harpy.

"Zara?"

She catches up to me, and I brace for a berating about how I enchanted her ex. Honestly, I wouldn't mind the scolding. Every moment with her eyes on me is a pleasure even if there's pain wound in with it as well.

"Did you mean what you said to Christian?"

My neck is stiff as I nod. "I don't regret a word."

Something miraculous happens.

Zara fists the front of my shirt and hauls me in for a kiss.

Is this happening?

Who fucking cares?!

Even if this is a hallucination, I'm going to enjoy the hell out of it.

Enclosing the woman I love in my arms, I kiss her back desperately, trying to sink into the sensation while memorizing every part of her luscious body in case this is the last time my lips touch hers.

When she breaks away, I chase her mouth, terrified of the end.

But her palm on my chest stays me long enough for me to realize Zara is smiling up at me.

"You really don't care that I'm a harpy?" There's a tentative note in her voice I want to obliterate.

"Of course I care." I hurry on when her hopeful expression falters. "I love that you're a harpy. Every form you take is utter perfection."

Reaching into my pocket, I pull out what I think of as my good-luck talisman. A shimmering black feather she left on the sheets after a night of passion. When I hold the piece of her up, Zara's eyes widen.

"Skin or feathers. Wear whatever. As long as it's you I'm with, I'm the luckiest witch."

Her mouth pops open in an 'o' before she snaps it shut and swallows hard. "You called yourself a witch."

Letting go of my tendency to tease is difficult, but she deserves a serious answer. "That's what I am. My childhood messed me up, but I'm working on it. My parents weren't like yours. They used magic in selfish ways, and my mother led me to believe I was nothing without it. So, I chose to hate it and myself by extension. But I'm trying to get over that. I don't want the toxic thoughts I've had about myself to spill over onto you."

Zara cups my face in her hands, and it's all I can do not to groan at her soft touch.

"I don't want you to think badly about yourself at all," she says.

I grimace. "That's a tall order. But I promise, every day, I'm working on it."

Zara reaches up further to delve her fingers into my hair, drawing my forehead down to rest against hers.

"I could use some work too," she murmurs. "How about we share the load?"

"I would love to give you a copious amount of my load." Despite the seriousness of the exchange, I can't help the innuendo that seeps into my voice.

And perfect woman that she is, Zara laughs and pulls me in for another kiss.

41

ANTHONY

Witches sure cling to some odd traditions.

Like velvet robes. Who wears these anymore?

I mean, I make it work. But still.

"Are we joining a cult?" I ask. "I feel like we're joining a cult."

Broderick elbows me out of the way, taking his spot in the floor-to-ceiling mirror so he can study himself in the floor-length black robe.

"Cult ... coven ... what's the difference?" he murmurs while retying the closure, not sounding concerned in the slightest.

"Well, I'm hoping there's less assumption of apocalypse and giving over of our worldly goods. Mor!" I call out, knowing she's only on the other side of the door. "Do we have to give this coven all our worldly goods?"

"Of course," comes her dry response. "Leave them with me, and I'll make sure to pass them on."

Ame peeks her head in the door. "How's it going?"

I affect mock outrage. "Have you heard of knocking? We could have been naked in here."

Her brow furrows. "You're supposed to wear the robe over your clothes. Did someone tell you to take your clothes off?"

"He's kidding, Ame." Broderick turns from the mirror. "At least, I think he is. Let's not ask for proof either way."

I smirk at them both, secure in the knowledge that I have pants and a shirt on under the oppressive weight of this cloak.

"Remind me never to join a coven in the middle of summer," I say as I stroll out of the room and down the stairs of the old Victorian house.

Even though the sun has set and the air-conditioning is on, the heat is stifling and will only get worse once we step outside.

My siblings follow me down the stairs, but we all pause in the large room near the front of the house. Zara and Jack sit at a table with drinks at their elbows and a card game between them.

"You off?" my mate asks, setting her hand down and smiling my way.

We're already running late, but I can't help rounding the table to press a kiss to her lips. "We are. Try not to miss me too much." I straighten. "I know this getup makes me irresistible, but you must find a way to restrain yourself."

She snorts. "How will I survive?" Still, she runs her palm down the front of the robe, as if she enjoys the soft material.

Maybe tonight, I *will* try the combo of this robe and my birthday suit.

"No idea," Jack mutters. Where my harpy sounded amused, the wolf's words come out with a touch of longing. The guy stares at my sister as if the shapeless robe were some scandalous bikini.

Ame smiles at her mate, hurries to give him a quick kiss on the check, then heads out the front door, Broderick and Mor close on her heels.

A warm hand clasps mine, and I glance down to find Zara with a concerned expression on her face.

"You sure you're okay with doing this? It's a big step."

Her caring is a gentle caress against my heart that makes me love her more.

I sink to my haunches by her chair. "It's a step I'm ready for." Scooping up her hand, I brush my lips over her knuckles. "Don't wait up for me."

Zara leans down, her forehead resting against mine. "You'll do great. And of course I'm going to wait up for you."

It takes more effort than it should to peel myself away from her, but I do, and I stroll out the front door before I make an excuse to linger.

It's not that I'm scared of this coven ceremony. It's just that I'd rather spend my night with my harpy.

But I do try to be responsible every now and then.

"All right"—I slide into the backseat of Ame's car—"let's go slaughter some goats or whatever witches do."

"The only goat slaughtering I've come across in my studies pertains to chupacabras. Not witches. Although voodoo practitioners ..." Mor leads us on a historical instruction of animal slaughter related to magic for most of the ten-minute drive to witch territory and the spot of the coven ritual.

Despite the lack of a working GPS, Ame seems to know exactly where to park, and the lot of us unload in our heavy black robes.

"These aren't a lot different from professor robes at graduation," Broderick points out as we hold up our skirts while treading a slim path into the forest. "Wonder if they get them made at the same place."

I lift my arm, bringing the voluminous sleeve to my nose for a sniff. "This is secondhand, isn't it?"

"Okay, let's get all the snarky comments out now." Mor glares at me in particular. "You need to keep in mind if you piss one of these people off, they could make you regret stepping foot in this town."

"Your pep talks are lovely, big sister. I don't know why I was ever afraid of magic in the first place," I mutter.

"Don't worry." Ame slows her pace until she's by my side, giving me an encouraging smile. "If anyone tries to work an enchantment on you, I've got your back."

The part-sweet, part-threatening sentiment eases a touch of worry I didn't realize was sitting like a heavy load in my gut. Ame might be younger than me, but she's a powerful force.

I'm lucky to have her on my side. To have her love and support.

I sling an arm around her shoulders. "And I've got yours. We're the Shellys. None can defend against our magical might."

Broderick throws a grin over his shoulder, and Mor raises a fist in the air.

"Hear, hear," she says.

Just as her agreement fades into the night, we step through a break in the trees and come upon a large gathering.

The mass of people waiting for us is eerie.

Every single one is dressed in the same dark cloak, only their hoods are up, obscuring their faces. We four are the only identifiable ones.

We're exposed.

"Ah. The Shellys have finally arrived." This cheerful greeting comes as a figure steps forward and pushes her cloak off her head.

Violetta Radeva. She gives us a toothy smile.

"I apologize. I didn't know we were supposed to be hooded," Mor says, speaking to Violetta, but her voice is loud enough for the group to hear.

"The hoods are not yet for you," another speaks. This one steps forward and pushes back her covering to reveal a gorgeous Black woman with short, curly hair and an agelessness about her. I recognize Selena, the witch council member. "Not all in the coven wish to reveal themselves to outsiders. Only once you've joined our ranks are you allowed to know your fellow witches. We're glad to have all four of you here tonight."

"Kind of a required package deal, right?" I snort, though I don't feel any more resentment.

Selena stares at me for a moment, brow creased in confusion. Then, her dark eyes flick to Violetta, and her expression turns to exasperation. "You told them all four have to join?"

As the meaning of her words sinks into my brain, I gape at the innocently smiling sea witch.

She winks my way and whispers loud enough for our group to hear, "I only said *I* wouldn't let you all into the coven."

"Vi," Selena hisses, clearly annoyed, "we talked about lying to new recruits."

"I distinctly remember *you* talking about it and me being too distracted by your beautiful face to pay attention." The sea witch kisses Selena on her cheek, then murmurs something in her ear that has the woman's dark skin flushing.

I wonder if Levi knows his fellow council member is hooking up with his mom.

Not my problem, and I decide to let go of any animosity about being lied to. Violetta is who she is, and things worked out in the end.

"Fine. Later," Selena says before facing the crowd. "Who here invites these four into the Folk Haven coven, taking responsibility for them?"

We need a sponsor?

I glance at my siblings and see they each have the same question in their eyes. None of us were aware, and I'm ready for a ringing silence.

"I invite the Shelly family into the Folk Haven coven." The sweet voice echoes strong through the clearing, and we four stare at Violetta, who smiles serenely back our way. "On one condition."

I roll my eyes. Of course.

Her attention homes in on me, and she crooks a finger, beckoning me to take center stage.

With a bracing breath, I force my feet forward, suddenly thankful for the large cloak that gives me more of a solid presence. The fabric helps me take up space.

"State your name," the witch commands.

"Anthony Shelly." My knees lock, and my spine straightens.

There's a challenge in her eyes. "And what are you?"

A month ago, I would have shied away from the question, denied the truth of myself. I would have let fear send me running from this group, abandoning my siblings to keep myself from falling apart at the seams.

But I don't run anymore.

And I'm proud of what I am.

Holding her sapphire gaze, I speak the words clearly, without a single doubt or regret. "I am a witch."

The night sky fills with the words, the stars bright above us as Violetta offers a satisfied smile.

"That you are. Welcome to the Folk Haven coven, Anthony Shelly."

42

———————

BRODERICK

She likes apples.

My sister found an apple.

Perfect conversation starter.

I smooth my hands over the fitted black button-up Anthony gave me. He insisted we look good in black, but I feel like the dark color is somehow too intense for me. I'm an earth-tone wearer. Give me a good green or brown any day.

But I need to change things up if I hope to catch anyone's attention.

Catch *her* attention.

I spread my papers out on the table in the English faculty lounge area. Technically, I could do my grading in the shoebox-sized office the university assigned me. Despite the small size, I like the cozy little room with its window looking out at the Chattahoochee National Forest.

But the lounge has a recycling bin. One that needs to be emptied every Wednesday afternoon.

Today is Wednesday.

At the familiar squeak of wheels, I straighten in my chair and try not to look like I've been eagerly awaiting this moment since this time last week.

The cart comes through the doorway first, a low, flat surface on wheels, holding two large, bright blue recycling bins with the Clean Haven logo on the side of them.

Next appears the most beautiful woman I've ever laid my eyes upon.

Ophelia.

Ophelia ... no last name. At least none that she's shared with me.

Not that she has to or that I expect her to.

Only I want to know every detail about her, so every hole in my knowledge leaves me wondering.

She enters the room with a no-nonsense gait, a long golden ponytail swinging behind her shoulders with every step. Ophelia is a white woman, but where I'm so pale that I need to worry about five minutes too long in the sun, she looks as though her skin lovingly absorbs the summer rays. She practically glows.

Her eyes, a golden hazel mixture, meet mine, and she pauses, then quickly looks away and heads toward the small blue receptacle in the corner.

"Hello, Professor Shelly," she murmurs, almost too low for me to hear. But of course I do because I'm straining to pick up even the lightest inhale from her.

Why does she fascinate me so much?

I'm not sure the reason, only that I was drawn to her, even when she was trapped in the shape of a rabbit.

"Hi, Ophelia. You can call me Broderick, you know. You're not a student. No need to be formal." Even though I really like hearing the title in her light voice, I'd prefer her to be comfortable with me.

She nods, but doesn't say anything else. Just reaches for the recycling bin and carries it over to her cart to empty.

If I don't say anything, she'll be gone before the minute is up, and I'll have to wait another week to see her again.

I stand abruptly from my chair. Too abruptly. The chair topples over backward with a loud crash.

Ophelia pauses in her task, staring at me with wide eyes.

"Uh, sorry. Leg cramp." I can feel my face turning redder than my hair as I pretend to massage my thigh muscle.

She offers a hesitant nod before returning to work.

Shit. Now, she thinks I'm a weirdo.

"You like apples?" I ask, slightly desperate.

Great. I just hammered the final weird nail into my oddball coffin.

Ophelia returns the small recycling container to the corner before answering, "I do."

"Do you know much about apples?" Somehow, I manage to keep my question sounding only mildly interested.

Ophelia gives me a curious stare, and I'm glad I don't bumble around this much with my words when I'm teaching a class.

"It's only"—I take a deep breath and order my thoughts —"my sister Ame found an apple. A magical one. A golden one, hidden in the walls of the library. And I ... we-we wondered if you've ever heard of such a thing?"

Ophelia takes a step toward me, head tilted as she considers my words. "A golden apple?"

"At least in color." I nod in a hard, jerky motion because I've forgotten how normal people move their bodies. "We don't know if it's really gold or something else. Would you like to see a picture?"

Maybe I shouldn't be talking to a stranger about unknown magical items in my family's possession.

But Ophelia doesn't feel like a stranger. Not to me anyway.

Especially not when she moves to my side as I tug my

phone out of my pocket and tilt the screen her way as I navigate to my photos. I hurriedly click on the apple picture, hoping she didn't catch sight of the selfie I took while wearing Anthony's nipple-revealing mesh shirt.

"Oh." She lets out the smallest gasp that still does things to me. Rattles my heart around in my chest and all that.

"Do you recognize it?" I ask while fighting the urge to lean over and sniff her hair.

That's what creeps do. Don't be a creep.

Ophelia reaches out and pinches her fingers on my screen to zoom in. "You said it's magical?"

"Definitely." I could feel the power radiating off it.

Her lips purse as she thinks over her answer. "I know stories of golden apples. But this might not be the same. And those were fairy tales. Bedtime stories."

"Could you tell me anyway? Just in case."

Ophelia breathes in deep through her nose before continuing, "There are tales of The Hot One having a garden. They grew the strangest plants they could find in each dimension and made their garden in a secluded stretch of land high on a mountain. They set a dragon to guard their treasures."

"A dragon?" I ask. "But those mythics are Of the Wing. Why would a dragon guard The Hot One's garden?"

Ophelia lifts one shoulder and leans closer to my phone, her soft breath puffing over my fingers as she studies the image. "Some say they are Of the Wing. Others claim to be Of the Flame. My aunt told me dragons were a collaboration between the two gods. Who knows? It's a story. All of it could be false. Do you want to hear the rest?" Her words flow on a fast rhythm, each sentence blending together in a way that makes the end sound like the abrupt finish of a song.

I want her to talk forever. About anything. About nothing. Just so I can listen to her lyrical voice.

But I only say, "Yes. Please. Sorry for interrupting."

Ophelia continues in her soft, mesmerizing tone, "In the very center of the garden was a silver tree that bore golden apples. A curious firebird heard tales of the fruit and wanted nothing more than to take a bite. They flew over the entire world, searching until, one day, they saw the sheen of dragon scales and the shimmer of silver branches. Stifling their flame, the firebird snuck into the garden under the cover of night, plucked an apple from the tree, and bit into the tender flesh." She pauses, leaving me on the edge of my seat.

"What happened?" I whisper.

Ophelia tilts her chin, blinking slowly as her eyes meet mine, capturing me in the intense, vibrant color in her irises.

"The Hot One appeared before the firebird, furious at the theft. They cursed the firebird to lose their wings and the heat in their soul. They were made mortal."

Sadness tugs at my gut. I've only ever seen Ophelia in her firebird form once, and the experience was glorious. The thought of someone having the power and losing it is too devastating to contemplate.

Only that's what happened to Ophelia, wasn't it?

My sadness morphs into simmering rage at the reminder of how a sorcerer kept her trapped for an unknown length of time. She was his prisoner and power source.

She's free now, I remind myself. And the sorcerer is dead.

"Is that what the apples do?" I ask, my voice rough. "Turn mythics into humans?"

Sounds like something Anthony would have wanted. Now, I'm not so sure. My brother seems to have come into his magic. Embraced it with gusto.

Ophelia tugs on the end of her ponytail as she thinks. "I don't know. Possibly. But that's just one story. There are others where The Hot One makes a gift of the apple. In those, the apples do great things. Grant wishes. Provide protection. Fend off death. But there's no way of knowing what your apple does.

If it is one of The Hot One's. But it *could* make you lose your magic."

That's certainly a warning label that should be attached.

"Thank you, Ophelia. For sharing your knowledge."

The firebird blinks, seeming to resurface from her storytelling, and hurriedly takes a step back. Away from me.

"Of course." She grabs the handle of her cart. "Have a good day, Professor Shelly."

And before I can correct her, she's out of the room, leaving only the squeak of the cart's wheels behind.

Dejected, I slump into my chair.

That was the longest exchange I've had with her, and I enjoyed every second. But what I have to admit, after that departing remark with the formal use of my name, is that Ophelia wants to keep distance between us.

She's not interested, and if I push, I'll be the asshole making her uncomfortable.

As much as the knowledge tears me up inside, I accept the truth.

Ophelia doesn't want me. I have to leave her alone.

43

ZARA

Three Years Later

I RECLINE on the couch with a boulder on my bladder. But I just peed a half hour ago, and standing seems like a lot of work, so I try to ignore the pressure and watch the wrestling match on my floor instead.

"Sin"—Anthony speaks to his familiar in a warning tone as he strolls into the room—"don't eat Bubblegum."

The snake lets the dog's paw slip from his mouth and raises his head, tilting it to the side, as if to say, *Who, me? I would never.*

Bubblegum—named for his pink nose and because giving pit bulls ridiculous names helps get rid of the aggression stigma the breed has—doesn't seem concerned about being consumed. He lies on the ground, panting and wearing a doggy grin. The mutt loves any kind of attention.

Anthony and I adopted the goofy pup after someone tied him to the front door of Folk Tails when it was closed and never came back to claim him. We put up posters and called the closest shelters, but there were no reports of a missing animal.

And Bubblegum was too sweet to give up.

Plus, we figured adopting a dog together would be a good couple-bonding activity.

Turns out, Bubblegum loves Sin more than either of us.

"Ugh," I groan, readjusting on the couch, trying to find a position where it doesn't feel like one of my ribs is about to snap.

A flutter of kicks responds to the movement.

"I think I just saw a foot." Anthony kneels next to the couch and presses his forehead against my distended stomach.

"Sure it wasn't a tentacle? I swear this baby has eight legs. Or appendages." I extend my arms, giving in to the demands of my body. "Help me up. Time for a bathroom break."

My loving mate expertly supports my weight, drawing me to my feet. With me less than a month away from popping, Anthony's had to become my walking, talking crutch on a regular basis now.

I wonder if my witch knew what he was getting himself into on that warm spring night two years ago, when we stood on the shores of Lake Galen under a full moon and spoke words of devotion during our handfasting ceremony.

Luckily, I can still manage to use a toilet on my own.

When I come out of the bathroom, only slightly more comfortable, I find him in the kitchen, making me a margarita.

No alcohol, just the mix.

But Anthony does up the glasses as if it were the real thing, and I wobble as much as a drunk person does anyway.

"Oh, that looks perfect." I hold out my hand for what I know will be a deliciously tart, refreshing drink. Exactly what I need to feel cool when this baby is cooking me from the inside and the Georgia heat is pressing on me from the outside.

Anthony has thoroughly enjoyed the task of stitching me

breezy—skimpy—maternity clothes. Now that I'm on leave from work, I spend most of the days floating in the lake to cool down and take some pressure off my feet. I make sure to tie my raft to the dock so I don't float away with the current, necessitating a friendly selkie's tow home.

Yes, that's oddly specific.

Yes, that might have been a lesson I learned from firsthand experience.

"Now, wait a moment." Anthony doesn't pass over the delicious drink. "Did you tell them?"

I roll my eyes and fight a smile. "Not yet."

"Come on, Zara. We talked about this." Anthony gives me his best attempt at a stern glare. "They need to know."

I give a big sigh, as if this is the most trying part of my day when, really, I love it. Bending my face as close to my big belly as I can manage, I make sure to speak in an overly loud voice.

"Hey, sweet little monster. This is your mother speaking, here with your daily reminder that if you decide to use your magnificent monster powers to decimate the population and rule the world, please remember your father, Anthony Ironfeather, was on board with the Monster Baby Plan from day one." I smirk at my witchy husband. "Happy?"

His proud grin holds all the love I've ever hoped for.

"More than words can encompass."

Anthony hands me my glass, and like every Monday night, the moment after I take my first sip, he steals a kiss.

Nothing better than salt, love, and witch on my lips.

EPILOGUE

MOR

Three Years Earlier

THE WOODS ARE lively today with the sun dripping through the canopy and limbs quivering as squirrels jump from branch to branch. I listen to the birdsong and the far-off lap of water from Lake Galen, trying to infuse the pleasant sensations in my soul. Build a shield around myself before this next task.

A chore I've put off for far too long.

There are times when patrons ask about the statue garden that sits a short distance away from the library. I've always told them that it is not yet open to the public. My excuse is that it's a very personal site for Delta.

But the truth is, the dragon never requested that we shield the collection from visitors. Delta never asked us to do anything with the space other than let her take the statue of her mother from it. I had no problems with her removing that sculpture or taking all of them.

Delta only claimed the one though, and Ame pointed out that the pieces of art could be a draw.

So, why haven't I incorporated the display into the library? The answer is simple and also complicated.

Simple because I don't like to open collections to the public without some type of organization or labeling system and I haven't cataloged them yet.

Complicated because I've had over a year to create that system and ample time to do it.

But still, I haven't.

The truth that I admit to myself and no one else is that the statue garden scares me. It is steeped in emotions. I tried to approach it one time before the sale of the house, and I couldn't get within twenty feet without my knees buckling from the agony and despair radiating off of the pieces of art.

The sensation doesn't surprise me. The statues were created by Delta's father, Dimitri Novac, after his mate passed away. Each one must have absorbed the pain he was going through while crafting them. Intentionally or not, Dimitri left emotional markers all over his work. Hard as I try to block them out, my shields—which are normally solid barriers against emotional turmoil—don't seem to work.

Maybe it's because I've only trained myself to block out the emotions of living beings. Dimitri passed away a few years ago. His emotions are now tied to objects, and it might be that I don't know how to block that type of aura.

What I do know is that it's time to stop avoiding something simply because it is hard. My family has shown me that with their everyday acts of bravery. Ame put her life at risk to save a mythic in need. Anthony has pushed past his fear of magic to learn to wield his power and even joined a coven.

Time for me to step out of my comfort zone and do what needs to be done.

I can do this. I can create an environment for the magnificent work of a heartbroken dragon to be viewed by the world. Or at least the mythical world.

This is what I tell myself as I pause just out of sight of the statue garden. There is a haze in front of me, only visible to my eyes, and I know that when I step into the space, emotions will batter against my mind and my soul. I will feel as though *I* am the one who has lost the one that I love.

One of the reasons that is so scary is because I've never even felt that kind of love for another person before. The kind that makes them your life partner. I don't have the happy memories to balance out the devastation. It's all twisted nightmares when I step into this cloud of grief.

"Just breathe," I coach myself. "Walk through them. That's all you're going to do today."

Realistic expectations.

With a firm step, I move forward.

My shoulders bow under the weight, my internal walls threatening to crumble.

It *hurts*.

"Breathe." I gasp the word and suck air in at the same time.

Sadness. Gut-wrenching sadness. Then fury.

Dimitri must have grieved with anger. It's not uncommon to rage at the loss of a loved one. I've felt it before from others.

"This isn't my pain," I remind myself, pushing the ache outward, but not running from it.

Eventually, I can take another step. The pain irritates my skin like nails against a sunburn, but it stays on that outermost layer, no longer flaying me on the inside. This is uncomfortable, but manageable.

Finally, I can visit the dragon's garden of statues.

Wrapping my arms tight around my overly sensitive body, I weave among the figures, admiring their beauty while also keeping the pound of emotion at bay. Like visiting an art museum while a hurricane rages outside.

The Pegasus in flight holds my attention for a moment, and I marvel at how the figure is made of heavy metal yet appears to be weightless.

Then, I move on to another and find myself pausing for an entirely different reason.

The piece has the same expert crafting as the others, so detailed as to be lifelike, but there's a difference.

This form is terrifying.

I stare at the beast, wondering what made Dimitri Novac stray into darker themes for this work while all his others remain light and airy.

Is this meant to represent his shattered heart? All that was left of his soul after losing the mate he loved?

I certainly feel the strongest push against my barriers here. As if it is the source of all the turmoil. The press is so overwhelming that my temples begin to pound.

"This isn't my pain," I mutter again. A reminder. A life raft to cling to.

Still, I need space.

This was a lot in one day, but a good first step. I swear to return later in the week, when I've shored up my defenses better.

But as I take a retreating step, my foot comes down on a stick I didn't realize was behind me. The fallen tree limb is large, and my sole slips off it instead of breaking the branch in half. Unbalanced, I fall on my ass, hands flung out behind me to brace for impact. I hiss at the sharp sting of a rock cutting into my palm.

"Damn it!" I growl.

Then, I gasp.

The unexpected tumble and jab of pain broke my concentration, allowing the deluge of emotion to spill into my brain.

But instead of a storm of sadness, I'm hit with a wall of pure fury.

Burns. It burns so hot.

Longing. And pain. And misery.

Each one a new flame, scorching my inner mind as I struggle against the onslaught, whimpering as I fight the urge to curl into a ball and protect myself.

This is too many, a logical part of my mind manages. Too many emotions to cling to an inanimate object.

I suck in breath after breath, rebuilding my walls a single brick at a time until I've pushed the turmoil outside of my barriers once more.

Then, in horror, I stare up at the monstrous sculpture.

A grid of emotions weaves over the surface, as intricate as any living being I've seen.

Which can only mean one thing.

"You're alive."

The End

~

Thank you so much for reading HARD FOR A HARPY. I hope you enjoyed Zara & Anthony's love story and that you leave a review! Do you want to spend more time in the mythic-filled Folk Haven? Check out the following books for more small town, sexy, fated mates romances.

SEDUCED BY A SELKIE

Folk Haven Book 1

Delta Novac hates Folk Haven, and as soon as she's done cleaning out her father's mess of a house, she's giving the town her taillights. But after she dives into the lake to save a drowning man that's not actually in danger, she finds herself with a sweet and sexy selkie shadow ready to do anything to get her to stay.

SUCKER FOR A SIREN
Folk Haven Book 2

Seamus MacNamara refuses to believe in the selkie mating myth: that his one true partner will rescue him from great danger. So, when the adorably beautiful barista he has a secret crush saves his life, Seamus ends up insulting her instead offering heartfelt thanks. Now he just wants a chance to redeem himself...and he's willing to go down on his knees to earn her forgiveness.

SWEARING AT A SEA MONSTER
Folk Haven Book 3

Moira MacNamara takes shit from no one, and that includes Levi Abadi, the enticing, infuriating monster who thinks he can dictate what she does with her own property. She makes a deal with him, sealed in blood. But now she can't help noticing how her veins thrum with heat every time he comes near...

SHELTER FOR A SHIFTER
Folk Haven Book 4

Ame Shelly found a cat, but this is no ordinary stray. She's almost certain her feline friend is a man stuck in an animal body. After years of searching, she's finally found the correct spell to release him from his fuzzy prison. Only, the man who appears in front of her demands two things: his witch mate and revenge.

If you enjoyed HARD FOR A HARPY, please consider rating and reviewing the book. Reviews help other readers discover my books, which helps me make a living and funds my ability to write more mythical romances for you!

Folk Haven stories will continue in 2024 with Mor's romance in
Waiting on a Witch.

Keep reading for a preview of *Fire Magic & Ice Cream*, Book 1 in
the Casual Magic series, where elementals try to find love while
controlling their powers...

FIRE MAGIC & ICE CREAM

QUINN

"This is a horrible idea."

I shouldn't have gotten out of the car, but I realized where we were too late. Harley already pressed the button to lock the doors.

"It's my idea, which means it's genius. This is exactly what you need, Fireball." Harley saunters across the steaming parking lot.

With another mighty tug, I try heaving open the car door. My effort is futile.

Cat hovers, dancing from foot to foot. "You told me you wanted to try this place."

Sometimes, I wish my little sister had more evil in her, like Harley. Then I could give her a proper glare for outing my secret longing.

"I said I *wanted* to try it, but that I *can't*. It's too much of a risk."

"Stop being so dramatic. It's not like you're walking into an ammo store, about to set off all the gunpowder," Harley growls at me, already at the front door. "It's an ice cream shop, for goddess's sake."

I know exactly what it is. Land of Ice Cream and Snow. The newest addition to the strip mall where I get my biweekly pedicures. Every time I hobble out of Tulip's Nails with my fresh coat of polish, the acid smell of acrylics clears from my nose, and I get hit with the most delicious scent imaginable.

Waffle cones.

Even though it's torture, I tend to take a roundabout route to my car, just so I can glance in the windows. Not that I ever see much. The interior is dimmer than the blazing Arizona sun.

The easy solution would be to walk into the shop, but I've never done it. Not once.

"I can't go in there!" I lean back on the car, arms crossed.

"Why not?" Harley glares, fists on her hips.

"You know why! The second I step through that door, I'll melt their entire stock. I'm a menace!"

"Oh Quinn. You're not a menace." The distress in Cat's voice almost makes me take the description back. Just to keep from upsetting her.

Harley stalks across the parking lot, coming to stand in front of me. "Listen here, little miss firecracker. You might not be able to control your powers yet, but I can. You start to spark, I'll shut you down. Now get your apple bottom in gear because I'm practically orgasming from the smell of that place, and I'm not about to rush through eating because you're pouting in the car."

We meet scowl for scowl, but I give up first. Probably because this ice cream shop has been taunting me for months.

"You really think you can keep my heat in check?"

My big sister loses her annoyance at my hesitant question, replacing her glower with a saucy grin. "Hell yeah, I can. Could help you out other times, too, if you weren't such a prude."

"Gross! I don't care how kinky your job is. We are *not* that kind of family."

She rolls her eyes. "I'm not asking to be in the room with you like some poorly written porno. I could sit outside your door, read a magazine or something, and make sure you don't burn the house down." Harley tilts her head as she looks me over. "Are you super loud or something?"

"Gah!" I cover my ears and sprint for the front of the shop. "Stay the hell away from me and my sexytimes!"

Through the earmuffs I've created with my hands, I pick up my sisters' laughter. Ignoring them, I take the step I've been holding back from ever since Land of Ice Cream and Snow flipped on their *Open* sign.

I grab the handle and slide in through the front door.

What greets me steals all words from my throat. My nose was already full of sweet scents when I stepped inside, but before my eyes can scan the room, my entire body focuses on the feel of the place.

Cold.

The sensation skitters over my skin, prickling tiny goose bumps and eliciting a shiver.

A shiver.

Shivers and goose bumps aren't for people like me with a constant fire sitting just below the surface of my skin. But here, in this ice cream shop, I experience the sensation of being chilly for the first time in my life.

The bell chiming over my head alerts me to my sisters' arrival.

I whirl around to clutch Harley's shoulders. "This is amazing! I didn't think you could control the fire this much!" I'm so moved that I rise on my toes to press a kiss to her cheek.

She stares at me with eyebrows scrunched together and her lips pursed in a confused smile. "What?"

"Oh my gosh. I've never...this place is so cool!" Cat's exclamation as she dodges around us breaks into my out-of-character thank-you.

Moving past my first experience with the sensation of cold, I finally take in my surroundings. No wonder I was never able to spy much from outside the window.

Most ice cream parlors are all bright colors and delicate furniture. Cute little shops that bring to mind quirky sprinkles or fragile ice sculptures.

Land of Ice Cream and Snow crushes the idea of delicacy under the heel of its heavy boot. This place resembles the homestead of some rugged mountain man or the headquarters of a Viking clan. Solid wooden furniture stretches the length of each wall, and the floor is dark oak. Lights hang from the ceiling, giving off a low glow—small areas of warmth in the stark terrain of the shop. I'm not even sure *shop* is the right word.

More like cabin. A cabin that sells ice cream.

A handful of people sit, talking and eating. I expect, if we came a couple of hours later, after dinnertime, this place would be overrun with sugar-hungry customers. A granite slab serves as a counter in the back of the shop, next to it the one familiar item all ice cream parlors possess—a glass container to view the offered flavors.

I take a single step before realizing the danger behind the counter.

A man.

But not just a man. This man is...well...a *man*.

I think I've found the Viking who pillaged and plundered and built this cabin of a shop with his bare hands. A black T-shirt stretches over shoulders wide enough for me to perch on one side and Cat on the other. His strong, ivory face belongs in a superhero movie. Sculpted cheekbones, square jaw, and enough golden stubble to leave a delicious burn on the inside of my thighs.

Oh shit.

The wonderful cold sensation drifts away as my inner fire senses a rising lust. Heat trails just underneath my skin, pulsing with a life of its own.

"I was right. This is a horrible idea."

But as I turn back toward the door, Harley wraps an arm around my waist. To onlookers, the embrace probably appears friendly and innocent. But in truth, her hold is stronger than steel as she drags me to my doom.

"Focus on the ice cream. Ignore the beautiful man."

"Ignore him? By gouging out my eyes?" I mutter, fighting an onslaught of lust and panic.

The ice cream god steps forward, his frosty gaze locked on the three of us. I watch with fascination as he slips a blue apron, the same shade of his eyes, over his head. The muscles in his biceps flex as he reaches to tie the strings behind his back.

At the display of his glorious muscles, I brace myself for another surge of heat. Instead, my fire remains stoked. The embers are there, teasing me, but they don't burst forth, causing mass chaos.

I guess Harley is as good as her word.

"How can I help you?" The ice cream god's words rumble out like tires across gravel as he watches us.

Not us, I realize. *Me.*

Being the middle child, I've often silently longed for a little bit more attention. But right now, I'm considering hiding behind my curvy older sister or picking up Cat to use as a human shield. All in the name of self-preservation.

As if sensing my cowardly plans, Harley gives me a shove forward, so I end up stumbling into the granite counter. My hands land flat on the surface to steady myself.

Cold shocks through my palms, racing over my skin, practically extinguishing my fire, if not my lust. To my utter embarrassment, my nipples tighten with a shiver, and my bralette does nothing to hide the reaction.

When ice cream god's eyes drop to my chest, I'm torn between crossing my arms over my boobs and attempting another escape or ripping my shirt off and asking if he has a bed in the back room.

I settle on the happy medium of staring up at his gorgeous face and losing the ability to form a coherent sentence.

Maybe, if he were a creepy perv, I'd be able to collect myself. Unfortunately, ice cream god almost immediately removes his stare from my overly excited nipples to look me in the eye again.

"Do you know what flavor you'd like?"

I begin to thaw with a shake of my head. The Viking man turns his back. Steady again, I drag my hands off the frigid counter, rubbing my palms on the sides of my jean shorts.

Not that I mind the cold. In fact, I find the sensation fascinating.

I'm never cold. I was beginning to think I'd have to be dropped in glacial waters or launched into space to truly experience such a low temperature.

But apparently, I just needed my big sister to crave ice cream. Despite her borderline bitchiness earlier, I throw a grateful smile over my shoulder.

In classic Harley fashion, she pokes me in the back. "Stop ogling the man candy and figure out what you want."

Feeling less generous, I stick my tongue out at her and then glance forward, attempting to kick my brain into gear so I can remember what flavors I like.

But I'm thrown off track again when I find a mini wooden spoon in my face.

"Flavor of the day: blueberry pie." Grumbly voiced ice cream god holds out the offering.

On pure instinct, I reach for the spoon. The tip of my finger brushes the edge of his thumb.

At the brief contact with the gorgeous man, I fully expect the utensil to burst into flames, forcing me to pretend I'm a street magician and my sisters are my camera crew and that everything has a weird but still plausible explanation.

But instead of heat, there's another trickle of coolness.

Harley is going to be exhausted after tamping me down. She'll probably pass out in the car on the way home.

Ice cream god continues to watch me, and I realize I'm just standing, holding the sample, and staring at his expansive chest. To my amazement, the sample hasn't melted. However it's headed in that direction with one and then two drips falling from the spoon onto the counter.

Desperate not to reveal my detrimental effect on frozen treats, I shove the flavor of the day into my mouth.

When I smelled waffle cones outside the shop, I kept my composure. When I set sights on the mountain of sexy behind the counter, I had a brief internal freak-out, but overall, I held it together. When cold visited my nerve endings for the first time, I kept my reactions on lock.

But this? It's too much.

"Oh, fuck me," I groan, not caring if there are children around, being corrupted by my involuntary reaction. In my opinion, no one under eighteen should be allowed in this shop. This ice cream is too sinful for young innocents.

I want to fashion a man out of this ice cream, marry him, and then devour him for as long as we both shall live.

The Viking ice cream man clears his throat in a glorious deep rumble as he crosses his arms over his chest, all the while watching me. The pressure of his eyes sits cool and heavy like the chilled treat currently melting on my tongue.

Would he taste just as delicious?

Continue reading Quinn & August's romance in Fire Magic &
Ice Cream!

NEWSLETTER SIGN UP

Get another Folk Haven romance for FREE! Sign up for my newsletter to receive *A Selkie's Secret,* a novella that tells the story of Isla, a selkie, and Finn, the human she refuses to fall in love with...

ACKNOWLEDGMENTS

Thank you to everyone who helped make Zara and Anthony's story a reality! Jovana, my amazing editor, is a grammar goddess and saves me every time. Neha Patel, you were a wonderful and supportive sensitivity reader, and only after working with you do I feel like Zara and Sanjay fully came to life. (Psst! If anyone is looking for a sensitive reader you should go check out Neha's website!)

Most of all, thank you to my readers. Your love for Folk Haven makes returning to the town a joy. I can't wait to give you many more magical stories!

ALSO BY LAUREN CONNOLLY

Find a list of all of Lauren's books on her website:

https://www.laurenconnollyromance.com/book-list

ABOUT THE AUTHOR

Lauren Connolly is an award-wining author of contemporary and paranormal romance stories. She has lived among mountains, next to lakes, and in imaginary worlds. Lauren can never seem to stay in one place for too long, but trust that wherever she's residing there is a dog who thinks he's a troll, twin cats hiding in the couch, and bookshelves bursting with the stories written by the authors she loves.

www.ingramcontent.com/pod-product-compliance
Lightning Source LLC
Chambersburg PA
CBHW051249210726
48287CB00002B/413